Jul

LOGAN-HOCKING
COUNTY DISTRICT LIBRARY
230 EAST MAIN STREET
LOGAN, OHIO 43138

D1261183

THE EDGE

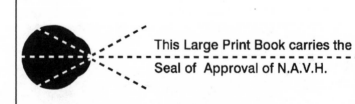

This Large Print Book carries the
Seal of Approval of N.A.V.H.

A SUPERINTENDENT MIKE YEADINGS
MYSTERY

THE EDGE

CLARE CURZON

THORNDIKE PRESS
A part of Gale, Cengage Learning

GALE
CENGAGE Learning™

Detroit • New York • San Francisco • New Haven, Conn • Waterville, Maine • London

GALE
CENGAGE Learning™

Copyright © 2006 by Clare Curzon.
Thorndike Press, a part of Gale, Cengage Learning.

ALL RIGHTS RESERVED
Thorndike Press® Large Print Mystery.
The text of this Large Print edition is unabridged.
Other aspects of the book may vary from the original edition.
Set in 16 pt. Plantin.
Printed on permanent paper.

LIBRARY OF CONGRESS CATALOGING-IN-PUBLICATION DATA

Curzon, Clare.
     The edge : a Superintendent Mike Yeadings mystery / by
Clare Curzon.
        p. cm. — (Thorndike Press large print mystery)
     ISBN-13: 978-1-4104-0583-8 (lg. print : alk. paper)
     ISBN-10: 1-4104-0583-4 (lg. print : alk. paper)
     1. Yeadings, Mike (Fictitious character) — Fiction. 2. Police —
England — Thames Valley — Fiction. 3. Thames Valley
(England) — Fiction. 4. Large type books. I. Title.
PR6053.U79E34 2008
823'.914—dc22   2007051725

Published in 2008 by arrangement with St. Martin's Press, LLC.

Printed in the United States of America
1 2 3 4 5 6 7 12 11 10 09 08

THE EDGE

CHAPTER ONE

Towards three o'clock the wind that had tugged all night at the shutters became possessed of a demon. Connie Barton poked her husband in mid-snore and continued prodding until he growled in protest.

'Somethun's blown loose,' she muttered. 'Best see to't afore it gets torn off.'

Ned groaned but dutifully swung his feet to the floor. ' 'Taint none of our shutters,' he claimed, cocking his head to listen. Through the customary creaks and moans of the old farmhouse this dull thudding made an alien sound. 'It'll be Hoad's stable door. Nowt to do wi'us.'

All the same he knew he'd be allowed no rest until the thing was fixed. He lumbered downstairs, shrugged on his market-day overcoat and sat down to pull on his boots.

The stable stood midway between the two dwellings, both Hoad's properties — although the older farmhouse came with

Ned's job as livestock manager. He would have ignored this overnight demand, except that dry fodder stored in the stable touched on his cattle interest. But by Sod's Law he knew that the minute he'd fixed the slamming door and regained his bed's warmth there'd be a call to attend Red Rose's calving. Best take a look in the byre while he was at it, and check the baby alarm set up there so's he'd be sure to have notice of the beast's increased restlessness. Not that he'd likely hear her movements above the noise of the storm.

Stepping out into the gale activated the yard lights' sensor. They made a difference, these modern-day devices. What usually let you down now was human error, labourers not being the steady folk of his younger days. Some lazy bugger couldn't latch a door right on this occasion. And the Hoads were playing at gentry with their ears buried deep in their duvets, passing on the effort to some other poor sod. 'Meaning me,' he grumbled as he stumbled out, and the wind gusted the words back in his throat.

His thinning hair was whipped into a grey quiff. It was a wind to lean on. Overhead black tatters of cloud streaked over the moon's gibbous face, strobing cold light across the rooftops like a kids' disco. He'd been right about the stable. Not a single farmyard noise wasn't intimately distinguishable after the thirty-eight years of his working here.

The timber door, swollen with rain, became heavy and there were times it took a good shove to drive it home. But for five days until this night's cloudburst the weather had been dry with the wind rising to gale force. In the downpour someone just hadn't bothered with the bolts. With the battering the place was taking, he'd need to drop the bar across besides.

He looked around for it, decided it must be inside, propped against the wall. Only it wasn't. He reached for the light switch, found it already at ON, but the stable in darkness. More bad maintenance. Nobody bothered since the horses had gone. He tried the switch several times before blundering across to feel for the nearest hanging bulb. His hand met jagged edges of glass. He swore as his fingers came away sticky with blood.

There was a storm lantern on the work bench. At least nobody had removed the matches for their fags. Ned lit the lantern, raised the wick and turned to look for the heavy timber bar. That was when he saw the straw bales dragged into the shape of a

9

crescent and the woman stretched out on it like a heathen sacrifice. Naked but for a coarse dark net spread over her chest.

She had to be unconscious. Any sleepwalker would be wakened by that repeated thudding of the door. He felt a dull beat of shock but, his mind still full of concern for the heifer, he acted from habit, struggling to free himself of his overcoat. Unwilling to disturb her but fearful for hypothermia, he went across to cover her.

It wasn't a coarse net stretched over her upper body. The glistening, dark tracks were drying blood. The face — he had to look away — was mottled and distorted, the tongue protruding. He lifted his head, gulping suddenly for air at the sickly smell of the abattoir.

Connie, who had rapidly exchanged her nightdress for a tweed skirt and sweater, filled a large kettle for unlimited cups of tea. Routinely fixed to the familiar, she could barely take in what her husband had gabbled as he rushed in to dial from the kitchen. She noticed blankly that in shock he'd forgotten the new mobile phone in his coat pocket. For that matter, he'd lost his coat too.

'I'll have to wait there till the police come,'

he said. 'I've tried the Manor number but there's no reply. You'd best have another go. Hang on till they decide to answer.'

Connie stood petrified with the instrument in her hand. 'Someone dead? But who?' she asked in bewilderment. 'What'll I tell Mr Hoad? He'll want to know who's out there in his stable.'

It took thirteen minutes from phoning for the first police to turn up. They were uniformed constables in a motorway patrol car. On arriving, one stayed in the warmth of the driving seat, chewing. The other, burly and stolid, was sceptical. 'You say there's no proper light, sir. Maybe what you saw was a bundle of rags. Or some kids been making a guy for their bonfire on the fifth. You stay out here with my colleague, while I take a look with my torch.'

He took just seconds to confirm what Ned had claimed and return sickly outside. He moved away to use his car radio, but his voice was blown back to Ned. 'Body of a woman, Sergeant. Violent, yes. Starkers. You want Hoad's Manor Farm, Fordham. Take the A413 to Bramall's roundabout then left and left again. There's a sign by the entrance. Got a picture of a cow on it.'

He listened for instructions, grunted ac-

11

knowledgement and returned with the driver. 'I'm to stay and guard the site. You'd both better get inside out of this gale.'

There was no more rest to be had that night with all the comings and goings. A white Land Rover and two unmarked cars brought more police, followed by the van with all their scientific paraphernalia and white-overalled Scenes of Crime Officers.

Connie had eventually abandoned the phone. 'Their line's gone dead,' she explained. 'It'll be the wind, see.' But when Ned offered to walk over to the Hoads' house and let them know, he was prevented.

'Sound sleepers are they?' a plain-clothes sergeant enquired dryly. He had a point. Even if the gale and the banging stable door hadn't roused them, the alien invasion of flashing blue lights must have done.

'Maybe they're away?' The man's round, blue eyes seemed to be probing him. He had a flat, puppet's face with a sharp, questing nose; made Ned think of that Pinocchio cartoon by Disney.

'They'd have let me know,' Ned assured the detective. 'Would've left instructions, see?'

Shortly after that the centre of interest moved from stable to Manor house. That was when finally the idea reached the Bartons that the body wasn't some travelling woman's, but someone they knew well enough. After the final vans and most police cars had left, a burly middle-aged detective arrived and reluctantly broke the full news to them. His craggy face was sombre.

'There's been a tragedy up at the house,' he said shortly. It seemed to have shaken even him.

'A killing. Counting the one in the stable, there's four of them altogether.'

By now some news of that kind was inescapable. Barton closed his eyes. 'The Hoads.'

'Four? Oh no! Not the kiddies too!' Connie whispered.

He nodded. 'So. It means that we'll need your help to fill us in on the family. But get some rest for now and I'll be back to talk to you about eleven.' He looked at his watch. 'That gives you just four hours. I must insist you don't get in touch with anyone outside for the moment.'

'Rest?' Barton queried bitterly. 'I've got my beasts to see to. Byre man's overdue and milking should be starting. There'll be no time for tattling.' He plunged out of the house, a leather jacket protecting his head against sleeting rain that dropped like a steel shutter.

■ ■ ■ ■

A crime of such enormity couldn't stay long under wraps. By midday increased activity at the morgue entrance alerted hospital staff. Phones buzzed. The press started to gather, roistering for details.

Earlier, Superintendent Mike Yeadings had been roused from his bed by his sergeant's call, and he informed him he'd attend in person. He drank his coffee scalding at the kitchen door, staring through darkness at the wrecked garden. Trees leant over the lawn littered with broken branches. The last brave October roses were stripped from the pergola and flower borders looked trampled in a stampede.

A demon night. And other demons had been let loose on human lives: the slaughter of an entire family as they slept. Or two slept, one vainly defended and one fled, half-naked, into the wild dark.

Major crime was his everyday concern, and violent death a part of it. But in Thames Valley, the UK's largest provincial force, murder made up a moderate statistic. Twenty-eight cases, he reckoned, in a bad year. But now — four in a night, and two of them children. A bloody massacre: surely the work of a madman.

He nodded to his wife who stood silent, understanding, walked blindly past his own two children, collected coat, car keys, and left with his head down, too conscious of little Sally in her nightdress staring out at the chaos of their garden, her blunt, puppyish Down's Syndrome face gone square with the effort not to cry. He wanted to stay on, help her stake up the battered dahlias, show her that disasters could be lived through, overcome. Up to a point.

What he found at Hoad's Manor Farm denied this. And it had been left to him to break the full horror to the Barton couple, standing stricken in their cottage, trying to believe that normal life could go on from where it was yesterday.

He looked at his watch, nodded to them, arranged to return after eleven.

The team was to meet at 8.50 a.m. Grim-faced, Yeadings went out again, into a drenched morning still streaked with the crimson of a bloody dawn.

CHAPTER TWO

A provisional murder team had been assembled from the Major Crimes Unit and CID of the local Area, where an Incident Room was already being furnished with a full complement of computers and office equipment. A whiteboard covered one long wall, to which an Ordnance Survey map, together with local press photographs of Fordham Manor Farm and the Hoad parents, had been affixed with Blu-tack. The assembled officers perched on desks and shared chairs or leaned against the farther wall, waiting to be tasked.

The dead had been named as Frederick Arthur and Jennifer Suzanne Hoad; their children simply as Daniel and Angela. The anomaly came to light as soon as the inquiry opened, because both murdered children were girls.

They had been killed sleeping side by side in twin beds; one dark-haired, the other blonde. Both were aged ten or eleven. Two sets of almost identical school uniform, scarlet and grey, were found hanging in the nearby wardrobe, and the clothes laid out for Saturday morning were equally uniform, being designer-label jeans, trainers, T-shirts and black fleeces.

Daniel, the son, was thought to be almost sixteen, tall, fair, willowy and said to look several years older. This description had been gathered from the Bartons. The boy was clearly missing from the house. Some weekends he was known to go camping.

The more solid little girl with thick blonde plaits had yet to be accounted for. Somewhere there were parents who still believed their young daughter was happily sleeping over for the weekend with her school-friend. They had to be found before news broke of the carnage at the Manor house.

Yeadings had phoned through to the SOCO team himself ordering an urgent search of the child's belongings. He nodded for DS Beaumont to continue his assessment of the murder scene.

'The boy's absence,' Beaumont said, visibly uneasy. 'Does that make him a suspect? He could have had access to the gun cabinet.'

'We keep open minds,' Yeadings told him.

'In any case he qualifies for Victim Support. We badly need to find him. Now let's get on to the time and circumstances of the crime.'

'Well before 3 a.m.' Beaumont said. 'That's when the thudding of the stable door got on Mrs Barton's nerves. It woke her some minutes before her attempt to rouse her husband. Apparently he sleeps more soundly and snores down opposition. When he did reach the first body, that of Mrs Hoad in the stable, blood from her stab wounds had had time to start congealing. Any wet smears found since then would have come from Barton's own hand, cut when he reached to the broken light bulb.

'Prof Littlejohn's up in Newcastle at a conference, but this case is spectacular enough to bring him back. He's flying into Heathrow tonight; post-mortem provisionally set for 4.30 p.m. tomorrow, Sunday. Until he gives us a lead we have no earliest time slot for the killings.'

'It has to be before the gale became so destructive,' Yeadings agreed. 'Otherwise the storm would have woken the children. There were broken roof tiles on the terrace under their window.'

'Some kids could sleep through Armageddon,' Beaumont countered. 'The parents' double bed was disturbed, with both pillows creased, so they'd retired for the night and then got up for some reason. Perhaps on account of the rising storm, or because there was an unexpected visitor.'

'There were no signs of a break-in,' DC Silver considered, 'so, unless Hoad let him in, maybe their killer was in the house as a guest, and he stayed up waiting for an opportunity to strike.'

'If so, he was cool-headed enough to remove his belongings before leaving. And no extra bed had been used,' Yeadings said. 'Whoever frantically chased Jennifer Hoad across the farmyard would hardly go back to clear his stuff away.'

'He spared time enough to rig a touch of theatre in the stable,' Beaumont reminded him. 'The straw bales had been dragged into a semicircle in the tack room and the woman displayed on top. That wasn't how Barton said he'd seen the place earlier.'

'Do we know yet if she was raped?' DS Rosemary Zyczynski asked in a low voice.

Yeadings hesitated. 'Dr Marlowe has reserved judgment on that. We'll have to wait for what the Prof finds tomorrow.'

There was an interruption as copies of the first crime scene photographs arrived and were handed around. A further set was pinned to the whiteboard alongside the family's particulars. The detailed horror made a shocked silence fall over the whole room.

'Something we still badly need is a likeness of the missing son,' Yeadings complained. 'Z, I want you to go back and join the SOCO team. See what you can turn up on that. Don't hurry back.'

For a moment she suspected he was blocking her out of some present action. Not that visiting the crime scene would pander to any imagined feminine frailty. No, she quickly decided, he simply meant her to catch up on the scene which the others had already observed.

Yeadings eyed her evenly. 'If you do find what we need in time, rejoin us for the next briefing.'

He looked round at the others. 'Right. Well, unless anyone wants to add anything, you'd better go your designated ways. After I've seen the Bartons again, mine is to interview the press. It seems the PR office is suffering a fit of the vapours. Regional Crimes will meet up with this augmented murder team at 3 p.m. when the Incident Room's fully prepared. Everyone reports then to Sergeant Wally Pierce as Office Manager.'

The meeting broke up. Yeadings was aware of Beaumont hovering, sleekly alerted and wearing his star-pupil expression. But he wasn't going to be awarded any gold stars for the moment. He clearly imagined that Z had been sidelined for him to receive an accolade discreetly.

Shuffling his papers, Yeadings waited for his tactful cough of reminder. When it came he looked up as if suddenly recalling the present. 'Oh, yes. The AC Personnel has confirmed DI Salmon's to stay on indefinitely. When he gets back from leave he'll be running the case as temporary DCI under me as Senior Investigating Officer.'

With that the DS would have to be satisfied. 'Ah, Beaumont,' said Yeadings, as if throwing a disgruntled dog a bone, 'I'll take you along, to talk to the Bartons.'

Rain was still sheeting down as they found Connie Barton scrubbing carrots in the kitchen sink. She hadn't forgotten their intended visit. In the dining room freshly baked scones topped with cream and raspberry jam, plus a tea-set of exuberantly floral bone china, were set out on a stiffly starched tablecloth. It struck Yeadings as almost indecent to make such an occasion of it. And yet he understood the woman's

21

need for some sense of decent normality.

'I'll jest call my husband,' she offered, went out into the still boisterous wind and applied herself energetically to the brass ship's-bell that hung in the porch. 'He's heard it,' she shouted as a distant double blast on a whistle replied.

'You probably reckernised it's a police one,' she said proudly. 'My Uncle Charlie was a copper up in Nottingham and he left it to me. Better than running up an almighty bill with them mobile phones.'

They heard Barton arrive at the back door, then splashings in the scullery's ceramic sink, followed by the wooden rumble of a roller towel. He joined them scarlet-faced. 'How'd it go then?' his wife asked.

'Fine. A healthy little heifer calf, pretty as her mother. And Red Rose made a good job of it, so she did.'

'There, then,' said Connie. 'I knew she'd be a breeder. Still, that's not what these gen'elmen came to hear about. We have to tell them what we know about the folks up at the house.'

Beaumont produced a pocket tape-recorder and found a place for it next to the scones. 'We'd like to use this, if that's acceptable,' Yeadings said, seeing the man's suspicious glance at it. 'It saves my sergeant having to take notes.'

Connie smiled confidently, hefting the heavy teapot. 'We're used enough to them things. Send messages that way to our grandchildren in New Zealand. Their Mum died last winter of leukaemia, so we make sure to keep in touch regular.'

It was clear to Yeadings that, shocking as news of the murder had been, this couple were accustomed to take life and death as a part of the expected. And as they explained how things were — they the real husbandmen while the owners regarded the herd as an investment or tax-deductible statistic — it appeared that beyond a normal countryman's deference for the 'gaffer', Ned Barton held no great opinion of the adult Hoads personally. Indeed, he and Connie seemed to have had more contact with the younger members of the family.

'Would you happen to know if young Angela had a special friend at school?' Beaumont probed cautiously.

'Not one special one,' Connie doubted. 'She'd invite a whole crowd over at once. They were great people for parties, the Hoads. A real worry it was to Ned when the kiddies all came flocking down and wanting to pet the animals. Most of them were town-

23

ies, wouldn't know a bull snaffle from a sprig o' cow parsley. We were always scared they'd get up to mischief and hurt theirselves.'

'Angela had a friend staying overnight,' Yeadings told them. 'Rather plump, with thick blonde plaits. Her school clothes had name-tapes sewn in: Monica and the initial J. Would you happen to know her surname?'

'Oh, that little girl. Yes, that's just what her name was. Jay, see. Like that screechy bird. Her dad's a lawyer up in London,' Ned helped out. 'They got a big place over at Ashridge. Her mother plays at farming, like the Hoads; only her herd's not a patch on ours. Mostly Friesians, see. Bulk producers, not quality like English Shorthorns and Channel Islands.'

Beaumont shot to his feet and left the room, reaching for his mobile phone. Slower to grasp the import of what Yeadings had said, Connie could barely wait for her husband to finish his derogatory comments. 'D'you mean there was this other little girl up there last night?' she asked, aghast. 'You said earlier on that there were just four killed.'

Yeadings nodded. 'So there were. At first we took Monica Jay for one of the family. It made four because the son was absent.

24

Would you have any idea where Daniel might be?'

There was an instant of horrified silence. 'Oh, Lor'!' Connie cried in anguish. 'What a terrible thing for him to do!'

So she'd jumped to the same snap assumption as Beaumont. It was odds on that the press would do the same. Under tomorrow's screaming headlines they could twist it deviously into libel-limit suggestion.

'He never done it,' Ned declared scornfully. 'Too much of a milksop.'

'We've certainly found nothing yet to make us think he did,' Yeadings warned, looking up as Beaumont returned. He passed to him the further information about the Jays, but his sergeant nodded as if he already knew.

'Did you ever meet Monica's parents?' Yeadings asked Ned.

'Took them around with a lotta visitors the first time. There was a party up at Hoads' and they came down, wanted to see the milking parlour. After that, Mr Jay always made a point of talking output to me.' Now Ned was certainly curling his lip.

'Bit of a bluffer?' Beaumont suggested.

'Not real country folk. Incomers, see?'

Both detectives saw. They'd met his kind: part of the Home Counties influx of busi-

25

nessmen playing at being squire: property developers, bankers, politicians.

Ned reached out a horny claw for a second scone. 'These are all right, Mother.'

Already, Yeadings thought, they were beginning to assimilate what had happened, seeing it as an event, however horrific, in a series dogging their efforts to get by. He guessed life hadn't been easy for them, and he appreciated that the Hoads — at least the adults of the family — might not have been their favourite people.

'So what will happen to the farm now?' Yeadings asked.

'We're still here, so it goes on working, and them going won't make no difference. Another lot'll come along to buy. Might even get somebody knows a bit about cattle for a change.'

He sniffed, ignoring Connie's murmured warning about respect for the dead. A practical man, he clearly hadn't had a lot of it for Frederick Hoad alive.

DI Salmon had materialised, suitably chuffed at his temporary promotion. At 2.30 p.m. the nuclear team re-assembled in Yeadings' office, less Z, sent to obtain a photograph of the Hoads' missing son. When they were seated the Boss surveyed

26

them grimly.

'Except for Acting-DCI Salmon, you've all been through the farmhouse, so you know the layout. I want you to see it happen. How was it? How many involved? — a single frenzied attacker assaulting the parents, killing the father, then the children before they could wake? Or more than one killer, fanning out to work room to room? And the woman escaping, running barefoot through the yard. Who pursued her, stabbed and mutilated her body? Possibly raped her, then left her displayed like a sacrificial victim on an altar? What kind of mentality was that?'

Salmon wasn't sure the superintendent was dealing with this in the best way. OK, so it was a massacre and the woman's death was overkill. It had knocked them all of a heap, but visualising the crime could clutter you up with a lot of wrong impressions. It was bald facts that counted, material evidence that would bring the villains finally to book. He harrumphed deep in his throat and the Boss's eyes swivelled on to him.

'If he did rape her . . .' Salmon began.

'We'll hope for DNA. There's one thing not to be known outside this office: even if he didn't penetrate the body himself, it appears he used a broom handle.' Yeadings was being atypically crude. 'Then surely he'd have masturbated. Traces on his hands. He'd have touched other surfaces. But we can leave that to SOCO.'

His face was grey, locked into grim lines. 'I don't need to say that catching this monster must be given greatest priority. A family at home, wiped out, overnight, in a matter of minutes.'

'And a little girl visiting,' DC Silver added in a low voice. 'Where does she fit in? Did the killer or killers know she didn't belong? Did they even look to see who it was?'

'That's important,' Beaumont put in. 'How intimately was the Hoad family known beforehand? Was it planned, or a random break-in? Would the killer know by now that one of the family had escaped? Sir, what are we doing about the missing son?'

'Enquiries are being made with neighbours and through his school,' Yeadings said tightly. 'Something should soon be coming in on that.' He looked at his watch. 'Time we met up with the extended team,' he warned.

They made their way down to the Incident Room. It was already crowded, with uniform and plain-clothes officers seated at tables and on windowsills. Latecomers had filed in to stand propped against the walls or sit cross-legged on the ground. When the conversational buzz ceased, Yeadings resumed, his voice depersonalised.

'Exit Wounds: a firearms subject you should be familiar with. On entering a human body, the bullet creates a neat round hole, like a mouth's small O of surprise. Once inside, the ravages begin, splintering bone, ripping cartilage, pulverising soft tissue. When it emerges from the body's denser pressure there's an explosion into open air, so the surrounding damage is extensive. Exit wounds look mightily more severe than what happened at the start.'

Yeadings paused, looking round. None of that was news to the extended team. But he'd a specific point to make about this massacre of apparent innocents.

'What we found at Fordham Manor Farm,' he went on, 'horrific as it is, should be seen as a single, extensive exit wound. Faced with that, we must work back to the point of entry, which eventually may prove far less momentous by contrast. And finally our objective must be to discover the first cause and the motive. Bear in mind that in any fatality the killer is the person, not the weapon.'

He was aware of a slight, restless movement in mid-room; the tensing of shoulders in barely smothered protest that he was making a lecture of it.

'I know that this is only partially a firearms case. The principal weapon was a knife, possibly knives. But the image remains true. Overall, we work backwards from exit wound to entry, all the way from massacre to intent.

'I do not need to remind you that in so complex an investigation no clue, no physical trace, no word of mouth, no implication is too minor to be disregarded. Search, expecting to find. Then consider whatever is found, however insignificant at first sight. Each of you has an individual angle on it; the next man a different one, so share your knowledge. Pass it on, include it in your report. All investigation is a mosaic.

'You are all, or at some time were, family men. This is a family destroyed. We cannot leave it — un . . .' For a split second his voice faltered.

Unavenged? Beaumont asked himself.

But after his burst of metaphor the Boss saw fit to rein in emotion at the last. 'Unsettled,' he said firmly.

Beaumont grunted aloud. So that's what they were to do — simply settle the matter.

Put it right? Could anyone?

CHAPTER THREE

DS Rosemary Zyczynski parked her blue Ford Escort sufficiently far from the house to allow her time to study it while she approached the front door on foot.

Amsterdam without a canal, she thought, confronted by the flat façade with its three gables, the central one fiddle-shaped and the outer two stepped. Maybe back in the seventeenth century someone had brought an architect over from the Netherlands.

At a later date an extension had been added to each end, and their horizontal rooflines balustraded.

She saw now that the Bartons' cottage, built of dark red brick and flint, typical of Buckinghamshire, had been the original farmhouse from the late sixteenth century. At some later point prosperity had struck, prompting the landowner to aspire to building a more impressive residence. Which this certainly was, deservedly a small manor house, the lordship to which its sometime owner had bought to match it, but ridiculously carried it away to a town house in Maidenhead. Since the incomer Hoad hadn't acquired those manorial rights, he'd been accepted locally as a gentleman farmer.

According to more of what Beaumont had picked up, he was actually a townie with an inherited fortune from manufacturing, and modest pretensions to joining county society. But now, whatever dubious glory the move had brought him was over. As the familiar words had it, he'd brought nothing into the world and taken nothing out. But there could have been a more merciful way of going.

She halted on the threshold, acknowledging the nod of the constable on duty, and rebuked herself for the disdainful attitude. She was herself a townie gone countrified from choice, and no matter what the dead man had been like, she knew her uncustomary bile was to cover up revulsion at the crime.

No bodies remained in the building, but chalk marks on the floor downstairs and the children's bloodied beds would be reminder enough of the Incident Room's first sickening photographs of slaughter. What she must investigate now was something too pitiable to be easily endured.

She stepped inside, zipped herself into sterile white overalls, pulled on plastic overshoes and latex gloves. Someone looked out from the door of an inside room and she recognised Ken Bates, a civilian photographer from Scenes of Crime. 'Still here then,' she remarked.

'If ever we get one right it has to be this one,' he said grimly. 'We're going for every minute detail. Sam's still upstairs bagging. Sing out before you go up and he'll tell you where you can tread.'

Rightly he'd assumed that her main interest was the children's rooms. Which didn't mean she'd spare herself the immediate death scene he was presently occupied with. She followed him back into the dining room, hands clasped behind to prevent touching any surface.

There it was total disarray with an overturned chair and the table crammed into a corner against a china cabinet with shattered glass doors. Behind them the once-elegant dinner and tea services were decimated and the rear wall spattered with shot.

Beyond a tall window was a second cupboard of the same style, or at least superficially so. It appeared to have been used for glassware displayed on shallow shelves backed by a mirror. But that entire portion had been swung out to show a steel cabinet behind. This in turn gaped to reveal a range of shotguns and rifles. Two sets of grips were empty.

One of the missing firearms, a double-barrelled, side-by-side twelve-bore, lay a few paces ahead of her, beside the outline of a body drawn in chalk on the polished floorboards. There was the distinct bloody tread of a shoe's toecap alongside. But no great quantity of blood, considering the number of wounds.

Z stood a moment taking it in. There was a storyline here but she needed to work out the sequence. Ken Bates resumed his work, focusing on the rubbed marks of wear on the cabinet wall behind where the guns were missing.

Z tried to get the picture. Hoad had run to defend his family with the gun and, being tackled to the ground, had somehow discharged its shot into the wall and china cabinet. The man confronted by the shotgun had then stabbed him several times, using a knife as on his upstairs victims, but at some point he too could have removed the second firearm missing from the cabinet. There was an immediate need to identify the gun taken away.

'What actually killed Hoad?' she demanded.

'Didn't you get the pics I took?'

'There was too much blood to distinguish every wound. And the Boss won't pre-guess the Prof's official findings.'

'Whatever else, there are plenty of stab wounds. He was lying face-up. Could have been blown backwards by a single shot, and then stabbed to finish him off. There was what could be a small entry wound in the chest. I never touched the body, and couldn't say for sure. If a bullet's left inside him you'll discover later at the post-mortem. Anyway nothing passed through; no bullet was found in the floorboards or walls.'

So, accepting Ken Bates's guesswork, the killer used a different firearm from the dead man's shotgun, because a spread of lead shot would surely have shown over chest or face.

If so, how did Hoad's killer get hold of the gun? Bring it with him or locate and unlock the steel cabinet before Hoad reached him? Unlikely. So perhaps he'd brought only the knife, hid away, then snatched a gun after Hoad had opened the steel cabinet. But one ready loaded? The ammo should have been securely kept elsewhere. Yet, if he'd been the first to fire, that would account for Hoad's shot going wide.

Later, had he chased the fleeing woman across to the barn with the same gun, but feared a shot in the open could rouse neighbours in the cottage? Or had he pursued and knifed her before remembering the unlocked armoury and coming back for the second, missing weapon? Doubly armed, he would be doubly dangerous.

As yet it wasn't clear at what point Hoad had been alerted and come downstairs. Before or after the others had been stabbed to death?

'Has any knife turned up?' she asked.

'Not to my knowledge. Best ask Sam.'

She gave the murder room another sweeping scan, then went to the foot of the stairs. 'Sam!' she called.

Bernard Weller, known generally as Sam, appeared almost instantly on the gallery above the hall. He too was now a civvy SOCO, an ex-sergeant from the force. 'Z, hi. Come on up,' he invited. 'Use the left side of the stairs where it's taped.'

She followed him down a short corridor to the large front bedroom where the duvet was flung back from the four-poster. One casement window was latched open and a rain-drenched curtain dragged aside. The central heating was full on. An open door revealed the en suite bathroom. The only lighting, apart from the SOCO's powerful torch came from one twin bedside reading lamp, the other of which was overturned. Weller saw her eyes swing to that, but he shook his head. 'The killer never did that. The woman must have knocked it over as she rushed out.'

'How do you know?'

'It's clean. There are blood smears from gloved hands along the gallery rail outside and lint from the woman's bathrobe caught on a picture frame where she pressed against it. She must have run out, got caught, broke free, perhaps kneed the killer, and was lucky to gain a few minutes and make for the stairs. Too bad that her luck ran out in the end.'

So probably she'd not been the first one attacked. But why run to the stables? Z wondered. To draw danger away from the children? Why not make straight for the farm cottage and protection from the Bartons?

'The girls' bedroom?' she demanded.

He nodded back towards the passage. 'Next one. You passed it. We've finished in there. You're free to look around. The brother's room is off the opposite wing, far door on the right.'

She went there next, putting off the worse option. She found everything normal, as untidy as any teenage boy would leave a room: magazines spilling from a chair, an old pullover slung over its back, and used underwear on the floor beside the bed. The door gaped open on his own bathroom where two dark green towels were abandoned on the tiles. Both had dried out and the smaller one showed smears of blood. Nothing excessive. A big lad of nearly sixteen, he could have nicked himself shaving.

Nobody had been in to tidy up after he'd left. And no clue to when that might have been.

Without touching them she read the titles on two of the magazines. One dealt with Information Technology. The other, more fingered, was a catalogue for camping equipment.

If he'd spent the previous night under canvas as intended he'd have had little sleep because of the storm. Maybe he was catching up with it now and would eventually return in a bedraggled state.

But, camping, he'd surely have been with

others in an organised group. There would be friends with him. A scout troop or boys from his school. Enquiries the Boss had already set in motion should turn up the necessary information.

She bypassed the bookshelves. That would require longer examination. On first sight they appeared to cover two interests: schoolwork and adventure fiction. She turned to look at the bed. There was an impression where a weight had stood on the feather duvet. Almost circular; perhaps a long, draw-top bag like the sort service men stowed their kit in?

The double doors of the wardrobe stood ajar. When she pushed at them they resisted closure. Inside there was a gap in the row of hangers on a rail and a confusion of shoes and boots on the floor. From a shelf above her head a leather travel case projected with a strap hanging down as if pulled forward when some other object was dragged from on top.

It all pointed to the boy, Daniel, having packed hand luggage before he left. But there was nothing to show whether his departure had been as previously planned, or if it was some spur-of-the-moment decision. In the three drawers of a tallboy clean clothes appeared undisturbed. She slid her hands in underneath but encountered no surprises, no papers or stash of cash.

He'd have needed both money and food, Z thought. A clue to what he'd taken must be looked for downstairs. She went down again, carefully keeping to the same side and not touching the banister rail. In the kitchen she put a tea towel over her fingers to open the refrigerator, not trusting the latex gloves to leave traces undisturbed. It was amply stocked, giving no indication of what could have been removed.

Somewhere in the house there would be a safe. She followed the sounds of Ken Bates's movements and found him in a smaller room furnished as an office. 'Have you come across a safe yet?' she asked.

He shook his head. 'Not all the walls have been checked yet. But it may be one of those under-floor ones. We're not touching the carpets until the rest of the team's arrived. So far there's just us finalising photo shots and bagging. Fingerprints are on hold until we're done. Your boss is a devil for preserving the scene.'

She went through to the long, low-ceilinged drawing-room. The keyboard of a Broadwood grand piano stood open for playing: no display of photos on the top. And none on the walls. But inside the boxy piano stool was a photograph album. She turned to the latest full page and removed a studio portrait of a blond, fine-featured young man she'd have taken for twenty years old. This, she guessed, was the son, almost sixteen, said to look older than his years. The slender, pale face and light eyes were the same as those in earlier photographs from toddler years on. His longish fair hair flopped over one eyebrow like a matinée idol's.

She slid the card into her shoulder bag. This was all she'd been asked for. The rest of the tour was a bonus.

And still she hadn't seen where the little girls had been stabbed to death in their sleep. Stoically she went back upstairs, observed the room, the bloodied sheets; then returned sombrely to her car.

At the Area nick she passed the boy's portrait in for photocopying and made her way to where Acting-DCI Salmon was still holding the floor, summing up Beaumont's presentation.

'Right then: approach and entry. Due to torrential rain overnight and the presence of our own vehicles, it's not been possible to identify any form of transport for the killer. But an approach on foot's unlikely, since the property is a quarter of a mile from the road, whether by driveway or through fenced fields and spinney. Both Hoad cars, BMW & Vauxhall Zafira, were found in a double garage, radiators cold. An elderly Jeep 4x4 in a converted stable had its rear fully loaded with fencing stakes, reels of wire, tools etc. According to the stockman, Ned Barton, whose cottage is nearby on the estate, it was ready for starting boundary work on Monday.

'Entry was not forced. The night caller either had a key or was let in by a member of the family.'

A hand shot up. 'Couldn't he have hidden inside during the day while the house was left open?'

Salmon looked to Beaumont for a lead. 'The building has plenty of rooms not normally in use,' the DS offered, 'particularly on the top, servants' floor. There's a live-in housekeeper, who was away for the weekend. Other servants, cleaners and so on, come in daily as required.'

He advanced on the easel covered in sheets of newsprint and drew an oblong in black felt pen. 'The original house is three hundred years old, facing south-west, with three Dutch gables at the front and later

A) Ground floor

Drawing-room with conservatory extension	Morning room	Entrance hall and stairs	Dining room	Study/office
TV and recreation room	Shower and cloakroom	Gun room	Domestic offices/utilities	

B) First floor

Master bedroom	Daughter's twinned bedroom	Gallery	First guest suite	Second guest suite
	SE corridor		NW corridor	Door/stairs
Bath and sauna	Wardrobe/ dressing room	Land-ing	Guest bathroom	Son's bedroom
			Son's bathroom	

C) Top floor

Two unused staff dormitories, housekeeper's suite, bathroom, darkroom, laundry, box room

extensions at each end. There are three floors.'

He drew in the rooms for each, naming them as he did so. Several officers in the elbow-to-elbow crowded room juggled with paper and pen, trying to keep up.

Yeadings nodded. Beaumont had acquitted himself well, now scowling impatiently while his audience's muttering covered efforts to reproduce his freehand sketch. In retrieving a dropped pencil one constable slid off the edge of a shared seat. A muted cheer from others at the back faltered and was covered by the shuffling of heavy patrol boots.

Yeadings shared their sense of awkwardness. Even for the most case-hardened this

43

investigation was nearly off the known scale. Little wonder the newer elements weren't at ease. He had trouble himself in confronting the callous and wholesale nature of the crime. For the present, emphasis would be on material evidence. Later, pressure must get worse as, with probing, the victims began to emerge as living, breathing souls. Some of the younger officers would resort to graveyard humour to get them through it.

'A restricted number of copies of this plan are for internal circulation only. Any leak to the press will be dealt with seriously,' Beaumont continued, grinding away.

M'm, Yeadings observed: a new ring of authority there. Did the DS have the energising scent of promotion in his nostrils? With Salmon's temporary shift to DCI, the need to replace a DI in Serious Crimes was more pressing. And overdue. So, would it fall to Beaumont or Rosemary Zyczynski? Both sergeants deserved it, were equally qualified, but he'd never get to keep either in his team once promoted to inspector.

He looked across to the door where Z had squeezed in as a latecomer. She caught his raised eyebrows and nodded back. Good, he thought. If the boy stayed missing, and nothing came of enquiries already under

44

way, that photograph would have to be publicised. Risky, though, if the boy's survival left him at risk of a similar fate. Also tabloid press zest for the horrific could suggest guilty involvement, and only God knew what trouble that could bring on. Best wait a few hours more. Whether he proved a suspect or under threat himself, Daniel Hoad's whereabouts would be safer handled discreetly.

Salmon left the room, leaving Beaumont penned in by volunteers eager for plain-clothes secondment. Yeadings cut a swathe through and found Z waiting outside. 'Daniel Hoad's photo is being copied,' she told him.

He nodded. 'Let's go and see if it's hit my desk yet.'

It hadn't, but he didn't appear put out, making straight for the coffee machine on his windowsill and spooning in sufficient grounds for four. It had barely begun its gentle burbling when a civilian clerk arrived with a box file of 8x10s.

Yeadings studied the shot. In seven-eighths view, Daniel appeared relaxed, eyes slightly amused, his maize-coloured hair longish but well-cut, falling in softly waved wings beside sculpted cheekbones. 'Arty pose,' he gave as his opinion. 'What do you make of him, Z?'

'As they said, he looks older than sixteen. Good-looking. Quite the golden boy. Nice smile.'

'A charmer's smile, and he knows it's a winner. He's going to need all that assurance when he learns what's happened at home.'

He turned back to the window. 'We've heard only one opinion on him as yet. Ned Barton wrote him off as a "milksop" — perhaps because he doesn't soil his hands like a farm worker. I guess at this lad's age Ned was earning a third of a grown man's wage and helping support his parents. There's more than a generation's gap between them. Also the difference of wealth and education. This young man could be more complex than Ned gives him credit for.'

'Is there news of him yet?'

'Only negative. The planned scout camp was wisely cancelled in advance of the storm, and the lads all dismissed an hour after they assembled. The scoutmaster interviewed suggested Daniel had gone home early with one of the other Explorer Scouts. He certainly wasn't there for roll-call. We're following up some addresses, to find out where he might have gone.'

Zyczynski slumped into a chair. 'But it's possible he did make for home. In which case, just what did he walk into? And where is he now?'

CHAPTER FOUR

Even without police cases, Professor Littlejohn was accustomed to multiple postmortems, due to the proximity of three motorways with the densest traffic flow in the South East. But this tragedy, a family group savagely slaughtered in their home, must give him special cause for pity. Yet the grey-bearded face bent over the first body showed no more than a frown of concentration, swiftly lightened by a gleam of curiosity.

He was taking them in order of age, the man first.

His assistant had shaved back the black, matted thatch of chest hair to reveal the long white scar of an incision for open heart surgery. 'He had that several years back,' Littlejohn decided. 'The pacemaker's a more recent job, quite a neat little Lucy Locket.'

Looking up, he caught Salmon's frown. 'Pocket, man! Use a little imagination.'

He wouldn't have been so brusque if the Boss had been there, Beaumont reflected. So Littlejohn, like Z and himself, wasn't particularly enamoured of the Acting DCI.

After the formal description of the body, he turned to the recent injuries.

'Aha! As suspected, we have the entry wound for a bullet under all that stabbing.' He inserted a fine steel tube into the wound.

'A single shot aimed at an angle, upwards through the ribcage to above the heart, then deflected and . . .' He probed. '. . . and finally lodged in the right clavicle.'

He removed a small bullet. Z recognised a .22.

Littlejohn was muttering into his beard. 'Interesting, that. One acknowledges, of course, the usual function of a pacemaker. But as a marksman's bull's eye, this is surely something else.'

'Dead, just the same,' Beaumont murmured.

'As you say. Certainly dead.' The pathologist's keen hearing had picked up the aside. 'The pacemaker's destruction would cause an immediate myocardial infarction. Since the single .22 bullet had been sufficient to kill him, the stabbings were mere ornamentation. Yes, comparatively little blood loss after the initial spurt, but sufficient to disguise the bullet's entry point.'

He squinted over his half-moon spectacles in Salmon's direction. 'As well as the number of knife wounds, you will be wanting the precise angle of the lethal trajectory. And that will be interesting, because the victim is by no means a tall man. Five feet five inches, as my assistant has informed us.'

He beamed at the group of CID officers. 'It may make your task easier if among your suspects is a pygmy.'

'Couch potatoes are commoner,' Beaumont suggested. 'Though murder's not a job to take on lying down.'

Zyczynski transferred her weight from one foot to the other. She could do without these tasteless quips. For distraction she moved a few paces away and turned her attention to the next body awaiting examination.

Jennifer Hoad, some three or four inches taller than her husband, had been of a slim build and long-boned; a classic fashion-model type. Agony had cruelly distorted a once-lovely face. She had long, shapely limbs and shoulder-length gold-blonde hair. Over torso and abdomen the network of blood had congealed in rivulets and pools in the hollows of clavicles and waist. She had been stabbed several times, probably while still standing, and again as she continued to bleed, lying on the straw bales, still alive. Not granted a quick death.

Z studied her face, the single vertical line chiselled between straight brows, the strong chin and jaw-line. This was a woman who had known her own mind and stood by it, authoritative and challenging. So what had drawn her into marriage with the small, dried-out, almost reptilian man who, more than anything, had reminded Z of a crouched brown toad? Yes, 'Toad', not Hoad, was probably the name other boys had called him at school.

Perhaps, alive, he'd had some special magnetism. A mellifluous voice? Great kindness? Whatever it had been, it was gone now and had left no record behind on his face. Not humour, she decided. Those heavy, dark-skinned features were never built for mirth. And Jennifer — what had made her smile? What sort of things could these two have laughed over together? In death it was unimaginable.

Z moved slowly on to the two smaller figures, but she found them less disturbing than she'd feared, so peacefully asleep, a white sheet drawn up to their shoulders, covering any injuries. Two school-friends as unalike as the two adults had been. The smaller one, Angela Hoad, was dark like her father, but had none of his heaviness. Instead she was elfin, in death the fine triangular face seeming almost to wear a puckish smile. The other child was harder to read, physically more developed but perhaps less aware of the world. In the way that children were drawn to each other at that age, she could have been the follower, a little slower, allowing the other to lead, perhaps cautioning when the Hoad child dared too far.

All of which supposition could be utterly wrong, Z warned herself; and went back to check on Littlejohn's progress.

The flesh had been given the Y-shaped main incision, the sternum was sawn through and the ribs opened out. Littlejohn removed the pacemaker in pieces, like a dismantled watch. There followed the ritual removal, examination, description and weighing of body parts, of little interest to the CID officers present, once the cause of death was established. But Salmon was impatient to know an estimated time of death.

He should have known better.

'That will be revealed in the written report, after due consideration of all aspects,' Littlejohn was pleased to pontificate. 'If you find your presence here wearisome, Acting-Detective-Chief-Inspector, do feel at liberty to return to more germane matters, or at least release your minions for that purpose. An initial exploration of the four cadavers will require at least a further two hours of my time.'

Salmon's down-turned mouth tightened. Z watched a scarlet flush spread up his bull-like neck. 'Beaumont, we can spare you,' he barked. 'Get back and see what's turned up.'

'Sir,' said the released DS with a nice balance of relief and distance.

Z watched him go with envy. For her the worst was surely yet to come.

Beaumont returned to base to catch Superintendent Yeadings, guiltily again at his coffeemaker. 'Should really stick to decaff,' he admitted, 'but who's to know?'

'Like the expert I've just come from?' his DS dared warn.

'God forbid . . .'

The internal phone on his desk interrupted them.

'Get that,' Yeadings ordered, waving a spoon in its direction.

'They're connecting me with Swindon,'

Beaumont murmured, the phone hugged between chin and chest while he reached across for a pen and paper. 'Yes, got that. Hang on, I'll ask him.

'Sir, they've traced the absent house-keeper, staying at her aunt's. Are they to break the news to her?'

'No. I warned them no action. This needs careful handling. I'll send Z down. You'd better get back to the post-mortem and relieve her. If Salmon objects, simply say "Women's work." He'll like that.'

My, my, Beaumont told himself, preparing to leave, our Acting DCI seems to have needled everyone.

Rosemary Zyczynski accepted her release without a flicker of expression. Out in the car park she punched a joyous fist in the air, remembered she was almost out of gas and pulled into the nearest service station for a refill.

The M4 was already buzzing with early rush-hour traffic, including heavy goods vehicles returning west and holding up streams of cars at the inevitable road works which that motorway seemed to spawn. Automatically she timed the journey and noted the trip-reading on arrival. Ninety-seven miles in an hour and forty-three minutes: not bad, considering.

Alma Pavitt's widowed aunt, Nora Bellinger, lived in a narrow, terraced house on the north side of the town centre. It was a typical Victorian development with a square, low-walled front garden barely large enough to hold an ancient bicycle, four slabs of paving stones and a few shrivelled survivals of autumn's chrysanthemums. The bike was a woman's, with a worn velvet pad to cushion the seat. A padlock and chain, attaching the machine to a staple fixed under the outer windowsill, was modest warning of the neighbourhood crime statistic.

It was the niece who opened to Z's knock. She leaned out to get the message with the door held close behind her, but failing to muffle the wailing of an older female voice from an inner room: 'Who is it, dear? I don't buy from travelling salesmen. You can't be too careful.'

'Sorry; what's that again? Did you say police?'

'Maybe I could come in and talk,' Z suggested, showing her warrant card.

Alma Pavitt examined it, appeared satisfied it was genuine, but looked slightly puzzled. 'Is something wrong? I hope there's not a gas leak and you're wanting Auntie to move out. She's got a badly broken leg.'

'No need to disturb her. Have you had trouble of that kind? Being evacuated, I mean.'

'A couple of months back there was a chemical fire and everyone had to leave for a couple of nights. She's still upset about it.'

'It's nothing to do with her, except that we really need you back at Fordham Manor. Is it possible for you to return with me?'

'I was due back there tonight, but I haven't yet found anyone to relieve me here. Auntie's quite helpless, you see. I rang the Manor to get extended leave, but the storm must have brought the lines down. Is there much damage?'

By now Z had eased the woman into a retreat to the kitchen, from where they could still hear reproachful complaints from the front room and an insistent banging on floorboards.

'You'd better sit down,' the DS advised. 'I'm afraid the news is really bad.'

Alma Pavitt listened in growing horror, clutching at her throat with both hands. 'Oh my God, that's awful. Awful. I can't believe . . .'

While she partially recovered, Z made tea. Women's work, she thought, echoing the unknown words Yeadings had sardonically used of perhaps the most hated job that befell the police.

'Universal panacea,' Alma Pavitt said wryly as she accepted her cup. 'Thank you. I'd better take Auntie's through and explain. She'll never keep quiet otherwise.' Already she was displaying her practical side. Well, it wasn't as though the Hoads were family.

She was away some ten minutes. The seesawing of voices, hers low, the other a protesting wail, came wordlessly through the partition wall. Z used the interval to phone the local social services and explain the position. Even before Alma Pavitt returned, Z's mobile rang and a male voice assured her someone was already on the way.

'I doubt we can cover the old lady's care at home,' he said, 'but we'll try and get her into a hostel where they'll take good care of her. You can leave it with us, Sergeant. What a terrible business at Fordham. We heard about it on the midday news.'

Apparently these two women had not. Z commented on that when Alma Pavitt came back.

'Auntie won't have the news on. Not since Iraq,' she said. 'I wasn't allowed to turn it on until *Neighbours*. She lives for that and *Coronation Street*.'

'I see.' Z explained about the arrangements social services were making.

'The old dear won't like it one bit. Not at first. But it's better than anything I could have fixed up. I'd better go and pack a bag for her. We'll leave telling her until someone arrives. Meanwhile, could you go and have a word with her? She'll want to know the far end of everything that happened at the Manor. I'm afraid, now she's over the first shock, she'll have quite a morbid relish for details.'

Zyczynski managed to confine herself to the outline permitted to the press and quickly passed on to enquire about the circumstances of the broken leg. Mrs Bellinger, by now delighted with her visitor, was even more keen to share her own experience: a fall from her bike, no less, almost under the wheels of a panting juggernaut.

'I might have been killed,' she said proudly. 'It happened Friday about teatime, when the first shower started and the roads were all slithery. There's nothing wrong with my bike, as I told them at the hospital. The doctor said I didn't ought to be still riding the thing at my age, but I'm pretty fit otherwise. Just a twinge or two of angina sometimes. Actually, more than riding, I mostly just push the bike and hang my shopping from the handlebars. It helps me get along. Only on Friday I was running late to go and pick up the laundry. Fridays they close early, you see.'

Z did, and stifled a sigh. 'You're lucky that your niece could drop everything and come to help.'

'Oh, it was already arranged. She was coming anyway. Providential, you might say. Got me straight out of that awful hospital once they'd set the leg and done me plaster.'

News that she was again to be moved on roused frantic protests, but these quietened on the arrival of a briskly assured woman who was to see to everything and offered transport in an ambulance-type van with an electrically operated rear loading ramp. Auntie was trundled out importantly in a wheelchair on loan from the Red Cross.

'Just you wait,' the comfortably plump woman confided to her. 'They're really going to spoil you when you get there.'

Alma Pavitt locked up the house and handed over the key. 'I'm sorry, Auntie, that I have to go. But you can see there's nothing else for it.'

They watched the van draw away, and Alma Pavitt turned with a grimace to Zyczynski. 'Now for the really grim bit. I'm ready to go, if you are.'

CHAPTER FIVE

'Did you drive down?' Zyczynski had asked while Alma Pavitt was collecting her things.

'I'd meant to, but the car had to go in for servicing. Nothing serious: the motor for the windscreen wipers suddenly went kaput. Imagine getting caught in that storm if I'd ploughed on without!'

'So perhaps you'd like a lift back?'

'I'd hoped you might offer.' Her grin was brilliant. A flash of very white teeth. 'I wasn't sure that was permitted, apart from carting off suspects.'

'There's no ban. And we even have moments when we think everyone's a suspect. It's my own car anyway. Such as it is.'

'What's wrong with it? Am I risking my life in accepting?' As she laughed, her voice rose and Zyczynski recognised the foreign lilt she'd caught before. The woman's English was almost perfect, or perhaps too perfect. Brits don't exercise all those facial muscles in talking.

They stowed her bag in the Ford's boot and Alma Pavitt took the passenger seat alongside Z. 'The car's sound enough,' the DS assured her, 'but sometimes I fancy something more upmarket, a touch of James Bond. It would make me feel I'm getting somewhere in the job.'

'I doubt he ever needed his ego reinforcing.' More laughter and a knowing flick of the head. The woman now seemed totally relaxed.

'They didn't tell me,' Z probed, 'if it's Miss or Mrs Pavitt.'

'Oh, either does. We're separated, Dennis and I. I could have gone back to my maiden name but nobody can pronounce it. I'm Hungarian by birth. Mother escaped with me in '56. I was only a toddler then.'

Which made her a good deal older than she looked. Her natural vivacity and careful make-up were deceptive. The black hair, braided and coiled stylishly over her crown, had no trace of grey in it. Her body was spare and lithe.

'I went to a provincial polytechnic, studied catering and while Mother was alive I worked in various London hotels, while she took rooms near wherever I was at the time. When she died I hadn't saved enough for a

61

home of my own, or not one that would appeal to my tastes. A bit like you are with your car, you see. So I decided to live in others' comfortable homes and leave the costs to them. I've been with the Hoads five years now. It's my sixth long-standing job.'

Again that lilting laugh and a little flick of the head. If she'd worn her hair loose she'd have been quite the siren.

'And somewhere along the way you married an Englishman.'

'Yes.' The gaiety left her. 'Are you married?'

'No.'

'Live with someone?'

'Not exactly.' Z was reluctant to open up. 'We have next-door flats,' she allowed. This was getting out of hand. The woman had actually started interrogating her! Z needed to get back on track. 'So how did you become housekeeper at Fordham Manor?'

'That was through my husband. Ex-husband. He heard of the vacancy and I just turned up on the doorstep. Mr Hoad was frantic for help, and his wife abroad at the time. You will probably hear everything about me anyway. Connie Barton delights in telling how I married her good-for-nothing nephew. What a loser! God knows where he is now. At sea perhaps or in jail.

He was not a serious person . . .'

The laughter died. Momentarily Alma became sombre herself. '. . . and fifteen years younger than me.' Her voice was bitter.

Well, if you take that sort of risk . . . Z told herself.

'It suited us both to go our separate ways, and I am comfortable enough with the Hoads. Or have been. But what happens now? Will Daniel stay on? Do I carry on looking after things there?'

Again the practical side had taken over. There appeared to be no sorrow, no regret. Not even horror, now that she was over the initial shock. Could she be so detached, as though what had happened was a story she'd finished reading, or a film she saw a week ago? When she encountered the reality back at Fordham Manor, would it strike her full-face? Would the collapse come then? For the present she was only concerned with her own immediate future.

'Who knows?' Z's tone was dry. 'Let's hope Mr Hoad's solicitor had some contingency instructions. I imagine he'll need to contact other family members, if there are any. Would you know about that?'

'No. Not the sort of thing they would share with me. No family ever visited, from either side.'

That seemed to give Alma Pavitt fresh cause for thought. Her animation subsided and she slumped in her seat, taking no interest in the scenery that flashed by. The earlier vivacity had disappeared, like a light switched off. But Z couldn't waste this unique opportunity to find out more about her passenger.

'So how does Mrs Bellinger of Swindon get to be your aunt?'

'She's no relation. Auntie's what we all called her when she was housekeeper at the Graythorpe Hotel. I went there as a young sous-chef after I took my City and Guilds in Catering. She sort of took to me, and recently I thought to look her up. Of course, by now she's a letter or two short of a game of Scrabble.'

But, blessed with a home, is useful to fall back on for a rest weekend, Z appreciated. Alma Pavitt had a way of employing available resources.

Acting-DCI Salmon admitted himself frazzled, but strictly to himself, since he was portentously conscious of the need to keep up appearances before the lower ranks. The post-mortems had drawn out long into the evening and he was continually reminded of his inadequate and rapidly swallowed lunch by a hollow rattle that punctuated Littlejohn's commentary on the two final bodies.

Both little girls had been in the best of health, the pathologist observed, apart, clearly, from being dead. Both his humour and Beaumont's were becoming blacker and more strained. Salmon summoned up the residue of a Methodist childhood to register silent disapproval.

Despite only a single deep stab wound to each, making cause of death indisputable, there was still all the dismal routine of dissection, removal and weighing of their healthy organs to be endured. And Professor Littlejohn appeared to be in no hurry to finish.

When eventually Salmon and his DS issued into pitch-dark and a flurry of windborne rain, neither was inclined to tarry over niceties of conversation. Beaumont's mobile phone warbled as he was halfway to his car. He snarled into it, recognising Z's voice reporting that she was at an inn-yard half an hour from base, and what did Salmon want her to do with the housekeeper?

'He'll need to interview her,' the DS claimed with vicious intent. That would go down like a pair of concrete boots with

Salmon after the prolonged session with the bodies. But why should the undeservedly promoted oaf be released from duty's shackles any earlier than he himself?

He shouted across the car park and waved vigorously. Salmon ploughed on through the rain, head lowered. Bull at a ruddy gate, Beaumont thought. Well, his own Toyota wasn't the bold crimson of a matador's cloak for nothing. Z's message should reach Salmon if it meant running him down in the process.

Her quoted half-hour had been understated because Alma Pavitt was determined to sample the inn's vaunted steak pie, where they'd stopped for a break. Meanwhile, Acting-DCI Salmon, equally fixated on the prospect of food, brushed off Beaumont's preference for a double Indian takeaway to be sent in, for fear of unseemly lingering scents. Instead he decreed ham sandwiches with chutney in the canteen. These had long been consumed when the two women turned up. Salmon, more than ready for bed, greeted their arrival with simmering rancour.

It surprised neither of his sergeants that the housekeeper's breezy confidence went down badly with him. Although Z was able to furnish a summary of what she had learnt from the woman on the journey back from Swindon, he insisted on questioning her minutely about her background (foreign, therefore dubious), relations with the Hoad family (claimed to be excellent, therefore suspicious) and private opinion of her employers (favourable, therefore most likely false).

She was required to write out her maiden surname, which Salmon found as contentious as Zyczynski's own, the date of her marriage, and details of the defaulting Dennis Pavitt. Alma repeated what she'd told Z about the reason for travelling to Swindon by train rather than in her own car. 'Wasn't it lucky I put it in for repair,' she said winningly, 'since that hellish storm was brewing up?'

Salmon declined to answer. Alma continued to flash him her wide, white-toothed smile. He demanded her house keys and reminded her that Fordham Manor was now a crime scene. She must put up elsewhere until such time as the police permitted reentry.

There he did succeed in disconcerting her. It seemed that the Bartons had begrudgingly agreed to take her for a few days at the old farmhouse, but Alma wasn't having any. 'Not in that hovel,' she objected. 'I'll check in at the Fletcher's Rest and charge it to the Hoads' executors.'

'You can always try,' Beaumont encouraged, knowing the solicitor involved and hopeful of an interesting outcome.

Scorning the offer of a patrol car to deliver her to the pub, she rang for a taxi and took her leave coolly, only nodding when Salmon warned he would need to question her more fully next day.

'How old would you say she was?' Z asked Beaumont as they stepped out into a fresh-smelling but puddled night where the rain had at last given up.

'Hovering over forty for the first time. Why?'

'She claims to be in her early fifties. At least that's what she must be if her story's true about coming to England as a toddler refugee in '56.'

'M'm, Hungarian. They're a lively lot, aren't they? Think of the Gabor sisters, flirty into their nineties. They've a certain *je ne sais quoi,* and don't wear out like English lady coppers do, Z.'

'Thanks a lot. Maybe you're right.'

She left it at that. All the same, schooled in England, surely by now Alma Pavitt would have lost that occasional slide into

68

foreign intonation. Unless at home her mother had always insisted on the use of her own language.

An interesting woman, the Hoad housekeeper. And a superb cook, according to her own evaluation. Z caught herself wondering how differently the outcome might have been on that fateful night if Alma Pavitt had stayed on at the Manor. Would there have been one more body to account for? Or might she somehow have contrived to get away and survive to give an account of what had happened?

Pausing as he started to unlock his Toyota parked alongside, Beaumont too had been busy with private ruminations. He came out with a personal question for Z. 'As a kid did you ever sleep over with a schoolmate?'

'No, my aunt wouldn't allow it.' Her tone was dry. Her aunt's concept of risk was tragically misplaced. The real danger had been in her own home, under the paedophile uncle's roof.

'But I did once have a friend sleep over when her mother went into hospital overnight. We shared my room,' Z conceded.

'So, d'you recall how it was? What did you get up to together? Something special, exciting?'

Z smiled, remembering. 'A secret "midnight feast". Like we'd read about in school-girl magazines. Innocent enough, but we planned and plotted for days beforehand. Noreen smuggled the goodies in with her overnight bag. Sausage rolls, jam doughnuts and a bottle of ginger pop. We took turns in drinking with a straw and thought we were no end wicked.'

She faced Beaumont. 'You're thinking Angela and Monica were up to something of the sort?'

'This is a more sophisticated age, Z. We found a half-empty bottle of Croft's Original under the bed. Also an empty box of chocolate truffles and wrappers from two lots of supermarket dressed crab salad with plastic teaspoons. Little wonder the storm failed to wake them. As Littlejohn discovered, their little stomachs were stuffed full.'

'And they'd be half-seas-over on the sherry.' That, and the innocent fun, made their end the more pitiable.

'You can bet that when the lab comes up with an analysis of stomach contents, that's what they'll find, plus whatever was the kids' official supper.'

'Was there anything of particular interest the post-mortems produced after I'd left?'

Beaumont assumed a cocky, know-all air. 'A note from the lab on something Littlejohn had requested in advance. Blood types. Not only was a small amount of blood, identified as young Angela's, found on Hoad's pyjama jacket, but it didn't match the group of either parent. Whether it was an accepted fact or not, the Hoad daughter could have been adopted.'

Z frowned. 'She could still be Jennifer's child. Carrying her unknown father's blood type.'

Beaumont had to agree, but his crowing revelations stayed in Z's head as she drove home through almost silent streets.

How could Angela's blood have reached Hoad's body? Unless he had been the one to stab her and so became contaminated. But 'a small amount,' Beaumont had said.

If Hoad had been the killer, surely his hands and pyjama cuffs would have been stained by both children's blood. At the morgue she'd seen that they weren't.

An alternative explanation was that the same knife had been used on both Hoad and Angela by a third party, and the children killed first. It wasn't the sadly familiar pattern of a family massacre, where the enraged husband went first for his wife, then the children — usually by smothering — finally killing himself. From his complex wounds, it was quite clear that Frederick Hoad had been totally incapable of that last act. He'd been shot dead with a single .22 bullet which she'd watched being removed from the body. His stabbing was post-mortem, as indicated by the amount of blood loss. But apparently the little girls had been stabbed in between.

Yes, she decided: a) Hoad is shot dead; b) the children are stabbed; c) the killer returns to stab Hoad. It must have been in that order. So where did the barn killing and mutilation fit in? As the mad, grand finale?

Hoad killed by a single small-calibre bullet. So was that a skilled shot, or a lucky one? With a small-bore gun, rifle or target pistol, using a bullet suited to pinging tin cans rather than murder, you'd expect the killer to empty his gun into the victim to make sure. But he hadn't. He'd gone away on a stabbing spree, then come back to mutilate the body. Unsure he was dead? Or as an act of frenzied hate?

Nothing in this hideous case made sense. Perhaps it was the wrong time to try. Have a nightcap, get to bed: your brains are blown, Z told herself.

She felt too weary to garage the Ford and left it outside to whatever ravages the weather might threaten.

CHAPTER SIX

As the two sergeants made for their desks in the CID office next morning, they found Superintendent Yeadings there before them, in his shirtsleeves. 'We've found family,' he told them as they came in together.

He paused. 'Or rather, the family's found us. Mustn't underrate so formidable a lady as the late Mrs Hoad's mother. Squadron Leader Anna Plumley, MBE, no less.'

'Joanna Lumley?' Beaumont couldn't resist mishearing.

Yeadings mouth quivered. 'An altogether different proposition.'

'And Daniel? Is he with her?' Z demanded.

'He's not. There's regrettably no news on him. For which the lady's prepared to hold us liable. I've spoken with her on the phone and have an appointment with her at 9.15 a.m., after which I shall be passing her to DCI Salmon and then to yourselves. This is at her request. She has experience, it seems, of working through hierarchies. The Deputy Chief Constable was called out of bed to meet her at 3 a.m.'

'Wow,' Beaumont breathed in awe. 'But formidable, man.'

'So long as everyone understands.' The Boss regarded them evenly. 'I've read both your reports from yesterday. Is there anything overnight that I should be updated on?'

They disclaimed, so he nodded and left for his own office.

'Where can she stay?' Z asked herself aloud. 'Alma Pavitt's booked in at the nearest pub. It's pretty cramped. I'd better ring around for an alternative, in case they don't hit it off together.'

'I've never met a RAF lady with clout,' Beaumont said wonderingly, 'though she's probably retired by now and just hanging on to her rank.'

'Why not? Male officers do.'

'Yes; most of them after some kind of war service. This one would have won no wings, flying a desk.'

'For all we know she could be one of the Red Arrows. You should leave sexism to our Acting-DCI,' Z riposted.

He shrugged. 'Well, if she needs chauffeuring, it's up to you, Z.'

'Your new Toyota's classier.' But Beaumont had already left, bound for the Incident Room. She picked up her file and followed, to find Salmon there attaching fresh photographs of the crime scene to the extended whiteboard. He was looking distinctly edgy.

'Hoad's mother-in-law is on her way in,' he thought fit to warn them, 'and she wants to know what we've discovered about her grandson's whereabouts.'

'Zilch,' Beaumont breathed sadly. Not only an officer in the Women's Services, but also a mother-in-law. She sounded more discouraging at every moment.

When the full investigating team assembled he made sure of a windowsill seat at the rear with a sideways view of the main entrance, confident that Salmon would hold the floor throughout the briefing. Any ancillary duties that cropped up could be delegated to Z, stationed at his elbow.

At precisely 9.12 a.m. Beaumont stiffened as below a taxi disgorged a well-built woman with a fuzz of hair like wire wool and wearing a tailored black trouser suit. Massive, Beaumont registered. The RAF could have used her to kick-start transport aircraft. Congratulating himself that forewarned was forearmed, he swivelled back and looked attentively towards where Salmon was in lecturing spate.

Yeadings had her wait in the reception area while he came down himself to escort her up.

'Superintendent,' she greeted him, instinctively picking up on his authority and holding out her hand. She had a beautiful voice, a warm contralto. And lovely tawny eyes, he noted, as they came face to face. For all that she'd been urgently demanding news of her grandson, she was prepared to be patient now, graciously accepting the offer of coffee once she'd quizzed the paraphernalia along his windowsill.

Busying himself with fixing the filter, Yeadings averted his eyes while he ploughed through his condolences. Though what bloody use were they in such an appalling situation? he asked himself.

She remained silent and he glanced up. She was waiting for him to get on with it. 'What's done is done, however . . . regrettable,' she told him grimly. 'My concern is for the future.'

'Your grandson.'

'The survivor. If, indeed, he still is?'

'We are following a number of leads regarding his whereabouts.'

'Peeing in the sea,' was her wry comment. 'I know how it goes when someone is intent on not being found.'

It shocked him. 'You think that's the case?'

'Nothing would surprise me with that young man. Well, perhaps almost nothing. He can be quite unpredictable. Not that I've had much personal contact with him over the past few years. Or indeed with my daughter. We inhabit different worlds.'

'It would help our investigation to know as much as possible about the Hoad family. Will you help us there?'

'No milk, thank you,' she cautioned as his hand hovered with a carton of Long Life.

She drew a deep breath. 'Jennifer was an early mistake on my part. Single mothers had it harder in my day, although I had been prevailed upon to marry the man. Who quite soon decamped. Took early retirement. A hushed-up fiddle with Sergeants' Mess funds.' The part-sentences were brusquely elliptical, delivered in that same mellifluous voice.

'So Jennifer grew up as a semi-orphaned "married-quarters brat". I was only a Leading Aircraftwoman then. The commission had yet to come. Humble background, you see: my father ran a south London gaming club. At seventeen I'd flown the nest, detesting smoke-filled atmospheres and being expected to scrub billiard tables. Joined the RAF for a more tolerable discipline.

'It wasn't the most stable background for her to grow up in. Jennifer, I mean. But as I said, "What's done is done". But I do have regrets.'

Small wonder if Daniel was 'unpredictable', Yeadings decided, with these genes to inherit. Every moment she seemed to produce contradictions.

Anna Plumley leaned forward to take the proffered cup and saucer. 'Thank you, Superintendent.

'Jennifer was a silly girl. But shrewd. She had brains, but preferred to keep them in a separate compartment from her everyday commitments which were frivolous in the extreme.

'She craved pretty things, so perhaps it's unsurprising that when she happened on interior decoration as a career, and actually applied her brains, she became very successful. Not until she had married Frederick Hoad, of course, and acquired the necessary capital to set up her own business.'

'Was the marriage a happy one?'

She gave an almost Gallic shrug and turned the tawny eyes on him. 'How many marriages are that, or only that? It has survived for some reason. For both it was a second attempt, so not a starry-eyed decision. Poor Fred never enjoyed the best of health and soon proved impotent to boot. He was pleased to take on a ready-made son. The daughter was a later cuckoo in the nest. He accepted her arrival placidly enough. To outer appearances he was a contented family man, only distantly involved in his inherited business, which was West Country-based, a foundry constructing and maintaining glass furnaces. It pleased him to relax as a Buckinghamshire country gentleman with a London club to escape to. To him the farm was no more than décor. I believe old Barton runs it rather well.'

The internal phone on the superintendent's desk gave a warning buzz. He reached across. 'Excuse me, Squadron Leader.'

The use of her rank produced a squawk of laughter from the redoubtable lady and a shake of her head.

'Yes, Z,' Yeadings murmured into the phone. He listened, nodded, and suggested she should join them in his office. 'One of my sergeants,' he explained. 'She's concerned about accommodation if you intend to stay on.'

'I certainly do. It's essential I remain in touch with your investigation. The truth is I feel responsible. For past neglect, if nothing more.'

They waited in silence for Z to appear. When Yeadings introduced her the visitor gave her a searching look. 'Anna Plumley,' she said, offering her hand. 'Zyczynski? As on the Polish Air Force War Memorial?'

'Stefan, my grandfather.'

'Before my time, of course. But I certainly know of him. I've made several visits to Northolt in the line of duty. There are still survivors of the Second World War who attend reunions and talk of the old days.'

'I'm glad he's remembered. My parents were very proud of him, as I am.'

'And now you're concerned about my welfare? Well, my dear, you need not be. I'm provided for. I have a mobile home. It's parked out at the nearby travellers' camp. They're looking after it for me until I get permission to move into Fordham Manor.'

Not so amazing, really, Yeadings told himself. He could quite easily see her thundering along at the wheel of a well-equipped caravan. 'Perhaps you'd like . . . er, Rosemary to direct you there?'

'I should be obliged. And perhaps she will give me a rather wider view of what actually happened than you've passed to the press. I promise discretion.'

She rose, indicating that the meeting was over. Yeadings nodded to Z. He had no reluctance about the DS wising her up. The formidable lady had been more than frank about her own unpromising background. She'd reached her retirement rank (level with, if not superior to, his own, he guessed) through her own efforts. He was confident she'd dealt in her time with matters that needed equal discretion.

He watched from the window as the two women left, disappeared round the side of the building and then a few moments later drove out in Z's blue Escort. It was then that he sent a text message to his DCI's mobile phone. 'Meeting with Plumley cancelled. Z arranging accommodation.' A suitable job for a woman, he was sure Salmon would consider it. He'd probably feel reprieved.

Five minutes later Salmon joined him. 'Briefing over,' he reported glumly. 'Anything useful from the mother-in-law?'

It wrong-footed Yeadings for an instant. He'd thought of Anna Plumley as the grandmother. Mother-in-law? Salmon was clearly regarding Hoad family relationships from the man's point of view. Natural to him, of course.

'She is quite a disquieting lady,' he warned the DCI. 'But shrewd. Her view of the family's a rather distant one, unfortunately. They've not recently kept in touch.'

'But now she's getting in on it.'

So Salmon fancied her as a vulture drawn to the corpses. 'I doubt if she is looking for financial control. More concerned about Daniel, as sole survivor. She described him as unpredictable.'

'That hardly helps,' Salmon grunted.

Unpredictable wasn't the word she used to Zyczynski. 'A charmer,' was how she described the small boy she'd known. 'Spent far too much time with his mother's silly women friends and learned to play them like wind chimes. Quite the harem child.'

She cocked her head, reminiscing. 'I had a Sudanese friend way back who described how it was. His mother was a Copt but married into a wealthy Muslim family. Multiple wives. Made a great fuss of because he was pretty. They used to dress him up, giggle over him, put kohl on his eyes. Rescued in time, thank God, by an uncle, who sent him to school in Alexandria, then university. He's a well-known microbiologist now, sexually straight, but he still has that appalling giggle.'

Z listened fascinated. She remembered that Ned Barton had described Daniel to the Boss as 'a milksop'. Implying a mother's boy?

They were driving in Anna Plumley's Jeep attached to the caravan. Z had expected a combo, but this was a distinctly superior turnout. 'Sleeps six,' Anna had introduced it, showing her around.

One of the Irish travellers on the camp had actually been installed in its lounge, with his dog tied up outside to keep off children's sticky fingers. Anna greeted him as though she'd known him all her life. 'Thanks, Sean, we'll be off now. Run into you some other time maybe.'

He'd grinned, accepting the banknotes she passed him and removed himself together with his crumpled lager cans and the dog.

There were two photographers hanging about the high iron gates to Fordham Manor, at least respecting the yellow crime scene tape. Mrs Plumley stayed at the wheel, impassive, as Z waved the men off, opened the gates and reclosed them behind the caravan. Now as they reached the end of the rising driveway Z observed the other police tapes had been removed. The constable on duty inside the gates came forward and spoke through the driver's window. Anna identified herself without reference to rank.

'Yes, ma'am, we were expecting you. There's a nice flat macadam area round the back suitable for parking, ma'am. Kitchen's been left open, so you've access to all facilities.' He handed over a key.

'Has anyone tried phoning the house?'

'The line's been diverted, ma'am. Do you want it restored?'

She considered. 'I've my mobile, but it's in case Daniel gets in touch . . . Yes, I'd rather he spoke to me than to a police station.'

'I'll report that in. There'll be a constable here twenty-four hours, ma'am, if you need anything.'

'Thank you. Have the scenes of crime specialists finished now?'

He hesitated, looking at Z for his cue.

'Well, have they?'

'I believe so.' He sounded reluctant.

Anna took charge. 'Then please ring Superintendent Yeadings and ask if Sergeant Zyczynski may show me around inside.'

Z smiled at the man, used by now to her directness. 'You do that. Then we're all covered.'

'Yes, sergeant. Ma'am.' He retreated, leaving room for the Jeep to sweep round the driveway and find its parking place to the rear. By the time the two women had alighted he was back.

'I'm to take note of both you ladies' mobile numbers, to pass to following duty officers,' he said gruffly. He handed over a ring of keys. 'These are for the locked rooms. I have to warn you nothing's been . . . er, cleared up yet.'

'We understand,' Anna Plumley acknowledged sombrely. 'I'm sure I've encountered worse before.'

But not family, Z allowed. Surely, sooner or later, the full force of the tragedy was going to hit the old lady. Nobody could remain so indomitable for ever.

CHAPTER SEVEN

In the caravan Anna Plumley wasted no
time, equipping herself with a white wrap-
around overall, a heavy electric torch and a
soft pair of house shoes.

'They won't have had the electricity cut
off,' Z assured her and received a tight little
grin.

'Dark corners. There are always dark
corners. Let's go in by the front door, which
I imagine was in general use.'

So it was to be a methodical examination.
Z considered herself rebuked and went
ahead. They began with a walk-through for
the visitor to get the general layout, Anna
following slowly with both hands clasped
behind her, holding the unlit torch. Z felt
sure it wasn't the first time that she'd
inspected a disaster area. Neither spoke at
first, apart from Z announcing the function
of each room as they entered. To begin they
turned left from the hall, unlocking the din-

ing room.

It was much as Z had seen it, except for the grey powdering of chemicals left by the fingerprint experts. The two women halted at the chalk outline of the body with its brownish staining of the floorboards. This area looked smaller to Z than she'd thought it on first shocked sight. Frederick Hoad had lost less blood than an average alley-way stabbing. But then, as Littljohn said, he'd been shot first and the heart stopped instantly. Why then all the unnecessary wounding later? Must they start looking for a sadist?

The shoe mark was only partial. They'd be lucky ever to identify and match it. There was no more than the toecap of a smooth sole, and not the ridged sort that would more easily pick up foreign matter and scars.

Had the killer walked over to make sure Hoad was dead? Gloating, or appalled? Or simply to follow up with the knife to make sure? She could almost see him dropping the rifle to kneel beside the body, savagely stabbing at it. If the initial shooting had been defensive, this last act wasn't. There had been passion behind it. Either hate for the man or the excitement of killing.

Anna went across to stare into the gun cabinet. 'Two removed,' she murmured.

Z returned from speculation to hard facts. She nodded towards the narrower chalk marks. 'That's where they found the shotgun Mr Hoad fired as he was hit.'

'Which accounts for the state of the china cabinet. It's put paid to the Royal Doulton.'

'The second gun, which killed him, could have been a sports rifle. It's still missing. The single bullet was a .22. Hoad's shotgun has been bagged as an exhibit.'

'Next room?' Mrs Plumley waited as Z relocked the doors behind them and restored the police tape.

They examined the large study/office which had two executive desks, one at either end. As well as its computer screen, that by the front window held a vase of pink and mauve asters wilting in a cut glass vase, tainting the closed air with decay. Brown, crinkled leaves had dropped on the tooled leather surface. There was opened correspondence in a wire in-tray, addressed to Jennifer Hoad. All of it personal letters, invitations and greetings cards. The business stuff would have gone direct to her Knightsbridge office.

Apart from its computer, the surface of the other matching desk was bare. The unlocked drawers held the expected clutter of pens, paper clips, stapler, rubber bands and stationery. There was even a small leather case criss-crossed with numerous old scratches and a peeling label written in ink that read 'F Hoad, IV B, New House'. It contained a geometry set: a unique memento of schooldays. There was nothing to show that he'd still used it.

The far wall between the desks held two steel filing cabinets, both locked, and more office machinery including a shredder and a fax machine. The rear wall was lined with shelves of books. For later examination, Z promised herself.

Back through the dining room, into kitchen and scullery, where Anna showed interest only in the contents of the dishwasher which she opened with a tea towel covering her hand. It was loaded with clean crockery and cutlery. A red light at the wall socket indicated it was still switched on from previous use.

'Newspaper accounts said that the housekeeper was away. That means the last meal would possibly have been prepared, and certainly cleared away, by the family. Which one of them, I wonder.'

'We could call the fingerprints team back.'

'Maybe. We'll think about that.'

Out again into the hall. 'Gun Room,' Anna read off a rustic notice on the door overhung by the stairs' landing.

'It would have been once,' Z offered, 'but following present rulings all firearms were properly locked away in the special steel cabinet.'

'Discreetly hidden in the dining room,' Anna agreed. 'I wonder how many people knew about the secret interior of the glass cabinet. This sometime gun room appears to be a glory hole, full of golf umbrellas, old slippers, gum boots and garden furniture for the summer. Judging by the scarred floor, I'd say it was the most usual rear entrance and exit. The outer door has a mortice lock as well as the Yale. I wonder how often they forgot to use it.'

'It was found locked when the first patrol men arrived. The whole house was secure. CID had to break in.'

'And the key?' Anna pointed to a cup-hook up by the lintel. 'Wouldn't that be the best place to leave it?' It was empty now.

In the cloakroom and shower room they found the U-bends had been removed by the forensic examiners. 'No blood traces found,' Z said.

'So the killer, or killers, went elsewhere to clean up.'

'There was a tremendous storm that night. Lashings of rain. It would have destroyed a lot of clues, tyre tracks included.'

'And covered up all sounds of departure.'

'Just the banging door of the old fodder barn.'

'Yes. I read about that. Too melodramatic for the press to miss out on.'

They passed more rapidly through the unlocked morning room and the drawing-room with its glassed-in conservatory extension. In the TV/games room at the rear, with its table tennis equipment and snooker table, Anna eyed the floor-to-ceiling cupboards. 'Plenty of space here for an intruder to hide and bide his time after Freddie was alerted. Perhaps the killer waited here while he went for his gun.'

Upstairs they walked through the bedrooms. Only two were locked, in the southeast corridor. When Z opened the first they met the stale, sickly scent of blood still trapped in there, although all the girls' bedding had been removed.

'Was any semen found?' Anna asked stiffly.

'No. It must all have been over in a flash. They were heavily asleep.'

Anna turned away, briefly looked into the parents' room, then walked the half circle of the gallery above the hall and went to inspect the two unused guest rooms off the opposite corridor.

'Daniel's room is across the way. It's just as he left it,' Z told her. 'He seems to have packed a kitbag or something similar. See the marks on the bed?'

They looked into his bathroom where Anna inspected the contents of the waste bin. Returning to the passage, Anna rattled the handle of a solid-panelled door at its end. 'What's through here?'

'Stairs to the housekeeper's quarters.'

'Have they been examined?'

'Yes, but I haven't been up there myself.'

'So let's look before she returns. If, indeed, she ever cares to do so.'

As they mounted the narrow stairs to the next floor Z explained how she had interviewed Alma Pavitt who had not questioned taking up her job again. 'She's staying at the local pub until she's given permission to move back in.'

'Not an oversensitive person then? Or perhaps lacking imagination?'

'Maybe both. She appeared barely affected by the time I got her back, but different people have different ways of reacting in shock.'

Z found herself on the point of confiding her impression of the woman, but stopped herself in time. Anna had fitted so well into her familiarity with senior women CID officers that she'd almost been accepting her as a colleague. Now she reminded herself that the ex-Squadron Leader was an outsider, a member of the victims' family, grandmother to young Angela whose blood still hung sourly on the air.

The top-floor rooms hadn't the lofty ceilings of those on the lower floors, but they were of reasonable size. In their early days several servants would have shared sleeping quarters, men at one side of the house and women at the other. The floorboards were bare and the old furniture had been removed except in one of these distempered rooms which held a collection of domestic junk and travel cases.

Two rooms only were decorated to modern standards, the housekeeper's bedroom with en suite bath, and her sitting room dominated by a wide-screen television and video player. There was audio equipment but no DVDs, and only a few cassettes, mostly of smooch music.

The long laundry room was a Victorian museum. A black-painted iron stove at one end supported a robust wire cage in which several heavy pressing-irons hung ready for application to a heated griddle. A broad table some eight feet long was still thickly padded and covered by a yellowed cotton sheet drawn tight and tied at the corners with white tapes. For almost the whole length of the room, which ran from front to back of the house, wooden racks were suspended from pulleys on the ceiling, for the drying and airing of damp linen.

'Either in days past the weather was more often inclement, or the gentry were easily offended by the public sight of bloomers and stays blowing in the wind,' Anna surmised, gazing up. Her voice was lighter, as though the break from sterner matters had come as welcome relief.

At the rear extremity was a closed door. Z opened it to disclose a well-equipped darkroom. The developing trays were empty, as was the drying line with its row of clothes pegs. Labels on the bottles of chemicals in the cupboard bore recent dates; so one of the family had been keen on photography.

'Have you seen enough?' Z asked. Anna was no youngster and apparently she'd been hard at it from the early hours. Time now, surely, to take a rest.

'Enough for the moment,' Anna allowed. She had opened a door in the outer side wall to view the iron staircase of a fire escape. 'I think we've earned some lunch.

Come and join me in my galley. You'll find I'm not the worst of cooks.'

DCI Salmon had summoned Bertie Fallon up from Bristol where, in addition to being Hoad's sole other director, he performed the duty of General Production Manager at the glass furnace foundry. News of the carnage at Fordham Manor had been broken to him by the scanty national television news available at weekends. Relaxing on Sunday with a few fingers of single malt following an abortive visit to his golf club where the fairways were still unfit for play after Friday night's country-wide storm, he'd been shocked out of his recliner. Incredulous and almost distraught, he had immediately contacted Thames Valley police and had the story confirmed.

'Look, what can I do?' he demanded. 'Freddie was the business head, the money man. Our functions were quite separate. Do I try to carry on, or what? Sorry to harp on about the works, but they won't run themselves. Poor old Freddie. My God, I still can't believe it. Who'd do a thing like that to him? And the whole family wiped out, you say? Must have been a madman.

'Eh, what? No, Chief Inspector, I can't just drop everything and come running.

95

There's a consignment of steel due in at the docks tomorrow. God knows what kind of cock-up they'd make of it if I wasn't there to oversee.

'No, the delivery can't be put off. There'd be storage charges and Finance'd go mad at the extra expense. We're a small operation and run a tight ship, as Freddie always said . . .

'Freddie . . . poor old sod; I just can't believe he's gone.'

Voices on the other end of the line had been switched. 'Mr Fallon, this is Superintendent Yeadings. I do understand what a terrible shock this has been for you, a colleague and friend to Mr Hoad. But we desperately need all information we can turn up on his background, both personal and professional. Who is in a better position to help us than you? The first few days of any murder investigation are of vital importance, so please sleep on our urgent request overnight. If you still find yourself unable to come here tomorrow I will send a CID officer to interview you at your home.'

Fallon complied. It didn't suit him to have police disturbing his domestic arrangements. He rang half an hour later to announce he'd made alternative arrangements for tomorrow's delivery and was already on his way.

Z, returning from her caravan lunch (garlic button mushrooms followed by a shared cheese and chives omelette; coffee, but no dessert), found the visitor in conference with Salmon and the Boss. Yeadings broke off to introduce her.

'Miss Zyczynski is one of my CID sergeants concentrating on this case. How did you get on at the Manor, Z?'

'Mrs Hoad's mother is taking it well, sir. She asks permission to employ professional cleaners, if SOCO have finished. I told her about the specialist team we sometimes use. She appeared unfazed by what she saw, but we didn't get as far as the stables. I felt the house was enough for the present. She intends catching up on lost sleep this afternoon.'

'Good. I want you to keep in touch with her.'

'It's too soon to dismantle the scene,' Salmon objected.

'We shan't until everything's covered. We can discuss that later. I'll let you know, Z. Thank you. That's all.'

She left and went in search of Beaumont who'd almost certainly be stealing a march on her.

■ ■ ■ ■

'Mr Fallon, just a few personal details, if you don't mind,' Yeadings continued.

'Bertie. Everyone calls me Bertie, Superintendent.'

'For the record, that would be Bertram?'

Fallon's fair skin flushed. 'Norbert, actually. My mum's French.'

He gave his age as forty-nine but looked considerably younger, being round-faced with a boyish manner. Yeadings could recall meeting only one man who'd had such ingenuous, wide-open blue eyes, and he'd been a mass rapist.

'When was the last time you saw Mr Hoad?' he asked.

'In person, that'd be a good fortnight back. More, maybe. But I briefly saw him Friday on my video-phone. We keep in touch that way and I fax him everything that comes in on paper: invoices, bills, receipts, correspondence. That's to say, my secretary does. Putting pen to paper bugs me, actually. Or finger to keyboard, as it is nowadays. We aren't a large workforce. Thirty-one in all, but we get through some business. Our name's getting well known. Just had a big order from Murano, Venice.'

There was unmistakable pride in his voice.

'And how long have you been with the firm?'

'Twelve years now. But I've known Freddie a lot longer. We met at university. He was a mature student doing business studies and I was a first year engineer. We met at Dramsoc. He had a talent for producing and I was into stagecraft. We went our own ways later and chanced on each other at a charity do his wife was organising in London. My sister dragged me there and I'm glad now she did. Freddie and I slunk off into the bar and made up for lost time. I let out that I wasn't happy working for a big conglomerate in Swindon and he suggested I should take a trip to Bristol and give my opinion on the firm he'd inherited from his dad. I had some ideas on technical improvements and we joined up. Been there ever since.'

The mention of Swindon brought Salmon out of his slump. 'Do you know a Miss or Mrs Alma Pavitt?' he demanded.

'No. Should I?'

'Or a Mrs Bellinger who also lives in Swindon?'

'Never heard of her. Anyway I didn't live in the town then. We were some eight miles outside.'

' "We" being?' Yeadings enquired, taking over the interview again.

'My mum and me. My dad scarpered when I was a kid, and my two sisters are married. One's in Canada and the other's in Cornwall.'

Forty-nine years old and still living with his mother; brought up in a family of women. How different did that make him? Yeadings wondered. 'How did you get on with the late Mrs Hoad?' he pressed.

'Jennifer? She scared the shit out of me. So bloody perfect. Could do everything better than anyone else. Couldn't imagine her slopping around in curlers like a normal woman.'

'Uncomfortable to be with?'

'Unless she set out to charm you. She tried with me at first, but quickly decided I wasn't worth the effort. Pity, because Freddie and I really hit it off, for all we're so different. Were different. God, I can't believe he's been done in. I don't suppose the poor sod ever hurt anyone in his whole life.'

At 4.15 p.m. Z returned to the caravan to take Anna Plumley for formal identification of the bodies. She found her sitting on the lowered steps outside, smoking a small brown cigar.

'Detestable habit,' she growled, throwing the remains of it down and scrunching it under one well-shod heel. 'I began it as an affectation, purely to annoy. By the time it had served that purpose I found I needed it in moments of stress. Better than hitting the bottle, I suppose. I'd hate to become an alcoholic and be obliged to give up drinking good Burgundy.'

Her tone was wry, but she looked more relaxed. It was a pleasant face, Z realised; almost pretty in a plumply determined way.

'Time to go?'

'If you feel ready.'

'I'll never be that.'

As she rose, her mobile tinkled out the first few notes of the 'Flight of the Valkyrie'. 'Plum dear,' she said, opening it, 'how're the fish rising? You did? Well done!'

She listened, smiling indulgently, then grimaced. 'No, it's much as we expected here. Daniel hasn't put in an appearance yet. A lot of waiting about, but we're just off to the mortuary. I'll ring you tonight, lovey. Mind that new speed camera on the hill. One of us must keep a clean licence. Yes, I do. Goodbye.

'My husband,' she explained, and catching a flicker of surprise on Z's face, 'My third. The first didn't put me completely off marriage. Sadly, the second died.'

She made shooing gestures. 'Come on then, if we're going. Let's get this over and done with.'

CHAPTER EIGHT

'If you're sure,' Nan cautioned him, placing the hot plate before him at the breakfast table.

Yeadings glanced up from the newspaper folded beside his coffee cup. 'Quite sure, thanks.'

He'd been only twelve days on the Atkins diet and already lost five pounds. So it worked. But Nan, ex-Sister at the old Westminster Hospital, clung to traditional wisdom, only agreeing to supply his dietary demands on condition that their GP monitored Mike's blood pressure and cholesterol levels frequently.

But so far, so good. All her earlier efforts to get his weight reduced had petered out, sabotaged at work, she suspected, by doughnuts fed him by his sergeants, like buns through zoo bars to bears. As high carbs, they were now on the strictly forbidden list.

Yeadings abandoned the *Telegraph*'s version of the carnage at Fordham Manor and turned with relief to the plate of tongue, beef and a small wedge of mature Cheddar. He poured cream in his coffee and let it swirl artistically. Nan couldn't begrudge him his slight sigh of pleasure.

But not contentment. How could it be, in the circumstances? Experienced as he was, he was letting this latest case get to him. Vicious murders did happen in leafy Bucks, but not wholesale slaughter, and there were two innocent children involved, one not even belonging to the family almost wiped out.

He had said nothing on returning that early Saturday morning from the crime scene. Simply slumped back on the bed for a further two hours and stomped off again, silent and dour. Nan had known better than to question him. Her first information on the tragedy came from the television news.

'Will you be going out there now?' she ventured to ask.

'It's up to the team. I'm SIO, deskbound.'

She imagined him padding like a caged lion between office and Incident Room, frustrated at the slowness of info coming in. Not satisfied with the old adage 'they also serve . . .', but impatient to use whatever came to hand, to collate and shape it into some sense — if any sense could come from such diabolical matter — and force some action that would point to a likely suspect.

'But I might go and check up on Mrs Plumley,' he conceded.

Nan nodded. He'd told her last night about her arrival: the grandmother who'd served in the RAF. 'Tell her if she needs anything to give me a ring.'

'Best not get involved, love. I've put Z on to nannying her. Not that she's the sort to need it. A real old warhorse. Nice with it, though.'

He finished his coffee and patted his mouth with his napkin, comfortably replete. That was the best thing about this new diet. You felt you'd really had a meal. There was something about the abandoned carbohydrates that had always given him a regrettable appetite for more. Now that he'd discovered you could actually eat to lose weight he merely had to resist the carbs' initial lure.

Before leaving he rang the Area desk to say where he'd be. Salmon had his mobile number if anything urgent came up.

The sky was crowded with low, dark horizontals of rain cloud, and as he drove from the garage the first drops began to fall, plinking on the bonnet and darkening the tarmac with large black circles. By the time he reached Fordham Village it was a regular downpour and the windscreen wipers were clunking away, one stiffly screeching. For a week now he'd meant to have it replaced.

The lane to the Manor and farm was narrow, first dipping and then rising with twists between high banks with winter-bare hedges, their breaks allowing occasional glimpses of chimneys and roof beyond. When he emerged into the open there were bollards with yellow crime scene tapes masking the pillared gates. The three-gabled house with its extended frontage glowered darkly behind. It looked empty. There was no guard on the front door.

Yeadings drove over puddled flagstones to the rear, to find Anna Plumley, in a hooded, shiny yellow waterproof, sitting out in the rain on the caravan steps and smoking a small cigar.

'Morning, Superintendent,' she greeted him, rising. 'Your young man's inside. I bullied him into taking cover. And a hot drink. So I'm standing guard in his place for five minutes.' She dunked the cigarillo on the wet step beside her and trod it flat as she rose.

Yeadings got out and followed her into the caravan's warm interior. 'I doubt there'll be any assault on the house while this torrent continues,' he allowed. He'd meant to cancel the duty, but that could leave the elderly woman vulnerable.

'How do you feel about moving into the house, once I've arranged for the housekeeper to come back?' he asked.

'To keep an eye on things? Why not?' She had to shout above the noise of rain drumming on the caravan roof.

The young constable had risen, embarrassed, from his place at the table. He was in his shirtsleeves. The odour of wet dog blankets came from his tunic drying out in front of the stove. 'Sir,' he said, his face flushing scarlet.

'I'll give you a lift back,' Yeadings said evenly. 'When you've finished your drink you can wait in my car, while I have a word with Mrs Plumley.'

'Always look after the ranks,' the lady said chummily when the two of them were alone.

'Quite so,' Yeadings agreed. 'Thank you.'

'It was only soup,' she said. 'Nothing stimulating. But I do have a single malt if you would care . . .'

He thanked her again and declined. Alcohol was still off-diet and it was too soon after his late breakfast. He hadn't risen that morning until after Nan took the children off to school and nursery class.

'Any developments?' she asked. 'That is, if you think I should know.'

They were seated opposite each other at the table. He faced the frank gaze of the concerned, tawny eyes. There were deeper ditches under them today. She'd spent a restless night. Would anything he had to say deepen her grief? Or could it offer needed distraction?

'I had a phone call from the forensics lab last night,' he confided, and explained how initial analysis indicated that Angela shared neither Hoad's nor Jennifer's blood group. Did Mrs Plumley know if she'd been adopted?

'No. She's Jennifer's all right. I visited her in hospital when Angela was born. So, surely with DNA you can later discover who the father is, if that's of importance. As I told you, Freddie proved to be impotent. With that as an excuse, Jennifer granted herself a loose rein.'

'I see. But also arising from blood analysis — Angela's and her little friend, Monica's — an unexpected level of alcohol was found.'

'So the children had been drinking.' It was statement, not question.

'Sherry, a good one. We found the bottle.

Part of a secret midnight feast, the evidence of which was hidden under Angela's bed. Judging by the amount missing it's almost certain they'd have known nothing of the attack on them.'

She was silent a moment, head bowed, before facing him again. 'Thank God, then, for kiddish pranks.'

'Amen,' said Yeadings.

He left soon after, promising to ring her mobile with information on Alma Pavitt's intentions. Certain rooms in the Manor must remain sealed for the present, until the professional cleaners saw to them, but as soon as Mrs Pavitt returned to her top floor a guest room could be made available for Mrs Plumley's use.

Turning from the driveway into the village lane, he came face to face with a lumbering refuse lorry. Instead of reversing as the scowling driver's gestures demanded, Yeadings braked and got out. He produced his warrant card and waved it up towards the open cab window. 'Detective-Superintendent Yeadings, Thames Valley Major Crimes,' he announced. 'Haven't you received instructions not to call here?'

'Nothing on me shift schedule, mate,' said the driver.

'Well, it's a restricted area. That's what

the yellow tape means. I'll let you past to reverse. Inform your line manager when you get back.'

He backed into the courtyard and waited while the oversized van made a five-point turn and re-entered the narrow confines of the lane, its sides brushing against twiggy hedges. When it was out of sight he phoned Area from the car and asked to be connected with SOCO.

'Who dealt with all refuse from the Fordham Manor case?' he asked after identifying himself.

He listened while enquiries were made and a name was offered. 'Put me through to him.' He waited until the connection was made.

'Did the Hoads use recycling bins? They did? Good. I'm interested in the paper and cardboard collection . . . No, that's not enough. I need to see for myself. Get it together. Then shall I come to you or . . . ? You will? Splendid.'

He snapped his mobile shut. They would deliver the recyclable paper to him at Area. At risk of turning his office into a rubbish dump, he believed he'd a chance of finding some lead there.

A civilian accountant was working through material retrieved from the two filing cabinets in the study, but there'd been little unusual paperwork discovered in Hoad's desk or waste paper basket. Maybe because it had already been dumped in the bin for recycling. And but for Yeadings running into the refuse van just now, it might well have missed his personal, meticulous examination. There was a point after all in abandoning the desk and taking to the field. Yeadings guessed that scavenging was one small area of interference which Salmon wouldn't eventually begrudge him.

DCI Salmon re-read Z's notes on the Hoads' housekeeper and decided she deserved a visit. He summoned Beaumont to drive him to the Fletcher's Rest. It stood a couple of miles to the far side of Fordham village and the same distance short of Fordham Green, an upmarket development of detached executive houses set amongst thin woodland in a central, triangle-shaped clearing.

He found Alma Pavitt smoking over a tabloid newspaper in the inn's cosy sitting room. His brusque approach endeared him to her as little as did her dismissive attitude towards him. No, she hadn't any identification on her beyond a driving licence. Surely that was enough for most purposes.

'Passport; marriage certificate; National Insurance number; Inland Revenue receipts,' he rumbled. 'Where do you keep all these then?'

'Some at the bank, but most in a drawer in my sitting room at the Manor, which apparently is out of bounds,' she told him distantly.

He stared rudely back, disliking her translucent, frilled blouse and the coal black hair with its widow's peak above strong, dark eyebrows threatening to meet over a slightly hooked, authoritative nose. Her mouth was mobile, twisting into a sardonic smile from a trout-like droop. He admitted that with those high cheekbones and hypnotic eyes some would call her handsome. For himself she had no attraction. Early fifties, Z had assumed. The woman looked younger, although well worn. Doubtless the hair was dyed.

She continued lounging in an easy chair while he stood over her, checking himself as he realised he'd started rocking on his heels. The questions he fired at her received a drawling response, always grammatical, but with that slightly un-English intonation Z had remarked on. He wondered if she'd been a more recent immigrant than she'd claimed, and marrying a man so much younger as a way of getting British nationality.

He learned nothing new about the Hoads. Once she moved back into the Manor it would do her good, he decided, to get a bit of disciplining from the ex-RAF lady. Her opinion of her dead employers was too guarded to be of any value, and she had left the house even before the daughter returned from school on the Friday afternoon.

She had no suggestions as to where Daniel might have gone once the weekend camp was cancelled. With a free afternoon, he was actually packing for it when she left, and had raided the freezer for provisions to take with him. No, she didn't know if his father intended driving him or someone would come to pick him up. As for the other little girl, that visit must have been a last-minute arrangement. She hadn't been consulted. The spare twin bed in Angela's room was always left made up.

'The Hoads' private life wasn't my business,' she said finally. 'I rather pride myself on being discreet. It's part of the job, if actually I still have one. However, if the old lady wants to move in, I'm happy to go back there, as a sort of guard dog or whatever.'

Dogsbody, Salmon thought to himself

113

with some satisfaction. He hoped the old lady would prove plenty demanding.

There was still no news of Daniel. That was what Anna had hoped — dreaded — that Yeadings' visit would be about. When the superintendent had left she remained seated inside the rain-buffeted caravan, staring from the streaked window, up-meadow towards the dark, cumulus outline of the wood on the hill.

She had never been there. Always, with the children, on her distant, rare visits, they had walked downhill over pasture with grazing cattle to the water meadows and the river. Her last, regretted, visit had been four and a half years back, when Daniel was about eleven and Angela celebrating her sixth birthday. Regretted because, despite her own efforts to be amiable, Jennifer had been even more withering than before.

Anna had never properly understood what made her daughter so inimical; but guessed at a long-held grudge from childhood. The distance then between single parent and only child had been one forced on them by the requirements of her service career. Jennifer, growing up ever full of expectations, could never accept the need to discipline her in her wilder moments, when Anna insisted no exceptions should be allowed by others for her rank.

Perhaps too there was something inherited. Could Anna's own distaste for her parents' way of living have actually passed into her genes? The grotesque idea made her smile.

She had come here that last time partly out of feeling for poor Freddie, the overlooked provider, the case-study example of woman's inhumanity to man. She'd felt a need to assure him there was someone out there who held him in esteem, because he got short shrift at home, the children constant in their selfish demands, the wife flaunting her glorious independence.

She could forgive Daniel and Angela, self-centred as all children are at the start. It takes a few years to rub the sharp corners off, learn consideration, finally compassion. Now they were cut off before the process could be completed; unfinished souls. It gave her a burning sorrow inside.

There was still hope that Daniel could have escaped total destruction. She needed that much of herself to survive. Her grandson, her genes; but also a person in his own right.

She remembered how they'd walked down to the river, and the meadow grasses, whipping at their knees, were thick with wild flowers: buttercups, centaury, white campion, poppies and sorrel. It had been high summer: Daniel bare-chested in cut-off jeans; Angela in a white tank top, and proud of her new fuchsia-coloured cords. When she lay face down, spread-eagled by the stream, sunlight had dappled their velvety surface in a jigsaw pattern of pink and purple.

She was flipping the water with a forked hazel twig, to tease the darting minnows. Under the overhanging trees the stream shone like dull pewter. Occasional rocks cut and tilted the surface to resemble overlapping slates with little foamy edges. Daniel waded out to sit cross-legged on a flat-topped rock, trying to look wise; superior to his sister's childishness. For Anna it had been an afternoon of lazy fondness.

The scene was crystalline, preserved forever in her memory. But now one grandchild was gone, the other at least transformed by the years between. And another little girl lost too, one she had never met. Over time Anna had grieved for crashed fliers, spoken with bereaved parents, devastated widows. She wondered about the family of the child who'd been invited for a weekend that abruptly closed her life.

Should she get in touch with them? Something perhaps to consult the superintendent on.

A new silence told her the rain had ceased. She looked out as a few pale streaks of sunlight lit the wet grass. Emerging out of the dark wood on the hill appeared the burly shape of a man, with a dog at his heels. She watched him come closer, skirting the trees until he was forced into the open. There was a rough shiftiness about him. The sack he carried seemed weighty. What she'd taken at first to be a wrapped shotgun under his arm turned out to be some other kind of object, probably a spade. Intrigued, she let herself out on the far side from him and waited until he was almost level.

'Good day,' she greeted him, stepping out into view and smiling broadly in welcome. 'That was quite a downpour. Really caught us on the hop, didn't it?'

He halted, suspicious, but careful not to give offence. 'G'day, ma'am. Takes more'n that to keep me from me rabbits.' He indicated the sack where a dark stain had begun to gather at the lower seam.

Ah yes, the honest poacher act. Not that he'd have shot them. More likely used snares. But then she doubted the sack bulged with rabbits either. Something larger, a single, much heavier shape.

'I could be a customer for some wild bunny,' she encouraged, holding out a hand.

'They're bespoke,' he said. 'You'd need to order in advance, like.'

She was watching the sack as the bulge stirred slightly; a dopey — perhaps stunned — creature coming back to life. The snorting grunt that issued was a sound she was accustomed to by night. 'Come in and rest yourself. I'll be making us a hot drink.'

He was anxious to be gone. She put a hand on his arm, and the dog — not a farm collie but a muddy Jack Russell — pricked up its ears, showing sharp teeth in a snarl.

'That's enough, you,' she addressed it.

She turned back to the man. 'I insist. You wouldn't want me blabbing about you digging out a badger's set, I'm sure.'

She laughed, making herself sound broad-minded, patting his shoulder as she ushered him towards the caravan's door. 'My name's Anna Plumley, by the way.'

He hesitated, reluctantly deciding that, although gentry, she wasn't a bad old girl. Country-born at least. Knew the way things were. 'Ben Huggett,' he admitted.

'So tell me about the wood,' she invited, once indoors and hefting the ever-boiling kettle over his mug. He had opted for

Bovril, and the salted beefy scent reminded her she'd eaten nothing since last evening. 'I heard tell from locals that it's haunted or something.'

'Bewitched,' he said with relish. 'There's all sorts of devilish things goes on there by night, especially full moon. Dancing and wicked feasting and casting spells. No one in their right mind will venture there certain times.'

Very convenient for such as him, she thought. He doubtless did his fair share of building up the superstitions.

Outside, the terrier had started yapping, dancing round the tumbled sack and darting in for little nips, then dancing free. One corner of the sacking showed a triangular tear where a heavy, vicious-clawed foreleg waved as the badger fought to free itself.

'Best let it go,' Anna advised. 'It'll be more trouble than it's worth now it's coming to.'

'That bloody downpour held me up,' Huggett complained. 'The clout's had time to wear off.' He slid a choke-chain over the dog's head and dragged him clear. Then, in high dudgeon, the man gave a surly nod and made off, towing the dog behind.

Anna left it to Brock to free himself, then consigned the bloodstained sack to her rubbish bin.

At least that was one of God's wild creatures that wouldn't be baited to death. She hoped that Huggett would regard her presence as good reason not to repeat the venture for a while.

Chapter Nine

'Miff' Smith, patrolman and outrider for Traffic Division, was an impressive figure, standing six feet five inches in his black leathers and biking boots. He wasn't unaware of the flutter he caused on entering Ward 5 to interview the now-conscious RTA case.

'Jeff Wilmott' the note told him: identified by his driving licence, a provisional one. So his bike should have had L-plates. Which it hadn't. Not that it was a powerful beast like his own Kawasaki, but a pootering little two-stroke.

Now that the lad was coming round Miff was prepared to make things uncomfortable for him. Particularly since his pillion passenger, the girl in ITU, wasn't offering much hope of recovery.

'Right then,' he said, seating himself in the chair a nurse had whipped under him. 'Let's hear all about it.'

'Everything's a bit fuzzy,' the patient complained. 'We were going along this lane, on the way home. No traffic once we'd left the main road. Then suddenly this fox darted out . . .'

Miff's pencil was poised over his notebook. 'A fox?'

'Well, it could have been a dog, I suppose. It happened so quickly. Anyway I managed to miss it, but skidded. Greasy road in the rain.'

'And hit a tree instead, side-on.'

'Yes. How about Charley? Is she going to be all right? Nobody tells me anything.'

'She's in another ward. Maybe you can see her later. We'll get this straight first.'

'Well, that's all I know. I must have passed out. I don't remember anything else.'

'You can start with your address. We have to inform your family. How many Ts in Wilmott?'

'Two, I suppose. Why? What's that got to do . . . ?'

'Jeff Wilmott. That's you, isn't it?' The patrolman regarded him with suspicion. If the lad remembered the skid and the fox, he surely hadn't forgotten his own name.

Now he was staring back, wide-eyed and ashen faced. 'No. my name's Danny. I'm Daniel Hoad. I live at Fordham Manor in

Bucks. But I know a Jeff Wilmott. He's a friend. It's his leathers I was wearing.'

'Which happened to have his licence in a pocket.' Miff Smith sighed. Now the little stinker would have the whole flaming book thrown at him. And the name Hoad clanged a very loud bell. It had been banner head-lines in the national press for the past few days.

This was the missing member of the slaughtered family. The sole survivor. He'd need to report in pdq to HQ Control.

Salmon growled low in his throat, suppress-ing his excitement. 'I'll send someone over,' he grunted, making it sound like a threat. He slammed the receiver back on the phone.

They'd been scouring the whole country to find him and the bloody boy was off sow-ing his wild oats. It seemed the girl in ques-tion wasn't going to make it. In which case young Hoad could end up facing a man-slaughter charge. And it was a dead cert that some bleeding-heart jury would let him off, because of what happened to the rest of his family.

He waddled into the corridor, stuck his head in the CID office and snarled, 'Beaumont!'

'Out, sir,' DC Silver answered instantly,

adding 'following up a lead.' The white lie should be good for a pint.

'It'll have to be you then. Get down to Ascot hospital. The Hoad boy's there, RTA casualty under a false identity. I want your report on my desk by 4 p.m. Details of everything he's been up to since Friday. Name and address of his girlfriend; length of the relationship; where they met; the lot. Oh, and try for witnesses to the accident. We need to know how he was behaving beforehand.'

It could be that the boy wasn't vital to the investigation, except to supply background to the family. He'd left home — as if for scouts, being an Explorer, some newfangled rank that hadn't existed in Salmon's own youth — well before the storm began, and now it appeared that, with the camp cancelled, he'd gone womanising.

Salmon wouldn't exactly have wished the accident on him, but his puritan cast of mind suggested a hint of justice in it.

He supposed he'd better wise up the superintendent on this latest development. With this in mind he made for Yeadings' office where the Boss, immersed in paperwork, shot a glance of exaggerated patience over his half-moon reading lenses. 'DCI Salmon,' he sighed.

'We've located Daniel Hoad, sir.'

'Alive?' Yeadings' back straightened.

Salmon explained.

'Have you notified his grandmother?'

'I was about to, sir.'

'Best leave it to Z. She can run the lady down to Ascot and double on interviewing the lad as soon as he's fit enough.'

'Silver's on his way there now, sir. And there's a girl injured too, Hoad's pillion passenger. They don't rate her chances high.'

'That's bad. Well, Silver and Z can cover it between them. What's afoot nearer home?'

'This man Jay, the other little girl's father. Seems he's a QC and he's throwing his weight about.'

'Yes. I've already heard of him from the Chief Constable. We have a meeting set up for this afternoon, at the man's home. I'll be taking a WPC along. You can leave the Jay family to us, Salmon. It's a wretched business altogether, and they're naturally very upset.'

'There are leads to follow up there, sir. Their little girl, Monica, supplied the eats and drinks.' His tone indicated the hard line he'd have taken with them himself.

'For the "midnight feast"? Yes, I'll be mentioning that. It's possible the mother was a party to it and provided the goodies

' — apart from the sherry perhaps.'

Salmon's mouth had tightened into a single line. He bridled every time the superintendent abandoned his desk to grab some action by rights in his own remit. But with the Chief Constable drawn in, there could be flak flying. So, just as well this time if Yeadings' broad shoulders were on the receiving end. That's what a super was paid for.

Salmon returned to his own office, soon to be further piqued by sight from his window of both Yeadings and Z leaving the building and separating to reach their respective cars. Beaumont was still missing, off on some scent of his own and leaving no hint of his whereabouts. When Salmon tried to raise him on his mobile it was still turned off.

One point continued to niggle at the DCI like a touch of tinnitus: the recurrence of the word 'Swindon'. Hoad's partner-manager Bertie Fallon, who once worked there, had denied knowing Mrs Bellinger, a resident, but no cross-checking had been done. He would drive down there and question the woman himself.

Passing Reception he observed several large open-topped cartons stuffed with crumpled paper being carried in. 'Who's that for?' he demanded.

'Superintendent Yeadings, sir. At his request. Recovered from Fordham Manor's recyclable waste, sir.'

Salmon's lip curled. He wished Yeadings joy of it when he returned from his outing, especially the large, tangled bundle of shredded typescript spilling over the edge of one carton like drunken party streamers. Gumming that back together could be more exercising for the mind, he reckoned, than a Sunday newspaper's puzzle section. For himself he'd rather hunt in Swindon for a connection between Hoad's business partner and the woman his housekeeper had been weekending with.

When Z broke it to Anna Plumley that Daniel had been located, injured in a biking accident, the elderly woman closed her eyes. 'Thank God he's alive. Has he been told how things stand here?'

'I'm hoping that will be left to us. A DC is already on his way to question him about the accident. I've tried ringing him to hold back, but his mobile's turned off. I'll try again on the way down, if you're ready to leave now.'

In the passenger seat Anna sat silent, hands clasped in her lap. Only when Z darted a sideways glance at her did she catch the little wobble of her chin as she fought against tears.

'He's been conscious for several hours now. There's no call to imagine he's in real danger. But he'd had a passenger on the pillion, and she's in Intense Therapy. I haven't heard what her name is or if her parents have been notified.'

'We should visit her too,' Anna decided.

Despite Salmon's instructions Silver was determined to confine his interview with Daniel Hoad to the RTA which had landed him in Ascot hospital, but he discovered that once the Traffic officer had had the name on the patient's clipboard corrected from Wilmott some unutterable oaf in the same ward had blabbed information on the family disaster. By the time he reached him the young man had become hysterical and been given sedation. With Daniel beyond questioning for the present, he found his way to ITU, tapped at the door, showed his warrant card and was admitted.

He sat alongside the unconscious girl, listening to the soft sigh and clunk of the ventilator that was breathing for her, and keeping his eyes off the gruesome assembly of equipment connected by tubes and wires to the comatose figure in the bed.

A nurse, mistaking him for a relative, brought him tea. When again he produced his warrant card she raised no objection to showing him the girl's personal effects.

The clipboard at the foot of her bed named her as Charleen Jenkins. Her clothes had consisted of flimsy underwear smelling strongly of perfume, a short black leather skirt, black knee-boots, a red and white horizontally striped sweater with a low neckline and a navy hip-length reefer jacket. All were stiff with dried-out mud and black grease. There was a rather scruffy red plastic handbag on a long strap which had snapped. Inside he found make-up, contraceptives, a mock-leather cover for a filofax which was empty and a Sainsbury's credit card from which the hospital had learnt her name. There was no address.

It wasn't lost on him that there was considerably more activity taking place around the other curtained beds than at this one, although a nurse checked every fifteen minutes and made a note of her readings. Eventually she turned to Silver and said, 'I'm afraid you're wasting your time. I can't say more until we've traced next of kin for her, you understand. And her doctor won't tell you anything definite.'

Which sounded pretty dire. They could be waiting for family to authorise switching off the life support equipment.

'No hope then?' he ventured. She said nothing, just tilted her head, eyebrows raised. Horribly discreet.

He supposed the Area police would be trying to contact family. At least they'd a name to go on, but she needn't be a local. Under the bandaging and bruises it was a pert little face with a tip-tilted nose. A frizzed bottle-blonde, she was young, but not as young as he knew Daniel to be. Perhaps early twenties. An older female to teach him the basic points of seduction? Prostitute or amateur; you couldn't tell by appearances these days.

A buzzer sounded. The nurse who took the call came across to them. 'Detective Constable Silver? Your sergeant's in Reception asking for you.'

There was another woman with Z. Silver guessed this must be the ex-Squadron Leader. She listened in silence as he explained how news of the carnage at Fordham had already been broken to the injured boy.

'Not your fault,' Z said quickly. 'How long has he been sedated? Could he be alert enough to interview?'

130

'I doubt you'll be allowed in,' Anna Plumley interrupted. 'I'm family. They'll let me sit by him until he's properly come round.'

Z considered this. Banned as a policewoman, she must leave all questioning to the other woman. But why not? She was a wise old bird and Daniel would speak more freely with her out of the way. 'Would you rather talk to him alone?'

'Can you trust me to report back fully? No, come in with me. To the nurses I could pass you off as my niece. You needn't say more than hello.'

Z followed in her wake. Outside the private room to which Danny had been moved she was conscious of the woman's pause, the stiffened shoulders, the deeper breath she took before opening the door. Her substantial figure cut off sight of the occupant in the hospital bed. As she moved to one side of the room Z glimpsed him petrified with amazement.

He made an effort to sit up, then fell back against his pillows. 'Grananna! You?'

'It's some years since I heard you call me that, Daniel.'

'Why've you . . . ? But, of course.' He swallowed desperately. His voice came out thin and uncertain. 'There's only us now. Have you heard?'

She nodded, sat on the visitor's chair provided and took his hand in both her own. 'I know.'

'Isn't it the most — bloody — filthy — thing? It can't be true, can it? They've muddled us with someone else. Who would ever want to . . . ?'

'Why else would I be here?' She sounded calm and reasonable, almost detached. 'I'll do whatever a grandmother can. Whatever you think I should. I've moved in and I'll stay on there for a while, if that's all right. Until you feel more settled.'

'Settled? I'm never going back there. I couldn't!' His voice rose shrilly. He had torn his hand away and shook both fists in the air, white-knuckled. 'Oh God, I wish I was dead!'

'Don't tempt fate. Your girlfriend nearly is.'

Z stared in disbelief. Where was the comfort in that? But it seemed to have brought the boy to his senses.

'Charleen,' he said in a choking voice. 'It wasn't my fault, Grananna. There was a fox ran out right in front. We skidded, trying not to hit it. She wasn't dressed for biking and I had to get her home.'

'And where would home be?'

'Her flat in Slough. I've been shacked up

there all weekend. She wanted to go to this rave down in Camberley. Insisted, really.'

'When did this happen?'

'Saturday night. Well, in the early hours actually.'

Some slight movement of Z's made him suddenly conscious of her presence. He darted a look across to where she stood against the wall. There was a flicker of some emotion, rapid like a camera's shutter. Then his face was prepared for her, young and pathetic. She recognised he was practised in this, conscious of his own angelic beauty, the power of his unfailing ability to charm. It didn't necessarily mean intention to deceive; just a habitual mechanism.

'Who's this?' he demanded.

'This is Rosemary. She's looking after me.'

'Hello, Rosemary.' He even smiled, a weak looping up of the lips under perfect cheek-bones unscarred from the crash.

'Were you wearing a crash helmet?' Z asked him.

'I — I think so.'

She was going to ask, did Charleen have one, but Anna moved between the two of them and gave a warning glance.

'It would have been worse without one,' Z offered limply.

He had an enchanting smile; defenceless,

little-boy-lost acting brave.

'So what do the doctors say?' Anna Plumley demanded briskly. 'How soon can we get you out of here and have you properly looked after?'

'Oh, it's all right here. They've been good to me.'

'Hospital's unreal. Fine as a brief interval, but you need to get your feet firmly on the ground again.'

Z marvelled at her callousness. That would have been part of Anna's received Air Force discipline: patch up the crash victims, send them up straight afterwards. She'd been treated the same way herself after a bad fall from a horse as a child. No truck with self-pity. Maybe that was right. It had worked with herself.

But this had to be different. Did Anna truly intend returning the boy to the house where his whole family had been wiped out?

'They want me to see a shrink,' he said in a weak voice. 'For counselling.'

'Nothing wrong with that,' his grandmother allowed. 'You don't have to stay here for it. There are excellent consultants in London.'

'London,' he said wonderingly. But she'd implied he had to go home. He frowned, seeming confused.

'Gran, do you mind? I think I need a rest just now. You will come again, won't you? I'd like you with me when the police come asking questions. They do badger a guy so, and I could get muddled.'

'We'll stay around,' she assured him. 'You can be certain of that; we'll both be coming back.'

As they left they passed a uniformed constable seated outside the door. Area, it seemed, were taking no chances.

'Coffee,' Anna briskly ordained. In the cafeteria Z pointed to a vacant table. 'I'll get the tray.' She queued for two apricot Danish, a cappuccino and a double espresso to cover all eventualities, guessing that the older woman would be grateful for a few minutes alone to adjust.

'He's just the same,' Anna said, as Z unloaded their crockery on the table. 'Only perhaps more so. Horribly spoilt.'

Why not? Z asked herself. He'd so many advantages that others hadn't: gifted with a secure family life, expensive education, a lovely home, moneyed background, good health and a talent to charm.

'Which makes it that much harder to confront the sort of thing that's happened. So much to lose at one blow, poor boy,' she offered.

'Yes. It's as he said. Now he's just got himself. And me, for all that's worth.' She sounded downcast. 'Maybe I shouldn't have come. It's taking on too much.'

'But he needs you, your strength. To know he's not entirely alone. Even his girlfriend — it's not certain she'll pull through.'

Anna stiffened, suddenly determined again. 'Yes. We must do something about her. Speak to her family?'

'DC Silver said they hadn't been able to contact anyone. No address was found on her. Nothing but a building society credit card made out to Charleen Jenkins. We'd need to ask Daniel. He mentioned a flat in Slough. He may know more of her background.'

'You're right.' Anna grimly surveyed the coffee and pastry as the next challenge before her, picked up her knife and tackled the Danish with aggression. 'As soon as Daniel has had his little nap we must set about tracing the girl's family.'

CHAPTER TEN

The WPC Yeadings took along with him wouldn't have been his choice, but Marion Peel was the only one available according to the uniformed inspector. She was a stout party in a tight uniform and with a bad complexion. Motherly she might prove, and therefore ideal for most dealings with a bereaved family, but Yeadings had misgivings about the Jays' immediate requirements.

He would be a channel for their denial and anger: their daughter's tragic death had no part in their successful lives. Grieving must come later. His present role was to bow his head and take what came. There was no call for invasive questioning, since the child's inclusion in the Hoad family slaughter had surely been accidental.

He found he was mistaken in considering only the man's anger already displayed in confronting the Chief Constable. There was the mother too. He hadn't quite speculated on her reaction. Mrs Jay opened the door to them herself, although a uniformed maid hovered in the background.

Her eyes were puffy and red with weeping. 'It's good of you to come, Superintendent,' she said, 'although God only knows what good it can do. Nothing will bring our darling back.'

She was a strongly built woman with an open face framed in wildly curling auburn hair. And humanly vulnerable, so that Yeadings had a natural urge to put an arm about her and gently rub her back for comfort. But she plunged away and they'd no choice but to follow, through the large, square hall and into an elegant sitting room. There was no sign of her husband.

'Please,' she said and motioned them towards twin sofas to each side of a log fire giving out the scent of apple wood. Over it hung a full-length portrait of a ballerina in a white tutu. She was an ethereal creature, slim and erect, possibly some thirteen or fourteen years old. Not the daughter, then. Perhaps there were other children. He should have enquired into that before coming.

Mrs Jay followed the direction of his eyes and nodded. 'I was crazy about dancing then, but I was growing too tall. Just never stopped. My father, an Ulsterman, said he should have put a turf on my head.'

Yeadings smiled. He'd heard that expression before.

'And my second love was cattle. So when Clifford came along and married me I grasped the opportunity. He indulged what he considered my whim. You may know I run a farm now. Friesians. They're amiable beasts.'

She was talking to keep off the subject he'd come about. A way of keeping him at bay. But he'd meant to offer comfort, however empty.

She caught the sound of a door opening and tensed. Then as the maid brought in a tray with tea things she gave a nervous laugh and settled to making room on a low table beside her. There were cups and saucers for three.

'Is your husband at home, Mrs Jay?' Yeadings asked.

'No. He — he's busy in town. Some urgent case that's come up. He left yesterday.'

Left her to deal with grief on her own.

'I think he blames me for letting M-Monica go for a sleepover. She'd done it before, with other school friends. She's a popular little girl.'

Yeadings found himself liking the absent husband less every moment. On an impulse he decided to unburden himself.

'I'm finding this difficult. You must forgive me if I seem utterly useless. In other cases there has always been some hope left, when I can promise we will do our utmost to find a missing child. But this time it is too late. All I can do is swear we will hunt down whoever has done this appalling thing, and bring him to justice.'

She shivered, staring into the blazing logs. 'That at the very least.'

'But it's never enough. I can't say how very much I feel for your loss. If it's any solace to you, Monica knew nothing of what happened. She was asleep.'

'You have children of your own.'

It was a statement, needing no reply. She started busying herself with pouring tea, and her two visitors drank without tasting it, knowing they should already have left. As soon as he could politely withdraw, Yeadings stood and offered his hand.

'You will let me know of any progress?'

'Certainly.' He noticed she had said 'me' and not 'us'. It sounded as though the marriage would not long outlast this devastating blow.

■ ■ ■ ■

Catherine Jay sat on for some twenty minutes while her tea grew cold. Then she rose and left the house by the kitchen, crossing the cobbled yard, past the row of stables to the distant milking parlour. The stockman was just herding her cows in.

She waited until Shula was opposite, then ran her hand over the velvety muzzle, drawing the great black and white body to her, breathing in her hay-scented breath.

'I'll see to this one,' she called, and guided the cow into a nearby stall. Not the impersonal, efficient Alfa-Laval system tonight. For Shula there should be hand-milking.

No, not for Shula: for herself.

The cow had a full, rounded udder, smooth like pink soap. The woman found a stool, pulled it alongside and sat, laying her cheek flat against the warm, sweat-greased flanks for solace. As she reached with both hands to squeeze out the sweet milk her tears began to flow. She remembered then that she had never been able to breast-feed Monica as a baby. It had left her feeling deprived. But nothing like now.

Her weight against the warm, breathing flanks, she milked and sobbed until both she and Shula ran dry.

'God, that's fabulous! A Granannavan!'

He leaned forward to clear the misted car
window with his sleeve and peer out as Z
braked and drew alongside the rear of the
manor. Despite his protests they had
brought him home. Anna had been ada-
mant, Z doubtful, but the hospital had been
happy to see him go, because of the hordes
from national and local press who were
finding ways of eluding the overloaded
security system.

Almost as soon as the car started moving
the boy had fallen asleep, his head lolling
on to his grandmother's shoulder. Through
her driving mirror Z had watched the
woman draw him closer, resting his head on
her ample breast and stroking back the
wayward lock of hair that flopped over his
forehead.

He slept all the way until they reached the
gates to Fordham Manor where a half-
dozen paparazzi, forewarned by phone, had
gathered with a battery of cameras. Flashes
lit the gloomy afternoon as they jostled to
get a view of the car's occupants. There was
even a TV van and a couple with furry
mikes, one brandished on a boom and
thrust at the driver's window.

'Police,' Z snapped, stopping while the duty constable operated the gates. 'There's no admission.' They drove through unimpeded and the gates were closed behind them.

Waking to recognise the close hedgerows and the windings of the lane, the boy had pulled away from his grandmother. A sound that was between a whispered groan and a whimper escaped him.

'You're going to manage fine, back among your own things,' the ex-Squadron Leader commanded. Z was doubtful, wincing as the woman went on, 'We'll go in by the gun room. I've brought the spare key.'

How could she be so unfeeling? But then Z recalled that the room had not been used to store guns for decades. It was more a dumping ground for garden furniture, golf umbrellas and muddy Wellington boots; as an entrance, probably more homely to the boy than most other parts of the house. But the name was unfortunate.

That had been the moment he saw the Jeep and the caravan. In an instant he was alert and fascinated.

'Mine,' Anna admitted shortly. 'I'm the peripatetic house guest, not always sure there's a welcome under my would-be hosts' roof.'

He flashed her his pathetic half-smile, there and gone in a second. And of course he knew what peripatetic meant. 'We've got two guest rooms,' he offered. 'There's beds for both of you.'

'Rosemary?' Anna raised a suggestive eyebrow. 'Like to stay on?'

'Thanks,' said Z, turning in her seat to face him, 'but I'm local, more or less. And anyway, Danny, you should know I'm police. Sergeant Zyczynski, CID.'

He stared back at her, eyes wide in an ashen face. It was anything but welcome news. She was aware of a new barrier going up between them.

'It was an accident,' he said weakly. 'A fox darted out and I skidded avoiding it.'

'That's Ascot's business,' she told him. 'Nothing to do with me. As your grandmother said, I'm here to help her in any way I can. But there's someone else who needs caring for. Your friend Charleen. We must get in touch with her folks. Do you know where they live?'

He continued to stare, his mouth slack.

'Did you give the Traffic officer her address?'

His reaction was delayed, but as he started to talk the words fell over themselves. 'She lives alone. It was a flat over a shop; number

7A, I think. I don't know the name of the road. It was dark when we got there and we had to get in out of the storm.'

So he didn't know her at all well. Probably a pick-up in some bar he'd risked entering, confident he looked older than his true age.

'This would be on Friday?'

'Yes.'

'That was your first meeting?'

He was young enough to blush. 'She seemed friendly; lent me change for the phone. I'd left my mobile at home.'

'And then?'

'Well, I had to stand her a drink, didn't I? Actually we had one or two. She was funny and we got on really well together. When I told her the camp had been cancelled she said I could come back with her; spend the weekend there.' There was a brief hint of cockiness there, while his expression stayed unsure.

'I was a bit doubtful at first, only by the time I'd given her a lift home she said I shouldn't be riding farther after what I'd drunk. So I said I'd stay.'

'And who did you ring?'

'Ring?'

'You borrowed change from her for the phone.'

'Oh, that was earlier. Yes. I rang home. Only there was no reply. The answerphone was switched on. They do that when everyone's gone to bed. To avoid being disturbed.'

'What time would that have been?' Her voice sharpened.

He looked vague, switched his gaze to his grandmother who was staring down at her hands. No help from that direction. What had he expected her to do — beg that the questions should stop?

'I don't know. It's all a bit foggy. Late, anyway.'

'Before the pub closed?'

'Of course.'

'So which pub would that have been?'

She caught a flicker of something like anger in his eyes. He wasn't used to being cross-questioned. His voice, when he answered, was superior, putting her in her place, a mere policewoman. 'Oh, the Swan or the Falcon or some such bird.'

'In . . . ?'

'Slough. I'd gone there to pick up my friend's bike. He was away that weekend on TA training.'

'Without his bike?'

'They'd sent him a rail warrant. To Bodmin. God, it'd have been really shitty out there on the moors. If the storm reached that far.'

'I guess so,' she conceded and managed a smile. No need to ruffle his feathers further. All he'd told her could easily be checked. 'Let's go indoors, then.'

'It should have warmed through by now,' Anna encouraged. 'I turned the heating up before I left.'

They all got out, Daniel hopping between the hospital's aluminium sticks while Z retrieved his kitbag from the car's boot. The women waited for Daniel to join them at the door. His face was chalky white and Z had further misgivings about bringing him home so soon. They filed through into the hall. As Anna turned on the lights he stared wildly around, his eyes drawn at once to the police tapes denying access to the dining room. Instantly he crumpled to the floor, his gasping cry followed by the clatter of metal sticks on the tiles.

'Out like a light,' Anna observed, whipping off her car coat and bundling it under his head.

There was the sound of rapid feet descending the stairs. 'The housekeeper,' Anna explained. 'She arrived just before you picked me up.'

Mrs Pavitt appeared. 'I heard your car. Oh God, it's Daniel. You've brought him back!' She sounded appalled.

She ran and knelt beside him, loosening his collar and chafing his hands between her own. 'We must get him to bed.'

'A sofa in the drawing-room,' Anna decreed. 'Rosemary, will you take his feet?' She stood back while the other two carried him through.

'Some water,' Alma Pavitt demanded, waving a hand at Z who disappeared into the kitchen.

'I think he's discovered a taste for something more bracing,' said his grandmother. 'Stop fussing and give the lad some air. You can get him a whisky when he comes round. Better still, make that three.'

Mrs Pavitt hesitated, darted an unfathomable look at the dragon, then walked stiffly from the room as Z returned with the water.

Anna took the tumbler from her and poured half its contents on to a potted aphelandra by the window. 'Mrs Pavitt is bringing us some scotch. There must be a kitchen supply. But I think he'd better not take his neat.'

In Swindon DCI Salmon had difficulty in finding the right house his quarry had been taken to. The M4 was clogged with traffic and he was twice held up at roadworks in sheeting rain which made his windscreen wipers almost useless.

His ballpoint pen had reached the blobby stage, and since he'd jotted down the address rain on his hands had smudged the end of each line. So he'd gone for Meldrun Road, been redirected to Meldrun Avenue and eventually located Mrs Bellinger's refuge at Meldrun Walk. The detour had not improved his social skills.

The retired hotel-housekeeper was matchingly foul-minded at having been deserted by her guest at a point when she needed a certain amount of physical assistance. The only bright relief was that Salmon could indulge her appetite for gruesome details of the crime that required Alma Pavitt's recall.

The DCI at his best was not effusive. At his surliest, as now, he saw information as totally one-directional. He made it clear that an officer in his position could not indulge a witness's morbid curiosity. Mrs Bellinger's jaw set stubbornly. Deprived of stimulating details of the Hoad family's disaster, she went mute as a clam. It was not until Salmon asked about her connection with somebody called Bertie Fallon that she perked up and demanded, 'Who?'

Challenged to provide info himself, Salmon resisted, simply repeating the name.

'Weel, I'm not sure,' the woman tempted, exaggerating her Lowland Scots accent. 'Now what would the mannie be looking like?'

Partially defeated, Salmon admitted that apparently he was of medium height, with medium dark hair, medium everything in fact. Then he conceded that the man had been a metallurgist locally.

'Eh? Would that be some kind of alternative therapist?' she enquired, cupping her ear as if slightly deaf.

Near explosion point, he was obliged to explain.

'Ah,' she said finally, after some thought, 'there's a lot of foundry workers around these parts. Not the sort of people I'd have any occasion to mix with, Sergeant.'

He wasn't such a fool that he mistook what she was about, so he didn't attempt to dispute his rank. If what she'd said was true there could be others much better qualified to give him some background on Fallon. He'd only to contact the local police and they could steer him towards men who shared Fallon's interests.

Better still he could leave it with them to follow the matter up, get himself a meal and be on the road home within little more than an hour.

CHAPTER ELEVEN

Yeadings sat grim-faced through the debriefing. For days uniformed men had combed the area round Fordham Manor for clues but it became increasingly unlikely that anything useful would come to light; a point the national press was having a field-day with. Neither the missing gun nor the knife had been found.

House-to-house enquiries in the village had produced no witness to any visitor to the estate on the night of Friday–Saturday. Who would be crazy enough to be abroad in that ferocious storm? Now, despite the outrageous nature of the crime, Superintendent Challoner was demanding his uniform men back for routine duties.

Salmon, the Boss had to admit, was doing nothing wrong. But he was getting nothing right either. He couldn't be blamed for not being Angus Mott, but surely by now there should be some spark of light in the general obscurity.

As the meeting broke up, 'My office,' he commanded, nodding to his two sergeants and signalling the DCI to follow.

'Now,' he said as they found places to sit, Beaumont cross-legged on the floor between desk and door, 'let's start all over again. Forget any pattern the investigation has followed so far. We need fresh eyes. What exactly is this wholesale slaughter about? Come on, tell me.'

'A total nutter.' Beaumont broke the sombre pause. 'Who else would rush from room to room killing anything that breathed?'

Yeadings grunted. 'There's no report of any such person loose in the vicinity.'

'He had to get inside the house, and he left without leaving a trace,' Z reflected. 'That took some organisation, which must rule out anyone truly demented, however crazy he went over the actual killing.'

'Someone known to the family, because there was no break-in. He was either there by invitation or they let him in on trust.' This was Beaumont's next contribution.

'One of them went suddenly crazy.' Salmon sounded unsure. Invited to break new ground he made a wild leap into fantasy.

'Four dead,' Yeadings reminded him patiently. 'That way the killer would have to survive his three victims and then dispose of himself. The children were asleep. No way could Hoad have shot himself with a sporting rifle while discharging a shotgun. And the rifle's missing. The woman certainly never half-strangled herself, and much of the stabbing was proved to be post-mortem. You can't deny there was another person present in the house. We have to discover who. But what I actually asked was — "what is it all about?" '

They all stared back, unwilling to offer a theory.

'Why all that mayhem? You've an open choice. Even a lunatic must have some kind of motivation,' he prompted.

'Bloodlust,' Z said simply.

'Possible. Anything else?'

'Hatred. Revenge.'

'Gain.'

'Sex.'

'Any of those,' Yeadings agreed. 'There's also fear. Fear of exposure or of actual harm. We have to consider each of the victims in the light of those options. One at least of them could have brought about the need to be killed.'

'But to wipe out everyone . . .' Z looked

away in horror.

'Perhaps that wasn't the intention,' Yeadings suggested slowly. 'Suppose the intention was to kill only one of them, but something went wrong, and the whole thing escalated out of control. It may have been Hoad or his wife. I think the children can be left out of this, but once something unexpected happened the killer panicked, had to finish off any possible witnesses.'

'Even — children — asleep?' Beaumont ground out in protest.

'Yes, in an almighty panic. We all know how obsessives, driven far enough . . .'

They sat in silence, unsure where consideration of a single intended victim could lead them. 'We've already been working on Hoad's background,' Salmon defended himself.

'We need to dig deeper. And the same for his wife. Had she a lover? What do we know about her business dealings? Even the missing son, Daniel. Suppose he was the intended victim but just happened not to be there.

'Because Hoad was the first to be killed, it doesn't mean he was the intended victim. Perhaps that was where it went wrong; right at the beginning. An intruder caught wrong-footed. All we know for sure is that someone removed another firearm from the locked steel cabinet and, confronted by Hoad with a shotgun, discharged it into him. The rest could have happened in a red mist. A simple scenario is often nearest to the truth. What's against it?'

Beaumont shifted uncomfortably on the floor. 'A rifle wouldn't have been put away loaded. Someone had to find the ammo first.'

'Apparently some .22 bullets were kept right there alongside. Hoad had failed to take full precautions,' snarled Salmon.

'His wife would know how to open the cabinet,' Z reminded them. 'She used to take part in their clay-pigeon shooting parties for her city friends. Why couldn't she have been the one to remove the rifle?'

'And accidentally shot her old man, mistaking him for a burglar?' Beaumont demanded sarcastically. 'Both of them wandering around in the dark because they'd heard a disturbance downstairs? This isn't a Tom and Jerry cartoon.'

'Imagine an intruder shocked into using the gun, finding he'd killed someone,' Zyczynski suggested. 'Wouldn't he normally make off, not set about wiping out the whole family?'

'Unless you were shit-scared out of your

marbles,' said Beaumont.

'If only we knew how the bugger got in,' Salmon complained, back to the original tangent.

'At least we know what we need answers for. There's plenty of scope for further enquiries,' Yeadings promised, preparing to wind up the meeting. 'Which is why the CC, in his wisdom, has called in a psychological profiler who will doubtless dog your footsteps and replicate what we've already discovered. However, in view of the case's importance, I expect you to cooperate with him, or her, as far as you are able.'

On this occasion denied the Boss's excellent coffee, the two sergeants retired to the canteen for its lesser version and sugar-loaded doughnuts.

'There's one good thing,' Beaumont considered, unloading their tray on the only free table, which Z had dived across to claim as they entered. She looked up at him expectantly.

'The press will go to town on the profiling. Slavering over a shrink should keep them off our backs.'

'Not if this one's glued to us. Honey for the wasps.'

'Well, let's hope it's not that starch-faced

old biddy from Reading Uni,' Beaumont prayed. 'You wouldn't remember her. It was before your time. Not content with early childhood memories, she was into exploring our sexual fantasies.'

'I guess you fulfilled her requirements in spades.'

He grinned impishly back at her. 'That would take all the fun out of it, going public.'

'So how did you handle her?'

'Went all solemn, tried to press a copy of the *Watchtower* on her. She decided a lifetime wasn't enough to get me sorted, so she gave up.'

Z's quick smile vanished as she tasted her coffee. 'This is undrinkable.'

'Yup. We have to get back in the Boss's favour. Which means a return to the galleys and hard graft. I wanted to talk to the boy; get him to dig the family dirt. But I guess he'll be left to the shrink. Who's your target?'

'The late Jennifer Hoad. Lovers, existence of; business skulduggery likewise. Just as the Boss said.'

'So a day in London? Are the Oxford Street sales on?'

She stood up, gave him a withering glance, hoisted her shoulder bag and left him to clear the used crockery.

There was one duty she must perform before taking the train. She drove out to Fordham and called at the Manor. Mrs Pavitt answered the front door.

'If you want the others they're out by the caravan.' She sounded put out, hardly the well-mannered family servant.

'Actually, this other is right here,' said Anna Plumley, stepping forward out of the hall's gloom. 'Good morning, Rosemary. I saw your car down the lane and managed to divert young Daniel. He's not ready yet for dredging up family history. I assume that's what this visit is for?'

'Not my job. I just called in to ask how things were.'

'More or less as expected.' She turned to the housekeeper. 'Thank you. Mrs Pavitt; don't let us detain you.'

They waited while she departed for the kitchen. 'Come upstairs,' invited the ex-Squadron Leader. 'We can keep an eye on my grandson from his bedroom window. He's out the back, splitting logs.'

'Your suggestion?'

'I said I fancied an open fire, and there was only big stuff available.'

Z smiled. That was good, keeping him occupied. 'How is he?'

Anna Plumley hesitated before answering. 'Confused and frightened. He — he's more clinging than I care for. This is the first time I've been able to leave him on his own.' They had arrived at the door to his room and went in.

'Last night he was scared to go to bed, so I told him I'd leave my door open. He said he'd do the same, but did I mind moving to the other guest room. I'd put my things in the one nearer the main body of the house. The one he chose was only a few feet nearer his own door, on the far side. I did as he asked. I heard him tossing and turning all night. Then at about two in the morning he got up and shut his door. I heard him dragging a chest across to wedge it fast. At least then it left us both to get some sleep.'

She crossed close to the window. 'And now, dammit, that woman's gone out to put him off his stroke.'

Z joined her to watch. The boy had moved round the woodpile and spoke over his shoulder to the woman who followed and reached out to touch his shoulder. He swung round and shouted in her face. They heard the anger in his voice but the words didn't reach them.

Normal victim behaviour, Z thought.

Sharing with her some of the survival guilt he felt for not having been here when it happened. However down-to-earth his grandmother's approach was, the boy needed professional counselling. The profiler could provide that.

'Isn't anger a good sign?' she asked. 'Progress, of a sort?'

'The victim's second stage, yes. But I think this is something else. It's personal. Those two are at daggers-drawn. I'm not convinced we need her around.'

Z wasn't so sure. Anna was just the absentee grandmother who had suddenly reappeared from his childhood days. Wasn't she taking over too forcefully, under the circumstances? Pavitt, after all, was the more familiar, the only one left from his routine home life.

'Don't you think they're suffering in much the same way?' she suggested, 'and that, once over the shock, they could comfort each other?'

Anna Plumley grimaced. 'Quite naturally Mrs Pavitt considers I'm usurping her position to some extent. But I am family. She's not, however much he's accustomed to her. I'm sure it's not good for us to force Daniel into being pig-in-the-middle.'

She grinned back at Z, quite unfazed by

the younger woman's presumption in questioning her wisdom.

Beaumont sat a while in his car before starting off to interview the Hoad son. The survivor, he reminded himself. And only a kid really, for all his photo made him look older and quite sophisticated.

He couldn't avoid thinking of his own boy in the same situation. Suppose, by some mischance — though perhaps less likely in a policeman's family than a gentleman farmer's — someone had broken in at home, armed, and murdered his parents while the kid was out employing some testosterone. What sort of state would he be in when he eventually reached home and learned about it?

Pretty shattered, he guessed, for all that they weren't a demonstrative family. It was the sheer incredibility of it, the destruction of all known security, that would hit hardest. It would take a special sort of guts to keep him from falling apart.

So the Hoad boy, Daniel, would barely be in a fit state to open up to an inquisitive outsider. Z could be right in dealing with him through the grandmother. His own best move would be to make it look as if he was calling to check up on her.

A hundred yards into the narrow lane leading to Fordham Manor and farm, he turned a corner and came bumper to bumper with Rosemary Zyczynski's blue Ford Escort. She wound her window down and leaned out, gesturing willingness to reverse, before pulling back in the gateway to a field.

He drew level and lowered his own passenger window. 'Thought you were off to La Belle Dame's office in London.'

'Had to pick up something here first. Mrs Hoad's mobile phone. It should have been collected with the computer. For some reason it had got itself into a kitchen drawer.'

Unlikely, but he didn't doubt Z. He wondered if Jennifer Hoad had hidden it there or someone had later tidied it away. He waved thanks for being allowed past and went on down towards the Manor, driving round to the rear where he found the mobile home parked behind a 4x4 and Mrs Plumley seated on the steps reading a paperback book.

He took his time getting out, conscious of her eyes following him. When he presented his ID she smiled. 'I had you pointed out at the station. I'm sure you know who I am.'

'Daniel Hoad's maternal grandmother.'

'Precisely. What can I do for you?'

'Fill me in a little more about the family. Explain, if you can, why anyone should want to do this to the family.'

'I can't. Nor can I understand how anyone could even consider such savagery. It defies belief.'

The round eyes in his wooden-puppet face were taking her all in. He didn't miss the title of the book in which she was marking her place with a surprisingly elegant forefinger. One of those portly women, he recognised, blessed with shapely legs ending in dainty feet, and with small hands to match.

'So you're reading up on the subject?'

'Ah, this.' She wagged the paperback casually. 'Found it in the boy's bookcase. Quite some years since I read it myself. An interesting study. Do you know it?'

'Not the book. Know the case, of course. Who doesn't? Charles Manson and the Sharon Tate murders.'

'Yes. A period crime classic. *Music, Mayhem, Murder.* The book gives a rational assessment of the man: obsessed by Beatlemania, stoned out of his mind, fed on pseudo-scientific, quasi-mystical superstition. Guru to a team of degenerates, LSD freaks, he was the prophet of doom, convinced a black uprising would end in rape, terror, carnage of the whites. Wanted to be the one to save creation, whether as Christ or Antichrist didn't matter. Simply the evil of the crazed, overblown self. At base a frustrated, pathetic soul soured because he felt his music was under-appreciated.'

'I guess I know more about what he finally did than what he was.'

'Which is how we all feel about the Twin Towers perpetrators. Every now and again stuff happens, as the saying goes. We face horrific deeds, fail to comprehend what possesses human creatures to commit such inhuman acts.'

'And that's how you feel about what happened here? I was hoping you could shed some light. Was there no way at all you could see this coming?'

She laid the book down on the steps and stood up, coming towards him. 'Sergeant, I am almost as much a stranger in this place as you are. I should have kept in touch. They were all that was left in this world of my blood. It is too late even for regrets. My business now is to stand by my grandson, do what I can to support him.'

'Was there some reason you kept away?'

'A long-standing difference with my daughter. She considered I always took her husband's side and opposed her.'

'So it was a divided marriage, husband and wife at loggerheads?'

'Not openly. There were differences of emphasis, of standards. Frankly, my daughter was a wanton. Freddie deserved something better than to be used as a cheque-book, but he accepted the way things were. Not that I ever believed their lives could end in such a tragic way.'

'End because of their differences?' He wasn't sure that she had implied that.

'Oh no. This is something else. What happened arose from some totally unrelated cause. I'm convinced of that. I wouldn't have spoken out otherwise.'

'Does your grandson think the same?'

'He doesn't know what to believe. He's avoiding thinking at all at the moment. I was just going to call him in for some coffee. Will you join us?'

She went to fetch Daniel while Beaumont riffled through the pages of the paperback. The boy arrived with his hands still wet from rinsing them under the garden tap, and there were fragments of bark clinging to his sweater. 'Been topping up the kindling for Gran,' he excused himself. His palms were red and sore-looking.

Beaumont kept his questions to a minimum, mainly concerning the date he'd booked for scout camp and who ran the show.

'Do you have to bother them?' the boy demanded. 'I'd rather they weren't dragged into family matters.'

'Probably shan't need to,' Beaumont allowed. 'We already know where you were that weekend. Routine questions we're obliged to ask everyone. Even your grandmother, while I'm at it.'

She shrugged. 'My alibi? I don't think I've got one. Home alone. My husband's down in Devon, fishing. I never go along. Sitting on a bank and waiting bores me to distraction, and he deserves a little time on his own.'

'Can you remember phoning anyone? Watching some TV programme?'

'I'd a heap of ironing to do. I'd left it to Friday night, and ran a couple of CDs while I was at it: Mahler and the Max Bruck Violin Concerto. Then I had supper and went to bed, sleeping through until almost four when the height of the storm reached us. It brought a tree down across the road about fifty yards from the house. Quite a crash.' Her gaze swept the caravan's interior. 'Thank heaven it missed this.'

CHAPTER TWELVE

Zyczynski was met at Miradec Interiors, Knightsbridge, by the person she had spoken to on the telephone. Until then she was uncertain as to his sex. His name was Hilary Durham, sleek and practised by voice, but less so in appearance.

He had tried hard. The suit was right, his silk shirt expensive, but despite that his efforts with them were incompetent. His collar bagged at the neck, the tie was knotted too tightly, his cuffs — too long — showed old stains inexpertly laundered. And then there was his hair, the colour and texture of straw, mostly greased flat but defiant at the crown, so that he reminded her of a tufted duck.

He apologised for the absence of Jennifer Hoad's PA, delayed in Paris, tying up loose ends. Mrs Hoad's death had been so unexpected they were all caught out, so to speak.

'So there's a French connection,' Z commented with apparent innocence.

'We have an office in France, yes. It deals with continental art imports. Not my department. I'm responsible for the planning and overseeing of work in hand. Well, I trained as an architect, but never sat my finals. Too much accountancy and law involved. Wanted to get to the nitty-gritty, if you know what I mean. Mrs Hoad called me her "Ideas Man".'

'She valued you, then.'

'I like to think so.' For all that, he looked uncertain. Z had never seen a man actually wring his hands but Durham was on the brink of it, clasping them together now as the words tumbled out, then beating one fist into the other palm until jerking them nervously apart like a small child reprimanded for a nasty habit.

'And what was Mrs Hoad's own function?'

'She made the contacts and ran the business side. She was very good with the clients. And she had wonderful taste.'

Z could believe that: the office was proof of it. An elegant archway led into a salon with off-white leather sofas and three giant screens, presumably for viewing videos of décor on offer. The walls were covered in matt paint: one jade, one turquoise, one muted orange. Vegetation overflowing high-gloss ceramics suggested rape of a tropical rain forest.

'Did Mrs Hoad have a business partner?' Z asked. 'I mean, who's in charge now?'

He turned a tortured face to her. 'There's nobody. That's what we need to know. What's going to happen to the company? We could all be out of a job.' His long, unhappy features flickered with angst.

'Don't worry. The executors will arrange to keep everything going until they find what arrangements Mrs Hoad had made.'

But were there any? Jennifer, fully occupied with the enjoyment of life had had no intention of yielding to untimely death. So what need for contingency plans? So far there had been no will lodged with their solicitor in Aylesbury.

The phone rang on the smaller of the two executive desks. Stuttering excuses, Hilary Durham scuttled towards it, halted with a hand over the instrument and seemed to pull himself straighter before venturing to answer. He took a deep breath and produced the sleek, practised voice Z too had heard over the phone.

He seemed to know his subject. Without consulting any catalogue he reeled off details of ornamental coving and fireplaces, gave advice, and appeared to placate what had been a doubtfully aggrieved client with a promise to visit next day.

Leaving him to it, Z moved into the salon and gazed through the broad, smoked-glass window into the road outside. A silver satin-finish Porsche had just driven into the vacant parking place opposite and a young man got out, flipped his jacket from the passenger seat and dived through the doorway of Miradec Interiors. His quick glance around took in the situation. He beamed on Zyczynski. 'How may I help you?'

May, not can: Z liked that. His appearance was as studied as his choice of words. Even as he slid his arms into the sleeves of his impeccable jacket it was for effect: boyishly caught out being casual, almost intimate.

'You may tell me a few things I need to know about your company,' she told him, opening her wallet to display her ID.

'Police. Oh God, Jennifer! It's about her, then?' His dark, handsome face crumpled.

'And whatever you can tell me about the business.'

He stared past her, considering. 'That's the simpler part. Jennifer herself was more complex. Look, take a seat. I'll get Hilary to run out for some coffee now he's stopped wittering on. There's a Starbucks almost next door. How do you like yours?'

'A large espresso, please.'

'Good. Two, then. I can't stand all that foaming milk on my lips that you get with cappuccino. Danish or muffin or something creamy?'

'Thank you, no.' She walked across to one of the leather sofas and sat squarely in the middle. 'Would you tell me who you are and how you fit in?'

He lifted a Swedish bentwood chair from a corner of the room, carried it across and sat on it facing her. 'I'm Justin Halliwell, Jennifer's partner. At least I'm that if she got round to making it official. There's a big difference, I guess.'

'Now that Mrs Hoad's . . .'

'Dead,' he completed. 'God, I can't believe it. She was so vital, lived every moment to the full. And not just dead, but — but savagely murdered.'

He was badly shaken, or a superb actor.

He sat hunched, forearms on knees, clasped hands dangling between, staring at the floor. Z was free to observe his dark curls cut close like her own, but his black while hers were a warm brown. On his face, too, the same black in his brows and the stylish, fine, bracketing line left unshaven from upper lip to chin. He was trendy, confident, took trouble with his appearance. Did that make him unusually vain? He was clearly Hilary Durham's role model, however incompetently imitated.

'So, if not her partner, what then?'

'Originally her PA.' He flashed her a wide smile. 'That means I shadowed Jennifer, represented her when she was elsewhere. Like any good PA, I was allowed to copy her signature.'

'I hope you can recognise the difference, especially on contracts and cheques; for when the auditors come in. I understood you were in Paris.'

'Running our office there. Until I heard what had happened to the Hoads.'

'When were you informed?'

'On Monday. I'd gone down to Geneva about an order for laminates. It was on my answerphone when I got back. Hilary, weeping his heart out.'

'And today's Thursday.'

'I came as soon as I could. There was stuff to attend to first.' He was beginning to sound needled. Not impressed by a CID sergeant? Or perhaps unhappy at being interrogated by a woman? He was, in his own mind, the alpha male of his little world. In which case, Z decided, one turns the proverbial Nelson's eye and sails on into battle.

'Can you account for your movements on the night of last Friday?'

'You're not serious! How can you believe that I . . . ?'

'A murder inquiry, Mr Halliwell. Routine questions of all closely concerned with the victims.'

'Not that closely.'

It was then, as the sharp denial snapped from twisted lips, that she realised: Jennifer Hoad wouldn't have denied herself this dishy younger man as a lover. Hadn't her own mother admitted to Beaumont that she was 'a wanton'? And Halliwell, clearly ambitious, would have considered the benefits arising.

So — softly, softly, from now on. 'Surely, Mr Halliwell, this isn't too difficult? When did you set off for Geneva? And by what means? Did you travel by train or plane?'

'I bloody drove down. Alone. Checked in at the Hotel des Anglais on Quai Wilson at a little after midnight. I'd phoned that I'd be late and they kept my room on. Does that cover the time you're interested in?'

'Perfectly, thank you. If we can obtain confirmation from the hotel.'

'They'll tell you it was a double, lakeside.

173

My friend was already there, waiting.' His smile was smoothly sophisticated, man of the world.

Hilary's arrival with the two coffees interrupted them. He was clumsy opening the sealed containers to transfer the hot liquid into bone china cups, spilling some over his hands. Which perhaps accounted for the stained cuffs on his silk shirt. When he withdrew to wash himself Z turned the conversation while they drank their coffee.

'Hilary tells me he was Mrs Hoad's "Ideas Man".'

'The nutter. Actually he's a bloody genius. I'll be keeping him on, if she got round to signing the partnership contract. First thing I mean to do now I'm back is trot round to Walker and Lillicrap to see what the legal position is.'

'Perhaps you'd give me their address. I need to know if they hold a will.'

Again they were interrupted. Halliwell reached in his pocket for a vibrating mobile phone.

'Excuse me.' He scowled at the recognised number and tapped out a text message. 'Arrived safely. Love you too, darling,' he drawled aloud.

He pocketed the mobile, rose and went through to the office where he wrote out the address Z required and saw her to the door. Since the phone call he was decidedly edgy and anxious for her to leave. Suspecting subterfuge, Z would have given a lot to examine the mobile.

Outside again, she walked a few doors down and stepped into a jeweller's doorway to look back. She saw Halliwell come out, the headlights of the Porsche flashing as he operated the key, and then he was pulling out into the traffic.

Zyczynski rang the Miradec Interiors number again on her mobile. When Hilary's practised phone-voice replied she identified herself. 'One thing I forgot to ask you, Mr Durham. When and how did you notify Mr Halliwell of Mrs Hoad's tragic death?'

'I rang him at the Paris office when I saw the midday news on Saturday. But he was away. So I left a message on the answerphone.'

'Why didn't you use his mobile number?'

'Because I don't know it. He's very cagey about who gets to contact him on that.'

Interesting. It seemed that Justin Halliwell kept two sides of his life apart. Perhaps business and personal.

Anna Plumley and her grandson were engaged in playing canasta. Very Fifties, she admitted, but a good challenge and worth bringing back in fashion. Caravan holidays were so often interrupted by downpours that she kept a stock of games to compensate Plum when deprived of his fishing.

Daniel had scorned Scrabble and wasn't up to the demands of mah-jong. He picked up the rules quickly, was a sharp player and remembered every detail of the discard pack. A pity he became petulant if she racked up a good score. 'Can't we go out on one canasta?' he demanded.

'No. Fifty-six cards, including the four jokers, and only two players. There's plenty of scope.'

They played on and, guessing he was holding two aces, she passed him one after freezing the pack. He fell on it avidly and melded with ninety, throwing in three eights for full measure.

Taking advantage of his temporary good humour, she murmured vaguely, 'Met a village local a day or so ago. Ben Huggett. Ever come across him?'

Daniel grunted. 'Bane of my Dad's life. Poached more pheasant than ever reached our table. In the end Dad sacked our gamekeeper and learned to live with it. Where did you meet him?'

Anna explained. 'Do you think your father

knew he took part in badger-baiting?'

'If he did he'd have blown his top. Blood sports used to get him really mad. That's why he didn't hunt. Never could see that poisoning or shooting vermin was dodgy; could leave them to die more slowly and painfully of gangrene.'

'He wouldn't have reported Huggett to the police?'

'Not him. He'd have waded into the old rogue himself. Trapping game was bad enough, but at least it was for eating. Anyway, who told you about the badger-baiting?'

'Nobody. I caught him with a beast he'd dug out. He'd clubbed it to keep it quiet. Persuaded him to let the thing go.'

'You what? Grananna, you're a bloody marvel!'

'M'm, not one of nature's gentlemen, is he? I fancy I'm not his favourite woman of the year.'

Daniel laid his hand of cards face down and stared at her. 'You were asking for trouble, however you did it. Makes me wonder . . .'

'Wonder what?

'Well, if he crossed swords with the Old Man . . .'

'You mean your father?'

'Yes. Then maybe . . . I mean, breaking in to steal isn't so much worse than plundering the same man's woods, is it? Just a sort of progression. And if there really was bad blood between them . . .'

'You think he might be the man the police are looking for.'

Daniel swallowed hard. 'The one who blew him away and then had to kill the others, once he was discovered.'

'It's a notion, certainly.'

'We should tell the police.'

'You mean I should?'

'They haven't a clue otherwise.'

She smiled, drew a card, found it was a black three and went out with three of the little beggars.

'Glad we're not playing for money,' said Daniel bitterly.

They had just finished reckoning the score when from the hall came the sound of a gong summoning them to lunch.

Their pâté and Melba toast were already in place. When Mrs Pavitt came in with the main course her mouth was a tight line. 'The cleaners have come,' she announced. 'They're at it now.'

This was the company the police had recommended, professionals accustomed to sanitising scenes of crime.

'Did they say how long it would take?' Anna enquired.

'All afternoon.'

'In which case we might as well go out and leave them to it.'

But her attempt at discretion came too late. The housekeeper had already killed any appetite the boy had. He pushed back his chair and rose from the table, white-faced. 'I can't eat anything. Oh God, why do we have to stay here? Gran, you said we could go to London.'

'I suggested a London shrink. He, or she, could have come here, but you wouldn't hear of counselling.'

'But a hotel, just for a while. Anything to take our minds off . . . what happened.'

'The police insist we stay close. It wouldn't be easy to avoid sympathetic neighbours if we put up at a local inn. No, you've broken the ice here already. I promise it won't get any worse than it is now. Believe me, each day it will ease just a little.'

'It's so shitty awful. I don't know what to do.'

'If you can't eat your lunch, which incidentally is really very good, why not go for a walk? Or, if you're feeling unwell, lie down. You can join me in the van later.'

He stared resentment at her, but she

continued eating. Better to appear callous than make things worse with sloppy sympathy.

When he had left she laid down her knife and fork, unable to face more. 'No dessert, thank you, Mrs Pavitt,' she called from the doorway.

From the gun room window she watched her grandson striding off uphill in the direction of the woods. She had never quite realised until then the physical nature of grief, the actual heaviness of heart, so much more than a poetical image. She felt her whole body ache with compassion.

At a little after three, a red Toyota swung round the corner of the house. Anna Plumley came down the caravan steps as Beaumont got out. 'Bad news, I'm afraid,' he told her. 'Where's the boy?'

'Gone walking. He should be back soon. Come inside and tell me what you've discovered.'

Perhaps Daniel had caught sight of the car from his viewpoint up among the trees. He turned up a few minutes later, eager to speak with the DS.

'Did Gran tell you about the poacher?' he demanded. 'How he's into badger-baiting, which would have made my father hopping mad.'

Beaumont listened with interest. 'Ben Huggett, you say. We've a constable lives in the village. He'll be able to tell us more about him.'

'But don't you see? My father could have threatened to report him, and Huggett'd know he'd get crucified in court. He'd want to get back at him.'

Beaumont regarded the young man evenly. 'Did Huggett have a key to the house? Because there wasn't a break-in. And your father was unlikely to open the door to him in the middle of the night, storm or no storm.'

'Maybe that was it. He called to say a tree was down, cutting off the lane. Or a high power electric cable severed. Anything to get in.'

'And then what? The man's a poacher, you say. Not a mass murderer.'

Even Anna Plumley blinked at such forthrightness. It silenced Daniel.

'Anyway,' Beaumont said, 'it's another matter entirely I'm here about today. I'm sorry to say your young lady didn't make it after all. She died during the night. So we need you to come down to the station for questioning. It could be a case for careless driving, or at worst manslaughter. A car will come for you tomorrow morning at nine-fifteen. You need to be prepared for staying on a while.'

'If he's charged, surely he'll get bail,' Anna pleaded. The sergeant was being unnecessarily brutal.

'In the lap of the gods. Or of Crown Prosecution.'

Bitterly Daniel turned on his grandmother. 'And you said it wouldn't get any worse!'

That night he was too weary to barricade himself into his bedroom. Anna was woken at a quarter past two by a wild cry of terror. She switched on her light and pulled a housecoat over her pyjamas before rushing in. Daniel was huddled against his pillow, one hand clutching his upper arm tight against his chest.

'A bad dream,' Anna soothed.

'No, it was real. I woke and she was there, standing over me. I was scared, lashed out at her. Pure reflex. And I've bloody put my shoulder out!'

Because he'd struck at thin air. Charleen was dead, and he'd been the cause of it. Small wonder he had nightmares.

CHAPTER THIRTEEN

Daniel wasn't the only one in the house to be haunted by dreams. When Anna fell asleep again she regressed some six years to when the children were small. But at that time she had never brought them a kitten as a present, knowing the farm had feral cats enough.

In this new version of her visit little Angela had been enchanted. She bent to scoop up the white, furry bundle and held it high over her head. 'Oh, aren't you the prettiest little thing!'

As she swooped, the edge of her briefs had shown in relief under the stretch jeans. Anna considered the tight-packed little backside. History had been made when girls started wearing trousers. She'd been a schoolchild herself then, defying her own grandmother's frequent disapproval. Even in the chilliest winters, with a touch of sciatica, old Granny Penfield had never overcome that early distaste. Anna, however, accepted that today girls were different and must be allowed to choose their own weekend uniforms. At least that hint of briefs had shown that Angela wasn't bare underneath.

Anna awoke smiling. Then she remembered. That child was no more. The world had changed too much.

The sadness stayed with her. At breakfast she found herself admitting, 'Last night I dreamt of your sister when she was little.'

'Hard luck,' Daniel growled, observed her surprise and added, 'Well, she could be quite toxic.'

Was she? Anna hadn't found her so. Impish sometimes, yes. Angela was the more daring of the two children, a tease in an attractive, elfin way. But then, as absentee grandmother, she had never seen them enough to know them well. She consoled herself that Daniel was at present feeling bad about his imminent visit to the police: it had soured the memory of his little sister.

When a patrol car with two unknown uniform officers arrived to pick them up he shied off it. 'I'd much rather go in the Jeep, Gran,' he pleaded, and although she picked up the reason for his distress she refused. Then, packed into the rear of the patrol car, she regretted it, sharing the feeling of being under arrest.

DS Beaumont kept them waiting ten minutes before taking them to a small interview room with four chairs and a table. As they settled, facing the detective, a second man appeared and seated himself in the fourth chair. Daniel darted him a wary glance. He was older, mid-forties, heavily built, had a lined, tanned face and mobile, dark brows like furry caterpillars.

'Good morning, Superintendent,' Anna greeted him.

Daniel was startled. Surely his misdemeanours couldn't rate anyone of that rank.

Yeadings introduced himself. 'We're thin on the ground at present,' he explained mildly. 'I'm just sitting in on this.'

Beaumont began by explaining that the boy wasn't under arrest, and asking about his relationship with Jeff Wilmott. Daniel explained that they had met through the scout movement.

'So you weren't at school together?'

'He's seventeen now, works at a garage. I was away at boarding-school first, then I changed to Wycombe Grammar. When I joined the local scouts he was what they called a Ranger then, but he's given up since.'

'However, you still keep in touch?'

'I ran into him in a caff a while back and we got talking bikes.'

There was a knock at the door and Zyczynski entered. Immediately Yeadings rose and they exchanged places. He nodded at Anna Plumley and left the room. Beaumont continued the questioning.

'He mentioned he owned a two-stroke? Which was when you asked to borrow it?'

'Hire it. He agreed I could have it the weekend he was away with the Territorials. He's training with them to take an HGV licence — that's to drive Heavy Goods Vehicles — and he wasn't taking the bike along.'

'So this was arranged in advance for that specific weekend, when you were due to attend a scout camp?'

'Yeah. And I gave him an extra tenner to borrow his leathers.'

'How much to borrow his girlfriend?'

Daniel spluttered. 'Nothing. I don't know what you mean.'

'Because she wasn't exactly his girlfriend? Is that it? He boasted about this prostitute in Slough and you fancied your chances?'

'I don't know where you got that idea . . .'

'From Wilmott himself. So did he give you her phone number and then you fixed a date?'

The boy scowled and appeared to clam up. Then, abruptly petulant, he burst out, 'Jeff told me what pub she sometimes picked up punters in, that's all. I was at a loose end and I thought what the hell.'

'When was this meeting?'

'Friday evening.'

'You must have impressed her if she let you stay over the weekend.'

Daniel smirked. 'She was expensive. I could afford it.'

'And now the young lady's dead. From a road accident. And we have only your word on what happened.'

'She was alive enough when I explained it the first time.'

'Alive, but unconscious. So she couldn't give her version.' Zyczynski had taken over from Beaumont. Daniel was struck dumb. He threw an appealing glance at his grandmother who elected to stay silent too.

'As it happens,' Zyczynski said, 'I've just come from your friend Jeff Wilmott. He too is in hospital, at High Wycombe. Another road accident. You having destroyed his two-stroke, it seems he borrowed a bigger beast and crashed into the rear wing of a car, shooting a red light.'

Beaumont gazed with mock innocence at the ceiling. 'Signally failed to stop.'

Anna stared at him with shocked suspicion.

'My colleague does puns,' Z excused him. 'We're so used to it we don't groan any more.'

'Right.' Anna managed to overlook Beaumont's defective empathy and demanded, 'But Jeff Wilmott, how is he?' His misfortune struck her as further jinxing that stemmed from the carnage at Fordham Manor.

'He's in an orthopaedic ward with an injured shoulder blade and extensive bruising, but should be out in a few days.'

Beaumont turned again to Daniel. 'Meanwhile,' he stressed, 'we are short of any witness to your presence at the girl's flat on Friday night.'

Daniel closed his eyes, mouth twisted sardonically. 'How could there be anyone? Do you think we invited an audience? And why Friday night? You can't think I'd anything to do with — with what happened at home?'

'Daniel, we all have to cooperate,' Anna cautioned. 'They asked me too, remember? I'd no alibi at all.'

'Well I've told them everything I can.' He turned on Beaumont. 'I don't see why I had to come here after you'd already questioned me at home. This is harassment. I shall complain to — to my solicitor.'

'Ah yes, I was coming to that,' said the DS imperturbably. 'You should think about consulting a brief with regard to any future charges concerning your biking mishap.'

'What charges are likely?' Anna asked tautly.

'Causing death by careless driving. Or maybe reduced to "without due care and attention". Then there's driving a vehicle underage, without licence or insurance. Possibly claiming a false identity at the hospital.'

'But it was a bloody fox caused the accident. I told you before!' the boy shouted. 'Why don't you listen?'

He put an urgent hand on Anna's arm. 'Gran, I haven't been arrested. We're free to leave. Let's get out of here.'

As he stormed through Reception with Anna in his wake, Yeadings was standing talking with a pale-faced man in a blue suit.

'Yeah, that's him,' the man said when they had passed. 'I noticed him special-like because of having the other chap's bike. I wondered if he'd pinched it, Jeff being away, like he'd said he'd be.'

'That would be Jeff Wilmott?'

'Yeah, I know him. A regular, like.'

'One of Charleen's clients?'

The man paused, unwilling to admit that

the pub served toms. 'A friend of hers, see. Look, I'm only a potman, clear the tables and wash glasses, like. I only noticed this lad because I'd slipped out for a smoke, and there he was riding up on Jeff's two-stroke with the red mudguards.'

'And you're sure this was Friday the twentieth?'

'Sure as my name's mud if I don't get home before me missus asks where I've bin. She's got a thing about police stations.'

Yeadings nodded. 'Thank you, Mr Barker. You've been very helpful.'

He joined his two sergeants in the corridor. 'Young Hoad is vouched for in Slough until 11.10 p.m. when he left with Charleen, on wobbly legs. So that should clear him for the Fordham business. He's still responsible for the girl's death. Traffic Division can send us their paperwork on that.

'Come up to my office, both of you. I'd like to discuss the pathology reports on the Hoad family.'

As they shared out copies Z demanded of Beaumont, 'You didn't seriously think Anna Plumley could be connected with the crime.'

'Is that a statement or a question? I asked her for an alibi and she hadn't one. Any reason she should be excepted from routine enquiries?'

'No. It's just that, if there's the slightest possibility she was at odds with the family, Daniel shouldn't be left alone with her.'

'Daniel as sole survivor,' Yeadings considered. 'You've spent time with them. Do you see any threat to him?'

'No. She's protective, in a robust sort of way. Won't let him feel sorry for himself. Keeps him busy.'

'And how does he regard her?'

'Naturally he depends on her. At the same time he resents the need for her. At present there's nobody else and, in shock, he's almost totally self-absorbed. Whether he's genuinely fond of her I couldn't say. But there's nothing menacing in her toughness. He's not cowed by her.'

'Then let's pass on to the path reports. I'll summarize. First, Frederick Arthur Hoad, fifty-four; cause of death heart failure due to a .22 bullet penetrating the left breast, destroying his pacemaker and being deflected to lodge in the right clavicle. The knife wounds were post-mortem. The bullet's upwards angle of trajectory was unusual, being at forty degrees to the horizontal. Dismissing Professor Littlejohn's whimsy of a pygmy, we're left with the choice of the killer crouched low or the victim already lying face-up on the floor.'

'The main light was found on in the dining room,' Beaumont reminded them. 'And there were only normal smudges on the switch, no blood. Can we suppose Hoad turned it on when he went for the gun? In which case an intruder, hearing him approach, would surely have hidden.'

'The heavy dining table was out of position,' Z pointed out. 'He could have been under it, waiting for the right moment, aimed from there and then disturbed it in crawling out.'

'But Hoad either saw or sensed someone there, aimed, and the shot went wild because he was hit at the precise moment of firing, thereby blasting the china cabinet.'

'So was the intention to kill him? Or did it become inevitable as a wild act of self-preservation?' Yeadings asked them.

'That's for Crown Prosecution to decide; not our worry,' Beaumont gave as his opinion.

'But it is,' Yeadings disagreed. 'Especially as we're to have a profiler on the case who will expect some input from you on the question.

'Anyway, so much for the report on Hoad's death. The rest concerns his general health: no mortal disease and nil toxicology. He had eaten an adequate evening meal some six or seven hours before death and drunk the equivalent of three units of alcohol.

'Next, the two children. Again no disease found; in each case death by a single stab-wound to the heart. Could be due to basic anatomical knowledge or pure luck. No sign of resistance, so no helpful residue under the nails. No indication of which was first to be killed. Full stomachs, several units of alcohol taken, corresponding with what was missing from the sherry bottle. Angela Hoad's blood group not corresponding with that of either presumed parent.

'Finally we come to the female body found in the barn.'

'The exhibit on display,' Beaumont insisted dourly.

'Yes. Different from the others. We'll discuss that later. Death was due to multiple stabbing preceded by an attempt at strangulation by a flat ligature, which was probably insufficient to cause complete loss of consciousness. While held helpless and upright, she was stabbed twice; once under the right clavicle and also on the left upper arm. Marks on the right side of the neck indicate that she was dragged by some kind of lead, possibly a narrow leather belt, to the bales of straw where the final stabbings took place. There were fifteen wounds in all. Other bales were then arranged into a rough semicircle with her at the centre.'

Yeadings removed his reading glasses, rubbed at the red patch they'd left on one side of his nose and replaced them. 'Actually, it was less of a semicircle than a horseshoe. I've wondered since how significant that was. A henge shape, connected perhaps with the primitive idea of sacrificial victims? Or some link with horses? All the family rode, of course, but only Mrs Hoad had hunted with foxhounds.'

'That'll be a field day for the press,' Beaumont muttered. 'They'll drag politics into it: urban vengeance on the country way of life. Further arousal of the hunting ban protests.'

'In such a case as this, we have to consider any idea however outrageous. There's more than a hint of madness involved; and reason seems inadequate to deal with the irrational.'

'But why was she treated differently?' Z asked. 'Was it because by then no one was left to interfere, and the killer had time for refinements? Or had she been the main intended victim all along, with the others simply getting in the way?'

Yeadings gazed round at the others, but

194

no one volunteered an answer. 'Final details: the dead woman had ingested roughly the same meal as her husband, but rather less in quantity and with rather more alcohol. Her blood test showed the presence of a small amount of cocaine.

'As to her general health, Professor Littlejohn detected the early stages of hyperthyroidism, which means she'd have suffered slightly accelerated heart rate with some sweating, a tendency to anxiety and tremor, also weight loss, the condition being due to enlargement of the thyroid gland.

'It's not certain she was aware of the condition, since the symptoms could have been accepted as stress-related due to personal or professional worries. The Hoad family doctor has stated he'd not seen her for over three and a half years, but she may have consulted someone privately in London.

'As we assume from SOCO's findings in the upper rooms, the killer disturbed her sleep. It's possible she ran to her daughter's room and caught him in there with the bloodstained knife, fled barefoot downstairs, pursued by him, and so out into the night. This was before the downpour: her nightdress and robe, recovered from the floor of the barn, were quite dry, and some bloodstains could have come from the killer's hands as he dragged them off her. Unfortunately neither fabric retains palm or fingerprints. The bloodstains contained minute samples from the three earlier victims as well as her own, and neither weapon — gun nor knife — has been found subsequently.'

'Time of death,' Beaumont prompted.

'Earliest presumed one 1.45 a.m. Certainly not later than 2.50 when the deluge started. Blood was congealed on the body when Barton found her soon after three. Rigor had not set in.'

The internal phone on Yeadings' desk buzzed and he picked it up, listened and nodded. 'Bring him up yourself.' He replaced the receiver and turned to Beaumont. 'Get yourself a chair, and two more for visitors. Our profiler has arrived.'

The man DC Silver ushered in was small and rotund. His suit was crumpled and a fringe of thin black hair stood up in disarray from a pale dome as though he had been pulled backwards through a thorn hedge.

'Dr Jolyon Abercorn,' he introduced himself breathlessly and bent over the desk to offer his hand.

Yeadings introduced himself and his team. 'I understand you're advised of the general outline of the case. To save your time,' he suggested, producing a tape recorder from his half-open top drawer, 'you may care to hear the point we've just reached.' He reversed to the start of their conversation.

'Ah.' Abercorn sat, crossed his fat little legs at the ankles and closed his eyes the better to concentrate. At one point he grunted, but made no comment. When the recording stopped he stayed silent until it seemed he might have fallen asleep. Then, abruptly, he sat up and swung round to face Beaumont. 'Displayed, you said. So this was more than a killer simply ridding himself of another human creature found bothersome. It was a deliberate demonstration. Perhaps a celebration. Tell me, was the late Jennifer Hoad a show-off herself?'

'You might say that,' Yeadings allowed. 'She has been variously described as "flashy", "overbearing" and "full of herself".'

'And your observation on the arrangement of the straw bales — a connection with horses? I'm not sure I go for that. Now "henge" — that's better. I wonder was she in any way superstitious or religious?'

'Evidence of that hasn't emerged so far.'

'Then I shall need to talk to someone who knew her well.' He smiled amiably. 'At least as well as her killer.'

'There's her son and her mother. At present both at the house where it happened.'

'Splendid. First I'll access your incident room information, then I'd appreciate an introduction, if you would set up a meeting with them.' He beamed on them all, accepted Silver's offer to escort him to the computer room and strutted out.

'Henge,' Beaumont said doubtfully when he and Z were clear of the office. 'Given that all shrinks are sad freaks, he could be dragging us into the zone of Druid sacrifice and mistletoe murders.'

CHAPTER FOURTEEN

Anna was pouring tea in the drawing-room, for the present suspending judgment on the visitor Zyczynski had brought with her. She was suspicious of such overt amiability, reminding herself he was a professional concealing an informed attempt to assess those he confronted.

He, for his part, beamed at her through steel-rimmed spectacles, observing and approving her decision to stay on the sidelines. As yet he saw no reason to doubt that she was what she appeared to be, reliable and commonsensical — which was by no means as common as the description implied.

The young man hunched in the armchair opposite was less comfortable. And why not? — traumatised by the double blow of the savage attack on his family and his own part in the death of a girl he'd sought out for sex. As the obligatory tea ritual progressed, with the woman detective handing round filled cups, Daniel kept his gaze on the carpet, bony knuckles strained bloodless on closed knees. Defensive, in denial; certainly resentful of the psychologist's presence. So, more anxious than angry?

The answer was almost immediate. Abruptly, he stood, almost pushing Zyczynski aside as she offered the little tray with sugar, milk and lemon slices, and turned on the older woman. 'I don't want any fucking tea. Sorry Gran, but I can't take all this faffing about. I told you, I'm not on for this counselling stuff.'

'As you wish, Daniel. You may leave us if you'd rather.'

That had him hesitating. He looked desperately between her and the fat little man absorbed in stirring his tea. When no one spoke further he shrugged, picked his way between the chairs and left the room. 'I'm going for a walk,' he called back from the hall.

'Don't apologise,' Abercorn said urbanely as Anna shifted in her chair, ready to spread oil on the waters. 'It is to be expected. Actually it's you I hoped to speak with, and preferably with only Miss Zyczynski present. If you feel able, I should like you to tell me about your daughter, Jennifer.'

Anna grimaced. '*Nil nisi bonum,* or must I

be frank? No, whichever, I'm sure you are capable of winnowing what you require.'

He smiled. 'Her childhood?'

'Sadly neglected, I confess. For the greater part her father wasn't there. I had a demanding career to carve out or we'd have been penniless. In married quarters, services children tend to buckle under or form groups and run wild, grow up too fast. And by nature she was independent, over-confident; like so many young things, thought she was immortal.'

'Took risks?'

'Led many of the worst escapades of her little gang, but usually managed to evade the principal blame. I worried that she was manipulative, but knew no way to reverse it. My world was one where you gave orders and obeyed them. Jennifer didn't belong there, and she let everyone know it. You have to understand that, even quite young, she was remarkably beautiful, could charm the crows off the trees, as the saying goes.'

'And grew up to become a successful businesswoman with artistic flair.'

'At eighteen she married a modern-day Micawber of her own age, and Daniel was born four years later. They had managed up to that point, but the arrival of a baby brought problems the marriage wasn't fit to survive, nor she to cope with. Peter left her and she started to drink heavily. Social Services stepped in. I obtained compassionate leave to look after Daniel rather than have him sent to a children's home, until suitable foster parents were found. I offered Jennifer a roof but she refused it. That left her free to deal with her own problem. She had two attempts at drying out and finally mastered it. She studied décor at college and seemed to have found her feet again. Although admitting she was an alcoholic, she has since allowed herself to drink, moderately, with meals. I know that's almost unheard of, but she's unusually strong-willed.'

'She must be. And Daniel?'

'Stayed with the foster parents who hoped eventually to adopt him. He was a beautiful child, sweet-tempered and always laughing. Later, when Jennifer took Freddie Hoad to see him she fell in love with the little golden cherub. He'd have been almost five by then, and I believe that Daniel was the main reason she agreed to marry a man fifteen years older than she was. Frederick had offered to adopt him.'

'The main reason?'

Anna paused. 'He was also wealthy. She'd lived hand-to-mouth long enough to see the advantages of that. He could afford nurse-maids, leaving her free to follow her artistic interests and return home to the child as a plaything. She had persuaded Freddie to finance the design firm she runs in London, Miradec Interiors.'

'And young Angela?'

'Born later. Was only ten years old when . . . this happened. It's unthinkable.'

'You know that her blood group is different from that of both parents?'

'She's not Freddie's, certainly. He was unable to have children. I don't know which of Jennifer's men friends would be the father. I didn't see it as my business to ask.'

'She was still running wild, as she did as a child?'

Anna nodded. 'Poor Freddie accepted the baby, seemed even to love her, as he did Daniel and their mother. If not passionate, at least it was an amicable marriage.'

'And your daughter found passion elsewhere?'

Anna bowed her head. 'I saw very little of them. At first Freddie insisted I spent my leaves with them, but naturally Jennifer found it unpleasant, associating me with so much that had gone wrong in her life before. And then grandmothers are suspect, the generation gap producing such opposing cultures.'

'You didn't approve of the way she was bringing up her children?'

'I was fearful that she was making a harem child out of her son, always including him in her girlie group meetings. I know as he grew older she encouraged him to dress up in her most exotic clothes, use make-up and wear a wig. She acted sometimes as if he were her spoilt little sister.'

'You didn't protest?'

'Once. After that it was made clear I should only put in a rare appearance, on sufferance.'

'And her relations with young Angela?'

'Cooler, on both sides. She was Daddy's girl, for all that they weren't related. Jennifer and she stepped gingerly round each other. As though they were afraid the other might encroach on private ground. She was old for her years. I suppose they were a lot alike, and unconsciously felt in competition.'

'Your daughter never wanted to become an actress?'

'She was an actress, in everything she did, but she'd no time for the hard graft required by theatre. You could say she was stagy, I suppose.'

'Superstitious?'

Anna looked hard at him. 'Why do you

ask that?'

'Some women read their horoscopes, won't walk under ladders, cross their fingers when they lie, consult mediums, believe in magic.'

'If she did believe in magic, it would be in her own magic. Not anyone else's. I know she used to organise great parties at Hallowe'en and dressed up as a black witch. Maybe that's what was behind the local superstitions about the hanging wood. An old poacher round here called Huggett tried to persuade me there were "goings-on" at full moon up there; a coven operating, so that locals were afraid of the place.'

'And did he persuade you?'

'I assumed he'd spread the rumours himself, to keep everyone clear of his traps.'

'Have you ever been there?' Zyczynski asked, at last stepping in.

'Maybe we should go and take a look.' Abercorn grinned, Puck-like.

'Actually,' Anna admitted, 'I had thought of dropping in on the folks down at the farm and seeing what they had to say about it. I could say I wanted to see the new calf.'

'Why not?' beamed the little man. 'But I like the idea of a woodland walk, perhaps tomorrow, if you could find some commission to occupy your grandson. Joining us wouldn't be in his best interests at the moment.'

'You want me to send him away somewhere?' Anna asked bluntly. 'I'm not sure he'd go. He steers clear of the village; naturally is keeping his head well down until he hears further from the police about the girl's death.'

'Yes. Perhaps an invitation from outside the family? Surely he has friends of his own age he can trust, and whom you can conspire with?' His face was impish, cajoling her into a fun thing and, although suspicious, she had to agree that it might be expedient.

'There's Camilla, a badminton partner,' she said. 'Four or five years older than Daniel, but then most of his friends are. She's a self-employed manicurist, so she could probably take time off if I paid her expenses.'

'Would you ring her? Emphasise how badly Daniel needs taking out of himself in cheerful company.'

Reluctantly Anna rose. 'I'd find it easier if I do this bit on my own.'

'But of course.'

While she withdrew to phone from the study, Zyczynski went across to look out of the window. 'He's going down the fields to the river.'

Abercorn was lying back, cup in hand and staring at the ceiling. He grunted. 'She's embarrassed,' he decided. 'Not being secretive, just not accustomed to acting deviously. That implies distaste for manipulation. I tend to share your opinion of the lady: she's not subversive. The boy has nothing to fear from her.'

'I never said what I thought of her.'

'You disagreed when your fellow sergeant suggested she'd need watching.'

Zyczynski stared back blank-faced. She'd need to be careful with this one. Too observant by half. But maybe he was what this complicated case needed. So long as he didn't let his cleverness run away with him.

'So you thought you'd warn me I'm transparent?' she accused.

'We're both on the same side.'

Just as well, she thought. I wouldn't give him the right to poke about in my brain.

'There's one little puzzle. I understood she hasn't visited for some years. How then does she know of Daniel's current friends?'

'Maybe this girl's more than a friend. He may have talked to Anna about her.'

'I don't imagine he's that open with her.' He said no more as they heard Anna's heels on the hall tiles.

She returned impassive, nodded and sat down again to drink her cooling tea. 'Camilla will ring him this evening, invite him out for lunch somewhere, maybe Oxford or Henley. I will ring later and let Rosemary know what time she'll be picking him up. That should leave us plenty of time to investigate Huggett's claims about the woods.'

She regarded the psychologist squarely. 'Actually Camilla sounded very keen. I'm afraid she may have a morbid taste for the sensational. I warned her to keep off the dreaded subject, and not to question Daniel. We don't need him further upset.'

'Unless the dam bursts and gives him relief.'

'I'd rather that happened here, where we can get the right sort of help.'

'You've been very helpful yourself, Mrs Plumley. Thank you. But now I'm expected by Superintendent Yeadings, so I must leave you.'

He handed back his cup and saucer, smiled at Anna and let Z lead him back to her car. Anna watched them drive off, saw Daniel in the distance walk out from a line of trees above the water meadows to stare after them.

When he returned she wandered in as he

shed his boots at the gun room door. 'Someone called Camilla phoned, wanting you.
She'll try again this evening. An invitation
of some kind, I think.'

He looked aghast. 'I'm not up to clubbing.'

'Of course not. Something rather different, as I understood it. Just a drive and
some lunch. Away somewhere. Make a bit
of a break.'

He considered this, pulling on his slippers. It would be a relief to be free of this
damnable house. Swap the grim grandmother for Camilla and her giggles. Pro-
vocative Camilla, teasing yet sexually bar-
ring him. Just the two of them. Maybe this
time he'd get lucky. It was more than time
something went right for him.

Dr Abercorn walked into Yeadings' office to
find his desk covered in crumpled pieces of
paper. A WPC, kneeling on the floor, had
separated others into five piles and was now
gathering them up in bundles.

'Historical archivist?' he asked benevo-
lently.

'In a way. Not without profit. SOCO had
examined bins in the house. This lot had
travelled a stage further but, thanks to the
recycling system, hadn't joined the stinkier
stuff.'

Abercorn hovered over the desk, after more detail.

'Some interesting results. Hoad was having problems at work,' Yeadings informed him. 'A whistle-blower had written to him, suggesting a review of the list of employees at the Bristol foundry. There have been recent sackings, and fictional names have been substituted on the wages lists. If that's true, Fallon, the partner, could be feathering his nest.'

'So what move did Hoad take?'

'The letter itself was torn into sixteen pieces, as if in angry denial, but the itemised phone bill I requested for Fordham Manor records a two-minute conversation with a Bristol number on the following day. This proves to be for Fallon's personal line. A short enough conversation to be a summons to meet, but not long enough to go fully into the matter and receive assurances that all was well.'

'Interesting indeed. So did they meet? And when?'

'That remains to be discovered. But other correspondence might also be germane to the investigation. A letter from Mrs Anna Plumley, Hoad's mother-in-law, who apparently kept regularly in touch. Computer-printed, so perhaps the envelope was too; so that unless the postmark gave it away, no other member of the family need have known the correspondence existed.'

'She spoke of him as "poor Freddie". More sympathy there than for her own daughter.'

'I think he kept her abreast of family matters, and even welcomed her advice.'

'An *éminence grise*. What a formidable lady. But that explains something I was puzzled by: how she was aware of what friends Daniel had. Hoad may not have been a blood relation, but he sounds like that rarity, a good family man.'

Yeadings nodded. 'I trust your visit was profitable.'

'Certainly interesting,' and he outlined it to the superintendent, ending, 'So tomorrow we take a walk in the woods.'

'Very refreshing.'

'You're wondering to what purpose. So, frankly, am I, but my question about superstition took that turn. I am simply going with the flow.'

'Uniform Branch reported there was nothing of interest there, but I doubt if they penetrated far. According to the Ordnance Survey map the wood's quite extensive. Nothing significant marked there.'

'We shall see. I just hope the weather stays

fair. I have an urban horror of rain.' He looked rueful. 'Also of cow pats and midges, if it comes to that.'

'See Z about borrowing some wellies, just in case.'

'Rubber boots? Ah, yes. Thank you.'

'As for the forecast,' Yeadings warned him, 'it's for showers and intermittent sunshine, with heavy winds rising to gale force by evening, blowing out overnight.'

'Oh dear,' said Abercorn, deflated. 'I wish I'd had advance knowledge.'

CHAPTER FIFTEEN

They had been lucky so far with the rain, but the wind had strengthened earlier than anticipated. Their jackets, unbuttoned for the climb, flapped behind them like broken wings. Anna strode stoutly uphill in mountain boots and with a shepherd's forked staff, observing how in silhouette a distant string of thorn trees toiled up the edge of the hill like bent and wizened crones.

My mind already exercised by covens, she thought dryly.

Rosemary Zyczynski lagged behind with the breathless Dr Abercorn, having kitted him out with wellies on loan from a strapping WPC who took size nines.

'I'll be glad,' puffed the little man, 'when we reach the shelter of the trees.'

Z smiled encouragement, thinking it might not be much better then. The tops of the nearest clump of ashes were rolling about as if in helpless merriment. Every gust brought a flurry of autumn leaves and the ground was already slippery with them.

They reached comparative calm in the darker depths of the wood, striking through to a clearing from which paths meandered in three directions. 'Do we take one each?' asked Abercorn.

'The left one's fairly fresh, little more than trodden undergrowth,' Anna pointed out. 'We could run into Huggett's latest traps that way. Let's stay together and tackle the other two in turn.'

After fifty yards of twisting, the central path ran straight except for circling a stagnant pond where two half-submerged logs lurked like wary crocodiles. A few minutes later it suddenly dropped away, zigzagging down a steep escarpment planted with pines and spruces. As the trees thinned they glimpsed patchwork fields in the valley below, its straggling lanes dotted with whitewashed cottages.

'Are we still on Hoad's property?' Abercorn asked.

'On the edges, I think,' Anna said. 'Just before the trees thinned there were the remains of an old fence. I imagine it was kept in proper repair when there were still gamekeepers. Shall we make our way back and take the other path? From here it looks as though that's the gentler side of the hill and the woods extend farther that way.'

They retraced their steps in silence, Abercorn easing his collar but making no complaint. Their second path was anything but straight, meandering between ancient beeches and eventually curving right, back towards the direction of the Manor, then plunging away left and opening out just above Fordham village.

'This could be the way the daily staff used to come on foot,' Abercorn surmised. 'I'm surprised it hasn't grown over, since the advent of bicycles and cars.'

'Maybe it's still used for picnics,' Anna suggested. 'And dalliance, of course.'

'Back to the clearing?' Z invited. 'Then do we call it a day or try the newish track?'

Halfway there it grew darker and began to rain. They heard more than felt it pattering on the foliage above. There seemed no point in breaking cover yet to get soaked.

'We might as well push on,' Anna decided. So they turned into the least trodden track, Anna clearing the way ahead with her forked stick. After some twenty paces or more she stopped.

'I was wrong. It's an old path, but grown over. Look, there are even flints tamped in underneath. This was certainly well used at some period in the past.'

Now and again they passed the shrivelled remains of wild raspberries, the canes dried brown and tangled like old brambles. The trees here were all deciduous and mature; no filling in with rapid-growth evergreens.

Anna halted again and produced her torch from a capacious pocket.

'What is it?' Z demanded.

'I thought so. A little way back I noticed something too. Wait till I scratch it off.' She bent and picked at the broad blade of a dock leaf.

'There. Tell me what that is.'

Abercorn peered close, touched the shiny surface. 'Wax?'

'Candle wax. Now why walk in a wood with a lighted candle when there are more convenient ways of picking out your path? I begin to think there really was a coven, or some kind of arcane gathering. The start of the path was deliberately concealed.'

That morning, just before eleven, Camilla's Toyota had slewed to a stop by the front door, throwing up gravel as she braked. Daniel, ready, waiting and stagy in an ankle-length black coat and leather riding boots, golden hair loose under a wide-brimmed felt hat, was taken aback to find three passengers grinning in the rear seats.

'Thought we'd make up a party,' Camilla said. 'You know Louise and Harry. That's Jack in the middle, playing dormouse.'

Daniel took the free front seat, disconsolate. The others' presence meant he couldn't demand to drive. It soured the day, because he'd hoped Camilla would be specially nice to him, out of sympathy.

They avoided the market-day crowds in Fordham and the narrow wriggle of Wendover's main street. Past World's End, straight roads opened up with boring shorn hedges and glimpses of corn stubble beyond. Camilla was being wary of the speed cameras, which irked him. The traffic grew denser and the pace ever slower.

'Right,' Daniel challenged, 'Let's get cracking. There was an old man of St Ives . . . You next, Camel.'

'Um', said Camilla. 'All right, then. Whose moggy had used up eight lives.'

There was a pause. 'Louise, we're waiting,' Danny sang over his shoulder. 'It's easy-peasy; yours doesn't have to rhyme.'

'One day it went mousing . . .'

'In inner-city housing . . .' That was Harry's uncertain effort.

The others all groaned. 'Doesn't rhyme,'

Camilla damned it. 'You've changed to a hard s.'

'Leaving me with the abominable last line,' Jack complained, wedged in the centre of the back seat. 'Hives, arrives, drives . . .

'No, I've got it. And ended on juveniles' knives.'

There was a horrified silence. Even a dumbo like Jack must have realised . . .

'Not one of our best,' Daniel said defiantly. For God's sake, hadn't they warned the idiot, don't mention the war!

Trying for cool, he felt sudden nausea, wanted to climb out and start trudging back home. No, not home. The way they'd come, that's all.

'Marked at two out of ten,' Camilla decreed, rushing into the breach. 'What's happening up front?'

Those in the rear craned forward. There was a tailback. At least twenty cars queued ahead, nose to tail. Red rear lights lit the darkening noon.

'Flock of sheep,' Louise guessed. But it was something more. An approaching siren demanded road clearance. Camilla ran the car on to the nearside verge. 'Oh Lord, we could be here for hours. And I'm ravenous.'

A second warbling note joined the other. Paramedics first, then Fire Service. Next there'd be police.

'OK. Looks like I get to start another,' Harry claimed sourly. 'A nautical traveller called Claud . . .'

'Spoke only English abroad . . .'

'Flawed, fraud, sawed,' Louise muttered under her breath.

'Shush, we're not there yet.'

'And we shan't be for a bloody long time,' Daniel growled. He'd reckoned on an hour for the journey, say one and a half for a meal. Now it could string out until dark. So much for his brilliant idea for when they reached a decent-sized town.

They edged slowly forward, only three or four car-lengths at a time with long pauses between, eventually reaching a narrow space past the emergency vehicles. As a fireman in a luminous jacket waved them over, Camilla ran the Toyota up on the grass verge, skimming the lopped branches of a giant oak that stretched across all lanes of the road. Its massive root ball reared over the far bank.

With windows lowered to gawk, they smelled dank earth and sap, heard the snarl of a chainsaw as it bit into the obstruction. Beyond it oxy-cetylene flared where a group of firefighters cut into the distorted hatchback of a small car crushed underneath. The entire front half, barely visible under the trunk's main weight, was staved in like a crumpled beer can. Paramedics from two ambulances sat strung out along the bank, useless as yet.

Without warning Daniel slid sideways. His head hit the window frame and he vomited over the seat.

Camilla drove on tight-lipped, the car lurching again from grass on to tarmac. 'Once we're free of this traffic,' she threatened, 'next pub we come to, all out and clean up the mess.'

Farther into the left-hand path through Fordham Woods less care had been taken to disguise the track. White scars showed where undergrowth had been recently slashed back. The path widened as though here people had walked two or three abreast. It ended in a second clearing with patches of scorched earth positioned in a large circle.

'Five stations,' Abercorn counted. They stood silently taking it in.

'Five,' Anna repeated. 'Isn't there something sinister about a pentagram?'

'Perhaps just the sum of those willing to take part,' the psychologist suggested.

'Take part in what?' Z demanded.

There was no clue to that beyond more heavily trodden patches, and a hole six or seven inches deep inside each of the scorch marks.

Z thought of the book Beaumont had caught Anna reading, about the Manson multiple murders and his reputation as a wizard. How soon had Anna caught on to the idea of witchcraft being practised in this place? If Ben Huggett's gossip about the wood had been the first she knew, how was it she already had the book with her, well thumbed and with her initials on the title page?

'Where do you think this path ends?' Abercorn wondered aloud. 'Shall we press ahead and see?'

They hadn't much farther to go, but without Anna's torch sweeping from side to side of the track they would have missed the hut, so overgrown was it with brambles, and Old Man's Beard hanging over the door like a misty curtain.

A contrived curtain, Z decided. The place was as deliberately hidden as the start of the track had been. Her curiosity quickened as Abercorn, token male of the party, tried the door and found it securely locked. 'It's solidly built,' he gave as his opinion. 'But quite old.'

'So what is it for?' Z asked.

'Not is, but was,' Anna decided. 'The family Freddie bought the estate from used to raise their own game birds. This would be where the eggs were incubated and the chicks fed before they were loosed in the woods. There are still a lot of pheasant here but now they're all wild. It's several years since Freddie gave big shooting parties, although he'd take out a gun and bag a brace or two when they were in season.'

'And still they keep it secured,' Z reflected. 'I'd say that lock's been renewed in recent months.'

'Quite shiny,' Anna agreed.

'Any chance we'll find the key handily slipped under a stone nearby?' Abercorn hoped aloud.

'No harm in searching,' Anna encouraged. 'Meanwhile I'll see if I can tickle it open.' She delved into the satchel hung from one shoulder and after scrabbling a moment produced what Z recognised as a picklock. It seemed the lady's skills knew no bounds.

'Perhaps, Sergeant, you would kindly direct some light on the operation?' Anna handed over the torch.

With such candour in acknowledging a police presence, how could Z refuse? And Anna was no novice at burglarious entry.

Abercorn was still poking about in the undergrowth when the old lady's jubilant cry came. 'Oh look, it's come open!'

Not only was the lock new, but the door's hinges were oiled. It opened without the least rheumatic creaking. They filed in, located a battery-operated lantern, and at once the isolated hut was transformed into a cosy interior with two rattan sofas, a card table and several cushioned chairs. Walls and the sole window were covered by dark drapes, behind one of which they found a set of shelves holding cardboard cartons. The first, close to hand, contained wine glasses and two slender carafes; the next held a number of wire hangers holding black gowns, a box of candles, coloured chalks, masks, and at the bottom a pack of large, square Tarot cards.

On the floor under the shelves lay a bundle of broom handles, each marked with soil at the base, and at the upper end an iron sconce packed with a pungent mass of material making it resemble a medieval torch.

'The games room,' Anna declared sardonically.

Abercorn was in his element. 'Not only a trysting place, but a theatre for witchcraft. So how serious did it get?'

'At least there are no chains or thumb racks.'

But the psychologist had moved on to other boxes on the floor. 'Plenty of ropes, though and — by George! — a rhino whip. Seen some like this in South Africa. Not so innocent after all. And a petrol can, half full. Now what's this little lot? Animal masks in papier mâché. Wolf, ram, serpent, cat, goat, eagle. Six creatures for five places. So one of them is special. I'm afraid it's the goat. Rather over the top, isn't he?'

Z examined a faint powdering of white on the gaping mouth. 'I think,' Z said firmly, 'we've interfered enough. I'm going to lock the place up and get our Scenes of Crime team in to examine it. Please don't handle anything else. Let's put our hands in our pockets and leave right now.'

Out again in the woods, they found the darkness deeper and the gale worsening. All round them boughs groaned and rattled.

'Best get back sharpish,' Anna counselled. 'I'll lead with the torch. Everyone keep a hold on whoever's in front.'

It seemed to take twice as long to reach the sloping field above the Manor, and there the wind burst on them almost knocking them off their feet. Overhead, smoke-black clouds streaked low, against a sagging, felty stretch of grey. Below, the distant house was in darkness. Then a diagonal shaft of bleak light briefly escaped the sky to pick out the flame red of Virginia creeper on the rear wall. The security lamp above the kitchen door burned feeble but welcoming, drawing them in.

As they watched, stumbling downhill, a single light came on inside the house. High under the eaves Alma Pavitt's window shone out against the premature dark. Then her arms reached up to swing the curtains closed.

At that moment the deluge began again. All three started to run and reached asylum breathless.

They shed their wet outer clothes in the gun room and went through to the drawing room where, at Anna's request, Dr Abercorn knelt to put a flame to the kindling under piled logs in the fireplace. As he rose he saw Z's eyes on the gold lighter. 'No, I don't smoke,' he answered her unuttered question. 'But many of my patients do. It helps them relax.'

She nodded. 'Excuse me. I have to phone for SOCO.' When she returned the other two had settled comfortably in armchairs by the fire.

'Strong coffee, I think. And a drop of

brandy wouldn't come amiss.' Anna instructed Mrs Pavitt as she came in for their orders.

'I'll bring a fresh bottle, madam.'

Was there a hint of something subversive in that last word? Z asked herself. And why the insistence on 'fresh'? Was she implying that someone — Anna herself, perhaps — had been knocking it back? Or was it that the only opened bottle was in the dining-room tantalus? Coming through the hall she'd noticed that, since the cleaning firm had been in, the seals were removed from that door, which was still closed. Had the housekeeper such a strong aversion to the place where her employer had been killed? Maybe everyone would avoid it.

Would Anna, with her stoic outlook, be insisting on her grandson's braving it soon?

They had been back barely twenty minutes when headlights swept across the uncurtained windows. They heard voices at the front door and Camilla made an entrance with Daniel trailing behind. They both looked drenched and exhausted.

'Thought I'd better deliver him in person,' she opened abruptly, tossing her wet hair. 'We've had a perfectly bloody time and a poor apology for a meal. Got held up for ages by a car crushed by a falling oak tree.

Single lane traffic to get past. Pretty bloody mess too. People still trapped inside. Danny was sick all over the place, wouldn't join us for lunch, so eventually we had to come back. Guessing there'd still be a helluva tail-back on the road round the accident, we opted for a point-to-point. Bad idea. We got stuck in a muddy field. Took just hours getting the wheels out of a bog, so it's been a bloody day all round, and my Dad'll go spare if I don't hose the car inside and out before he gets home. So must rush.'

'How very kind of you,' Anna murmured. 'I'll show you out. Daniel, don't stand on ceremony. Hot bath and dry clothes, then join us. Mrs Pavitt shall get you some soup and toast.'

Z looked across to Abercorn who was playing the interested spectator. 'Time we left, perhaps.'

He levered himself out of the comfortable chair. 'If you say so, Sergeant.' He followed her meekly to reclaim his soaking Burberry, boots and pork-pie hat.

Anna followed them to the door, and while Abercorn settled in her car, Z asked, 'Are you all right?'

'Don't bother yourself about me. It's Daniel who matters. If only his mind could let it all out, the way his stomach did. It's more than time we got him to talk.'

Abercorn had picked up on it. He leaned out of the car. 'I could try tomorrow,' he offered. 'Latish in the morning, if that's convenient for you?'

'The sooner the better,' Anna agreed. 'Thank you, Doctor.'

Chapter Sixteen

Z finished typing her report and waited for the printouts. Reading through, she knew it was incomplete. Although containing details of all said and done on their little expedition, it was depersonalised, giving no hint of the underlying unease she felt.

And doubt had struck her before they set out, at the moment when she'd connected Anna's eagerness to search the woods with her possession of the Manson book. Not that it had been Anna who suggested the search. That had been Z herself, and Anna had almost countered it by mentioning her intention to question the Bartons about the reputed goings-on.

But hadn't she first brought the subject up, mentioning the woods after Abercorn's question about Jennifer and superstition? Then, after Z suggested a search, Anna had more or less taken over. Was she, in fact, working to direct police attention, and influence the investigation?

What after all had Anna come here for? Was her consciousness of shared genes enough to justify sudden renewed interest in her grandson? Or had she a special fondness for Daniel as a person? But then, after a death vultures gathered, didn't they?

As sole survivor the boy would surely inherit from both parents but, being a minor, required someone to control his finances. Since Freddie Hoad had never envisaged such wholesale loss of family he'd probably made no provision against it in a will. Did Anna see herself as officially filling the vacancy? If so, from what motivation? — family responsibility or avarice? She appeared comfortably off, but in Z's experience few ever thought they had enough to live on.

She collected her three copies of the report, knocked on DCI Salmon's door and delivered his. He barely looked up, grunted, nodded towards his in-tray and waited for her to leave. It seemed that Beaumont had been sent off on some mission more vital than any Salmon would ever task her with, and she badly needed to talk over her new misgivings about Mrs Plumley. However, by good fortune Superintendent Yeadings was in the Incident Room as she delivered her report for the office manager.

'And one for me?' he asked, reaching out a hand. Then, 'I've sanctioned your request for Scenes of Crime to go in at first light tomorrow. Come upstairs and we'll look through this together.'

In his office he made no move towards the coffeemaker, intent on scanning her face. 'You're uneasy about something, Z.'

'Maybe you should read my report first.'

'I will, if you won't think me sexist in asking you to make the coffee.'

She felt colour flooding her cheeks. 'Am I that transparent, sir? Spiky?'

'No spikes. Just occasional ruffled feathers.'

It wasn't a rebuke. He didn't actually say 'understandably', but his tone implied it and she relaxed, spooning coffee grounds from the foil packet into the filter. Nevertheless this was her second warning of her expression revealing her thoughts. She'd need to cultivate something like Beaumont's po-face.

At the conclusion of his first reading the Boss grunted and went through the report again. 'So you think there's a cocaine connection. It seems we have another element to consider which may or may not affect our case. Five participants. Or even six.

How many of the Hoad family are involved, do you suppose? And are numbers made up by house guests or people from the village? I'm afraid the time has come to disregard young Danny's sensibilities and pin him down on how life was lived at the Manor. I doubt if Mrs Plumley is sufficiently in the picture for that.'

'Enough to have brought along her own copy of the Manson massacre account. A well-thumbed one, at that.'

Yeadings' black caterpillar eyebrows shot up to his hairline. '*Music, Mayhem, Murder.* That book? Almost a police textbook of its time.'

'You've read it, sir? I only sneaked a quick glance at her copy, but the mention of witchcraft . . .'

'The book's not as sensational as the title, which was probably chosen to boost sales. It makes clear that Manson was a pathetic misfit, victim of a crazed mixture of drugs and hippy culture. He'd spent most of his life in prison, just escaped the death penalty for murder when it was abolished in California; then, finally released, tried to make it as a musician and a guru collecting nubile young girls, deep into acid culture.

'He was a punk icon dealing drugs and ingesting effluvia from the Beatles' "Helter

Skelter" theme. All before your time, Z. At certain levels America was on the boil just then: violence and bloodshed following the love-and-peace flower-child period. Robert Kennedy and Martin Luther King were assassinated, the war intensified in Vietnam and there were student uprisings at home. Flunking it as a musician, he found a slot as Prophet of Doom, preaching a mishmash of Armageddon and ranting against the ordered way of life, wealthy and successful people. Drawn to the glitz of Hollywood, he found ready victims near to hand.

'Roman Polanski, then away in Europe, had directed the horror film *Rosemary's Baby* about a Satanist plot to bring the Antichrist into the world. Film buffs love disaster, so it minted money. Polanski's pregnant wife, Sharon Tate, was living ostentatiously within the cult's reach and, fired up by drugs, the Manson sect broke in on her household, committing wholesale slaughter. He had longed for universal chaos which only his nihilist elect were to survive. The gothic rock star Marilyn Manson later thrived on the cult, but by then society had picked up the real Charles Manson. Sad it wasn't sooner.'

'So are we dealing with a copy cat massacre here?'

'I devoutly hope not. It would take a very sick mind to pick on Charles Manson for a role model. But we can't risk dismissing the set-up in Fordham Woods as simply props for kinky play-acting. That sort of thing can push unstable people over the edge. Much may depend on what forensic specialists find there. Fortunately our right to search already covers all Hoad's property.'

He took the coffee she passed to him and stirred in a sweetener. 'You're still unhappy about something.'

'Mrs Plumley bringing the book with her. I accept that the reason for it being well-thumbed could be that she'd picked it up second-hand; but doesn't bringing it imply she already knew there was some Manson-like cult being practised at her daughter's home? And she pretended the book wasn't hers. According to Beaumont she claimed she'd found it on a shelf in Daniel's bedroom.'

'It's possible.' Yeadings didn't sound convinced.

Zyczynski hesitated before pressing further. 'We can't be sure what her motivation is for coming to the Manor. She's settled in, taken over thoroughly. With Daniel in such a mess, can we trust her not to bring too much influence to bear . . . ?'

'We haven't a choice in this. For the present there is no one else. She'll probably apply to become the boy's guardian. I doubt if it's a case for the Official Solicitor to intervene. Frederick Hoad's will still isn't in our hands, and it's doubtful his wife ever had one drawn up. We must leave Daniel to the grandmother, and any lawyer they see fit to employ.

'Meanwhile we keep to the universal rule: believe nothing on first hearing, trust no one, check everything.'

So where does that leave me? Z asked herself silently. Was I initially too ready to trust the old lady? Am I swinging too far the other way now?

'There is some progress in the case,' Yeadings confided, to change the subject. 'A widening of the investigation. I was careful to say Hoad's will isn't yet with us, but among the recyclable paper we've been examining was a rough draft Hoad made shortly before his death. It was handwritten, so probably the fair copy was as well. He wouldn't have wanted it left on his computer, however impenetrable he considered his password. Connected with this, correspondence which our IT specialist did lift from his personal computer included a letter to a W K Stanley at a London address;

who, we now find, is a retired solicitor and a member of Hoad's Jermyn Street club. The letter, discreetly enough, spoke of "bringing things up to date".

'An officer from the Met known to me has called on Mr Stanley who confirms that he recently drew up a revised will for Frederick Hoad from such a draft. He sent two of his one-time clerical workers to deliver it and witness the signature on two separate copies, returning one to the new head of his old Chambers. In the continued absence of Hoad's own copy Beaumont has gone to collect the other.'

'So there had been a previous will as well as the new draft? And we haven't found either.'

'Which means Hoad was cunning in keeping certain papers under wraps, or else one or both were removed by a person unknown. In which case he was right to be wary of someone in his own household.

'Another little gem I found from grubbing through the recyclable waste is an anonymous, computer-printed letter from a whistle-blower at Hoad's Bristol foundry, suggesting a check on staff actually employed there. It reported sackings over several months, and fictitious names substituted on the wages lists. Fallon, as Managing Director, is accused of cooking the books to feather his nest, to thoroughly mix the metaphors.'

Yeadings went on to explain that although Hoad had torn up the letter, he must have seen fit to act on the information, and that a meeting with Fallon had probably been arranged by phone.

'We don't know if such a meeting actually occurred. Hoad's phone call was made on the Wednesday. By the early hours of Saturday morning he was dead. We need to account for every movement he made in between.'

Yeadings started moving papers on his desk to signal he was almost done with bringing her up to date. 'Fallon will be putting in an appearance here tomorrow afternoon to give his version of the matter.'

Z waited. Was she to be allowed in on the interview?

'Acting-DCI Salmon will question him along with DS Beaumont,' Yeadings explained shortly, killing her hopes. Then he relented, cheeks crinkling and eyebrows soaring. '. . . while, after lunch, you and I take a trip to Bristol to look into the matter for ourselves.'

Beaumont had expected the document he

received from the London Chambers to be sealed against his own prying eyes, but not that it would be addressed to Graham Dent, a solicitor in Aylesbury. Even the Boss had been left out of the equation. Apparently Stanley was one of the old school who set great store by observing protocol. The will would be disclosed first and formally, by a member of his own profession, to members of the deceased's family. Which, failing other interested parties suddenly appearing, meant Daniel and his grandmother.

Yeadings, advised of this, approved. 'No cause to rush things,' he said. 'But when the will's read after the funeral, I'll need to be around.'

So the Boss had something more pressing in the meantime. Beaumont put on his prize pupil face and waited to hear where he'd feature in it: as back-up to Salmon, he learned, when Fallon arrived from Bristol next afternoon for a further interview. It sounded as though the Boss accepted by now that Z was out of the running.

Beaumont caught up with her later at her desk in the CID office and, relaxing to switch off competitive mode, suggested a pub meal. 'Unless you have to rush back and do the culinary thing for Max. How is he by the way?'

'No, no, and yes,' she answered, eyes still on the computer screen.

'I get the noes, and gather I'm turned down, but what's the yes for?'

'Max being by the way. Rather a long way. Sudan, in fact. Not much of a culinary treat out there, it seems. The people are starving.'

'So you're free. Why refuse an invitation? You need to get out more.'

She turned to look at him. 'I understand that's a little dated as a sophisticated insult. Actually I'm busy.'

'On what?'

She flicked off the screen as he circled to scan it. 'Oh, women's work, you know. Nothing to trouble your mighty mind with.' She smiled frostily at him.

Touchy, he thought. Salmon's really getting to her. But she needn't have turned down the offer of a meal: soon she would need all the friends she had. Especially when he took over as DI.

'Salmon's having another go at young Danny early tomorrow, about the Ascot death crash. I'm to fetch him. And we're pulling Fallon in again after lunch tomorrow,' he confided.

'Yes, I heard he could be fiddling the books. But is that serious enough to give a motive for murder?'

'Depends how deep in the mire he is. Needed to shut Hoad up before he went public on it and dissolved the partnership, maybe. Fraud carries a sizeable sentence.'

'So would he wipe out the whole family while he was at it?'

'If he went totally barking, why not? Somebody did.'

'That could be where our friendly neighbourhood shrink plays his master card. What do you make of him?'

He grinned. 'I've not had him on my couch yet. Have you?'

Z smiled. 'We took a little walk together in the woods today. He hadn't a lot to say. Nor I, for that matter. I think he plays his cards close to his chest.'

'Ah, building an impressive silence before uttering the pedestrian obvious.'

'He did seem interested in relations between Daniel and his grandmother. I'd like to know what he made of them.'

Beaumont rolled his eyes, backside hitched on the edge of her desk. 'He'll be working on a theory they did the job together, despite the physical impossibility. Family wipe-out to swipe the Hoad millions.'

He shrugged again as she stared at him. 'Salmon had me check the boy's alibi with the Ascot potman, and it holds. Also there were no dabs from Granny P found in the house before she was officially allowed in. But our DCI always susses females who throw their considerable weight about. So be warned, Z, and stay sylph-like.'

Z scraped her chair back against the wood-block floor. It covered the sound of a gentle snort. Fat or thin, all women got short shrift from Salmon. If anything, he treated her worse the harder the work she put in. She wheeled on Beaumont, forced a grin.

'I'll be thoroughly female-indexed and change my mind. Not a meal, but certainly a drink. Hang on a minute while I fetch my coat.'

Anna Plumley put off going to bed until almost one o'clock but still she didn't sleep right through, too conscious of muffled sounds of distress from the open door across the corridor. She'd left her own ajar on purpose, then regretted it, knowing it would humiliate the boy — the young man — if she went to give him the hug that was needed.

When finally she awoke she thought it must be late because light already showed between the curtains. Crossing to the window she saw a sky clear of clouds. High white diagonals crossing the pale blue were vapour trails of jets stacking for entry at Heathrow. The rising sun struck silver on a plane's fabric and she was consumed by longing to be up there. For her the sky had always been the limit; nothing ever coming close to the sense of rightness in controlling altitude, take-off, landing. Without flying, her early life would have been as empty as — as — as her grandson's now was.

She sighed, put on her housecoat and made for the guest bathroom, passing Alma Pavitt with a tray for her early morning tea. 'Lovely morning,' she greeted her.

'Amazing,' said Pavitt. 'But it won't last. Do you want your tea with you or . . .'

Anna had higher hopes of the weather. 'Just leave it in my room, thank you.'

Anna finished soaping herself, rinsed off and lay back in the bath to do her cycling exercises, observing she still had good ankles, and straight toes untrammelled by ever wearing fashion shoes. Then, with her feet propped on the taps, relaxation. Just a couple more minutes . . . She closed her eyes.

There was a sound outside. Someone in the corridor. Actually coming in. She hadn't thought to lock the door. It was the guest bathroom and the only guest was herself.

The door was behind her head. With her feet cocked high and her shoulders low she couldn't turn to see who had entered. The intruder moved across towards the window and she saw it was Daniel. He seemed unaware of anything amiss. Perhaps accustomed to walking in on private ablutions. Casually he drifted past to sit side-saddle on the bath's edge.

At the feet end, facing her.

Anna's back had stiffened and she lacked the balance to move her legs down. Vulnerable ankles. He had only to grasp them and lift, then she'd be helpless, face underwater, breathless and drowning.

For a moment a flicker of some emotion crossed the boy's face. Amusement? For once free of defensiveness, he was authoritative, coolly in control. She knew he was enjoying her discomfiture.

Anna planted her elbows firmly on the bath's curved rim and forced her back upright, bent her legs and removed her feet from beside his bare thigh, where the terry robe had fallen open.

Sitting bolt upright, she flipped a hand, batting a floating island of foam to cover her genitals, aware of the unsightly bobbing of sixty-seven-year-old breasts. 'Daniel, perhaps this isn't the time or place for a conversation.'

But he hadn't spoken, had he? Just looked at her. And made her afraid.

'Maybe not,' he drawled, stood tall, then leaned over and splashed a wave over her chest. 'Don't take a chill.' Then he left.

Anna sat on, shivering, water drying on her skin. Was she crazy to think there was menace in his actions? He'd meant to mock, certainly. He'd succeeded in humiliating her — ugly, aged flesh exposed to youth's beauty. It was shaming.

But did that matter? It was her spiritless reaction that had betrayed her. Just two words would have sufficed: 'Get out!' And she'd failed to say them. The realisation un-nerved her further.

She looked in on her grandson as soon as she was dressed. He answered her knock with a groan and she found him, legs dangling from the side of his bed, hands gripping the mattress edge, shoulders stiffly hunched. His face was grey and taut, a totally different person. Stricken.

Such contrast alarmed her. She had to stay cool. 'Bad night?' she asked. 'Me too.'

But it was more recent than that. 'Look.' He held out one shaking hand. Clenched in it was his mobile phone.

Anna reached for the glasses suspended on a chain round her neck. The text message she read was simple enough: 'U NEXT.'

Warning or threat? Either way wickedly cruel.

'Who would do that?' she demanded. But then who could commit such an atrocity as his family's slaughter? She felt her heart beating high in her throat. She must let the police know at once. They could trace the call.

'I've got to get away. Disappear.'

'You're safe enough here. If you run you're more vulnerable. We can arrange for protection.'

Even as she spoke, she questioned her own advice. This message might be a malicious hoax. But if a real threat, then the slaughter hadn't been indiscriminate. There was intention behind it, and the entire intention was still unfulfilled. Killing Daniel would complete it. Madness like that couldn't be lightly brushed aside.

'I'll phone the superintendent,' she said. 'From downstairs.'

Yeadings, an early riser, was in the garden, muffled in a polo-neck sweater and enjoying the day's brightness while confronting the still soaked ruin of his dahlias. At least the kitchen plot no longer resembled a paddy field. A few fine days and the damage of the past ten could be repaired. There'd be fresh growth.

He gazed at the clean-swept sky. It promised to be one of those stupendous golden October mornings when the sun was still warm on your face.

Nan, in dressing-gown and slippers, called to him from the porch door. 'Telephone.'

He waved back, picked his way across the squelching lawn and took the call outside. Mrs Plumley, not at all happy, but resolute, wasted no words.

'It could be an unpleasant hoax,' he offered, but she'd arrived there already.

'But if not, we must take it seriously,' she insisted. 'Daniel is for running off and getting lost. I've told him he's safer here where we can control things. I thought of hiring someone to keep an eye on him. Alternatively, I suppose he could go back to boarding-school, but a different one. It appears he was asked to leave Stowe. Some trouble with a housemaid. In any case arrangements like that can take time.'

'Will you leave it with me, Mrs Plumley? I have an ex-constable in mind who might stand in as bodyguard.'

'Equally I could find someone ex-RAF, but he needs to be fit, not too old.'

'The man I'm suggesting is all of that, Mrs Plumley. If he'll take it on he could be with you tomorrow. Even later today.'

She felt reassured, laid down the phone and stood thinking how she might distract Daniel from his panicky state. She'd forgiven him the bathroom intrusion. It was understandable, the boy-man resenting the way she'd taken over. He'd needed to take the wind out of her sails, reinstate his own dignity by humiliating her. She must put it behind her, look forward, plan something special, a diversion.

But he wasn't a toddler to be distracted with a candy bar or toys. And yesterday's outing with Camilla had turned into the proverbial lead balloon.

She glanced out the window again. Wet grass sparkled like gems. Hillside's dew-pearled, she thought. Snail's on the thorn; that Pippa Passes stuff. But all was not right with the world. How could she fix it?

She made a second call. 'Caspar?'

'Plummie, you just caught me. I'm flying to Morocco at noon. How's everything with you and the venerable Plum?'

'Plum's gone fishing in Devon and I'm

fine too, thank you. No need to ask how you are. Have you closed down for the winter here?'

'Yes. I'm taking a fortnight's break, while the gear travels out by freighter. Then in mid-November we start up in Marrakech.'

'Sounds wonderful. I'll wish you a good season. I had hoped you'd a week or so left here. And for once it's a glorious day.'

'Is this personal?'

'Myself and grandson.'

'You've kept him under covers, Plummie. How old is he?'

'Sixteen, but passes for older. Actually I'm temporary guardian. I was wondering if . . .'

'Look, although I'll be away myself, Jeremy's hanging on with some of the gear. Let me find out if he can get a mate to help out. Then maybe, if the weather holds. Why not? I'll get him to ring you on your mobile.'

She thanked him, sat in a patch of sunlight and waited for the return call. It came a quarter of an hour later. Satisfied with the result, she was almost purring as she joined Daniel at breakfast. 'We have a little expedition arranged for this evening,' she announced. 'Something to look forward to after your talk with Dr Abercorn. Did I tell you he'd be dropping in to ask about your mother?'

CHAPTER SEVENTEEN

Waking was a let-down for Rosemary Zyczynski. She had dreamt they had a puppy; dark, smooth-coated and rolled into a little, soft ball, asleep. They had been Max and herself. They'd seemed to be living together.

This morning the sky was empty of clouds, deceitfully halcyon. But reality was less honeyed, with Max thousands of miles away. His apartment, across from hers, lay silent. For her it was a working day and the case showed no signs of breaking.

Get going, she told herself. Go and soak in everything available in the analysis room. Maybe lightning illumination will strike.

At Area she had to deal with Acting DCI Salmon first. He accosted her in the corridor and snarled a demand for coffee and a bacon sarnie, in his office, asap. A man who hadn't breakfasted and was in a hurry going nowhere.

She delivered the order, found he'd no

other use for her. What new in that? Seating herself opposite the longer wall of the analysis room, she tried to see all the whiteboard data as new; nothing she'd been grinding over for days.

There was the Hoad family in the middle. From it lines reached out in all directions like a starburst; one towards the Bartons, physically close to the crime but fully involved with farming and their antipodean family. Or so they seemed. They'd had opportunity; could have had a key to the Hoads' back door; might have had cause to hate the man's guts. But it took a leap of the imagination to see them as mass murderers and superb actors to boot.

A second line led to Bristol and the inherited foundry from which Hoad derived his wealth. He appeared to have a detached interest in its activities, or at most a purely financial one. So was Bertie Fallon, or some other with easy access, fleecing Hoad there, and panicking when threatened with exposure? But surely wiping out the whole family, except for the absent son — that was insanely over the top?

Insane. She considered the word, which featured at the end of another line with a question mark alongside the capital letter X. Wasn't that the solution you fell back on when logic, sweat and hard graft failed readily to turn up the true killer? — a random mass murderer who just happened along at that particular time, secure in anonymity and unconnected with his victims? No, she couldn't accept that. All crimes she'd come across so far had been subject to recognisable cause and effect. This had to be the same.

Another line on the whiteboard led to the family of the child visiting the house overnight. That she found she could accept as a random fact. How could young Monica's presence have been a factor in causing such carnage? It must be irrelevant to the overall crime.

From Jennifer Hoad's name a line ran out to the company Miradec Interiors in west London, which she'd visited herself. She recalled the two men there, the self-assured fashion-plate Justin Halliwell and the insecure Hilary Durham, proud to be called Jennifer's 'Ideas Man'. Halliwell manned their European office in Paris. He was concerned with import-export. From all accounts the company was a successful one. Certainly the Knightsbridge set-up implied as much and, according to her mother, Jennifer had made a fortune for herself once Freddie had financed her start.

Crack cocaine had featured in the raves that went on in the woods, and Z suspected its source was more likely London than anywhere local. Thames Valley had its share of dealers, but drugs were less easily accessible in villages like Fordham. Jennifer, a user, might well have been supplied by contacts regularly visiting the Knightsbridge office. Or from the ultra-sophisticated Halliwell, probably a sexual — if not officially a business — partner.

He was arranging to call in auditors, to present updated accounts for Jennifer's executors. The results could take a while, but there was no reason why she shouldn't pay Miradec Interiors a visit and enquire how far things had gone.

She made for Yeadings' office but he wasn't there, so it had to be an approach to Salmon, who snarled at her, phone clamped to one ear.

'If you don't need me, sir . . .'

He waved her away. Better leave a note for the Boss, she decided. I could be taken by aliens and Salmon would never make a move.

Fleetingly she remembered that sour thought as, taking the steep curve down towards Halton Air Base, the brakes failed to respond. Futilely her foot pumped at the pedal. Every movement was in agonised slow motion while her brain raced. She reached for the handbrake. It held, but, skidding on the frosted road, she had a blurred vision of the Vale of Aylesbury spread wide in mist far below, and then the car was sliding sideways over the edge.

'Where's that dratted girl?' demanded the DCI.

'Sergeant Zyczynski?' Yeadings enquired after a second's thought. 'She's gone to check up on something in London. Do you need her specifically?'

'London? Beaumont went there yesterday, to fetch Hoad's will. He could have doubled on it. Now that's two lots of expenses they'll put in for.'

'She's gone by car. Much the same mileage as a day spent footling around our patch. My worry, anyway. Not yours, Inspector.'

'According to Chief Superinten—'

'Yes, I know. Expenses. I still bear the scars. What did you need Z for? Use one of the DCs.'

'Have to, I suppose.' Disgruntled, Salmon took his leave.

This stalemate's getting to him, Yeadings silently observed: it has us all on edge.

■ ■ ■ ■

Upside down, with her seatbelt searing her shoulder, Z wriggled her mobile phone from one pocket. She had to beat the airbag down to get her breath before she could press out the number. It took fourteen minutes before she heard emergency vehicles and voices on the road above, and all the time she was aware of small slithering sounds as the soggy earth gave way a little more. Too much movement on her part and the car, nose down, could toboggan farther downhill on its roof. Was it water below or trees, she asked herself. This way up, it wasn't easy to work out exactly what point she'd reached.

'No brakes,' she gasped, as soon as they'd smashed the rear window to pull her out. But the Traffic officer wasn't one to mutter 'woman driver' under his breath.

'We'll get you sorted in two shakes of a lamb's tail, miss,' he assured her.

'Sergeant,' she insisted. 'I'm in the job. Regional CID. I want the car examined for tampering.'

'Right, Sergeant. Bob here'll give you a lift to A&E.'

'I don't need hospital. I want a car. Or a train to London.'

They argued, but she got her way. The aforementioned Bob delivered her to Wendover station and bought her a return ticket for Marylebone.

It was in the train that the shivers started.

I could have been killed, she told herself. Who the hell wanted that? The car had been serviced a week before and given a clean bill of health.

In the toilet at Marylebone station she examined herself. There was a livid band of red on her lower neck from the seatbelt, and a bruise was already starting to show over her left breast.

Not so serious as it might have been, she decided. She applied fresh make-up, thanked her stars that she hadn't phoned ahead to fix an appointment, and queued for a cab to take her to Knightsbridge.

Two hours before the expected visit from Dr Abercorn, DS Beaumont arrived to take Daniel off for interview. A Traffic officer had come up from Ascot, one the boy hadn't met before, who proposed a charge of Death by Dangerous Driving. Police bail would be arranged at a reasonable sum which Anna could cover, and a duty solicitor appointed to the case.

Daniel appeared sulky and uncommunicative. Cover-up, Anna guessed, for the very real fear he felt at the death threat. Up until now he'd shown no hint of remorse for causing the unfortunate girl's death.

As they manoeuvred the narrow passage back to Reception they ran into a grey-haired couple being escorted in. Anna barely recognised Ben Huggett accompanied by a straight-backed woman who could be his wife. The poacher wore a well-cut dark blue suit with hand-finished lapels, but never tailored for him. It pulled diagonally from collar to armpits over his barrel chest, and the trousers had been inexpertly shortened.

'Ma'am,' he said, standing aside for Anna to pass. Best Sunday manners as well.

'Mr Huggett, how are you?' She observed his wife's outrage at finding herself in a police station.

The woman eyed her sourly. 'You the lady staying at the Manor?'

'My wife,' Huggett apologised on her behalf.

'How d'you do, Mrs Huggett. I'm Anna Plumley, Daniel's grandmother.' She would have moved on, but the policewoman with the Huggetts was in no hurry to cut short any interesting exchange between them. Her considerable body blocked the way.

'I'll have you know,' the poacher's wife declared in high dudgeon, 'that we're respectable folk. I don't know why you should stop my husband walking in Fordham Woods. It's not trespassing, since he never did no harm there.

'Just ask our neighbours. They'll tell you. We're decent folk what pays our bills prompt, and goes to church at Easter and Christmas. And I run the jumble sales for Age Concern,' said Huggett's wife importantly.

It explained her husband's suit. A smidgen of time sacrificed to charity can repay in scooping cream off the benefits. Wifely duty, you might say, securing perks from the job.

'Well, quite,' said Anna, smiled at them both, removed the policewoman with a hard stare, and passed on.

'Did you grass on him?' Daniel demanded, nearer to cheerful than he'd been all morning.

'Just suggested he might have some information on what went on in the woods,' she said serenely. 'The police are interested in a hut up there. The old pheasant-raising place. I doubt he had any recent connection.'

'Why?' he asked, perhaps too keenly. 'I mean, why the police interest?'

'I'm not in their confidence,' she assured him. 'But it seems they found something unexpected.'

Daniel fell silent. In the police car which returned them to the Manor he sat hunched, his face averted. 'I'm going to my room,' he announced on arrival.

Anna heard him trudge upstairs, and then the slam of his door. She let herself quietly out of the gun room and stared up, flattened against the outer wall. She heard the boy unlatch his window. He leaned out, field-glasses to his eyes.

Simply curious about the police activity? Or disturbed on account of involvement with what went on in the woods? He'd be none the wiser in any case. The forensics team in their white coveralls had long gone, carrying off their trophies in black plastic sacks.

'Coffee,' she reminded herself, and went indoors to have a word with Alma Pavitt.

'It's not an interview,' Dr Abercorn insisted as he shed his coat in the hall. 'More in the nature of a medical consultation. So there isn't the need for a responsible adult to be present.'

He waited a few seconds before adding, 'Unless I'm considered to be that myself.'

His chuckle was practised but feeble, as if he was tiring of the well-worn joke himself.

'I'll fetch Daniel down,' she offered. 'He's been resting.'

The boy entered belligerently. 'You know my life's been threatened?' Anna heard him challenge as she closed the door between them. Go for the shrink's jugular before he picks at your brains, she thought. Demand why he's here and not a tough bodyguard.

He had a point, but there was a deal of anger dammed up inside Daniel and a whole lot of secrecy as well. She had got nowhere trying to get through to him. Maybe the professional would be more successful.

She went through to the kitchen where Anna Pavitt started lifting objects and putting them down elsewhere with unnecessary firmness. Invasion of the woman's territory, Anna admitted, but on what other ground could they meet for any sane discussion?

'Mrs Pavitt, something has to be done about your wages. And free time too. We've been trading on your good nature too long already. I should like to make up what's owed you, until such time as my son-in-law's solicitor takes over.'

The other woman stiffened, with her back to Anna. Then she turned, suspicion in her eyes. 'I was paid to the end of the month, so I don't need charity. But I could do with a break, if only to go and get my car back. They can't deliver, with a police guard on the entrance gates.'

'I'm sorry, I hadn't realised the difficulty. But they should certainly let your car through. It's only the press and other prying eyes they're meant to keep out.'

'Well, the garage people tried and were turned back. Now they're being shirty about it.'

'So by all means take time off to fetch the car. Why not now? Take the rest of the day. Daniel and I will be out until quite late in any case and won't be needing a meal.'

Saying thank you must have cost the woman, but she was clearly less disgruntled now. 'I could, I suppose. There's only Melba toast to make for the pâté. The goulash is simmering for lunch and it's a chilled dessert. I made plenty, if the doctor wants to stay on.'

'Splendid,' Anna decided, beamed on her and left. Twenty minutes later the front doorbell shrilled. Through the study window Anna saw the housekeeper, wrapped in a burgundy-dyed sheepskin coat, escorted to a waiting taxi by the cabby. This time, it seemed, the gate police had been less rigid in their duties.

All seemed quiet in the drawing-room. Perhaps Dr Abercorn was patiently waiting for Daniel to open up. Anna leaned close to the panelled door and caught the sound of low sobbing. She nodded. It had taken a stranger to get through.

She felt little better herself. It was the same grief: his mother, adoptive father and half-sister dead; her child, her grandchild, poor Freddie. There was always a sense of guilt over the old surviving the young.

From her own soured experience of Jennifer, she knew there'd be plenty the boy must have regretted, however intense his love for her. Quite early on he'd struck her as almost Oedipal, with Jennifer's behaviour fuelling his obsession. He would never be free of his mother; had even less chance now she was dead, an ever-present ghost to haunt him.

Anna returned to the kitchen to look in on the goulash, a rich brown with little peaks of red peppers, bubbling gently. Perhaps a tad heavy for midday eating, but the aromatic scents should tempt any reluctant appetite. She reached for baking potatoes from the vegetable rack, slit and seasoned three of the largest, ready for the oven.

Again the doorbell shrilled. She opened

up and found a lanky figure in shabby brown leathers towering over her. He had a lean, curved, Don Quixote face with shaggy brows and an enormous, limply drooping, reddish moustache. The eyes, assessing her, were a bright blue, clear as a summer sky. Under one arm was a black helmet. Behind him, parked at the bottom of the steps, gleamed an enormous Harley.

'Ms Plumley?' he enquired. 'Superintendent Yeadings sent me. I'm known as Charlie Barley, but my first name's really John.'

The bodyguard. She held out her hand. 'I'll use Charlie, if I may. I'm Anna.'

The gangling figure followed her in, produced ID. A DC taking six months' sabbatical, he explained. She couldn't help wondering why, but wouldn't ask outright.

'Something smells good.'

'I wasn't the cook, I'm afraid. You'll join us, of course?' She took his wide grin for assent and went to prepare a fourth potato.

In the event, while Daniel again slunk upstairs, Dr Abercorn made a swift departure. At least as far as his car, where he remained, presumably making notes, then just sitting, staring up at the cloudless sky.

Anna turned from the window and was startled to find Barley looking over her shoulder. He was a silent mover. She stepped away. 'How well up on this business are you?' she asked.

'Mr Yeadings briefed me, but I could do with more detail. That was the shrink leaving?'

She nodded. 'I imagine he'll report back to the superintendent?'

'Yup. Dr Abercorn's right in there with the team now. He's good. I know him.'

'You've worked together?'

The droopy moustache quivered, curved up at the ends. 'He sorted me out.'

Anna managed not to blink at the admission. The fact that Barley could freely offer it meant surely that the other had done a good job on him. Discretion, she warned herself: don't pry. I've known others go through personal hell and come out on the right side.

'I hope you've an appetite. I'd calculated on Dr Abercorn staying for lunch. Would you care to call Daniel down? He might not hurry for me, but your voice will make him curious.'

The conversation over their meal was mainly gentle probing on Anna's part and a droll recital of 'funny things that happened in the job' from Barley. Occasionally Daniel showed slight interest. Eventually, as she brought in the cheeseboard, Anna heard him burst out, 'They're making such a bloody fuss over that bike crash. And the girl. She was only a fucking prostitute, for God's sake.'

'A life's a life,' said the detective. 'Has to be followed up.'

'As if you care. Just a statistic.'

'Like your family,' Anna ground out, disgusted with him.

It caught Daniel unprepared. He blanched and swung on her, mouth agape. Almost choking, he managed to get the words out. 'That was a tragedy. God, I'd give everything for that not to have happened.'

'Can't turn back the clock,' said the man. He was rolling out the clichés with monotonous detachment.

Daniel stared at him. 'It's nothing to you, is it?' More curiosity than anger now.

'It's my job. Happens all the time.'

But it doesn't, Anna thought. Murders aren't that common in Thames Valley. Wholesale slaughter almost unheard of. What was the man up to, gutting the boy?

But at least he was getting a reaction. She decided to take a step or two backwards and leave them to each other. 'Why,' she suggested, 'don't you both make the most of the sunshine and take a turn round the grounds while I fill the dishwasher? The housekeeper's got the day off, but I'll serve coffee soon. After that we're going out for a drive. I've something to show you.'

The other two looked at each other. Daniel shrugged, took out a coin from his pocket, flipped it several times in one hand. 'Uphill or down? Call for the river.'

'Tails,' said Barley.

'It's heads.' Daniel held out his hand with the coin in it. 'Uphill then. We'll go to the woods.'

He pranced to the door, turned, twirled an imaginary moustache. 'Aha, to the woods, me little darling!' — delivered in a theatrically villainous voice. Then a child's piping treble, 'No, no! I am only thirteen, sir.' A gruff, 'This is no time to be superstitious!' A frantic wail, 'I shall tell the vicar!' Most villainous of all, 'But I am the vicar!'

A faint flicker moved the detective's own moustache. Anna turned away, uneasy: you try to treat an adolescent like a grown-up, and then in an instant he's a child again. Really I am fit only to deal with adults.

'You'll need stout boots,' she said shortly to Barley. 'It won't have dried out up there.'

'These'll do,' the man said.

Daniel went upstairs to change from the clothes he'd worn for the police interview, and Anna appealed to Barley. 'He has a rather morbid interest in the woods at present.'

'I guessed he would have. Which is why I bid tails for the river. There are a few double-headed coins about and he was a tad too cocky. I've yet to see a double-tailed one.' At the door, he stopped. 'May I ask where we're bound for later?'

Anna smiled. 'I arranged a little treat to distract him.' She explained.

'That's novel,' he said. 'It'll be a first for me as well.'

So he would be coming too. Just as well, perhaps. He and Daniel might yet hit it off, man to man.

CHAPTER EIGHTEEN

When the cab dropped Z at Miradec Interiors a young couple with a small boy were just going in. She fell in behind and let Hilary Durham take her for one of the group. He was far too occupied with pleasing the couple to notice, let alone recognise, her. They had come by appointment to view the computerised ground floor layout for an impressive Georgian town house.

Not to the manor born, Z noted, and a later mention of 'Our Good Luck' was clue to a big National Lottery win or a Premium Bond turned up trumps.

Hilary was earnest and slightly bumbling still, but he knew his stuff. I'd have consulted him myself, she thought, falling instantly in love with the graceful staircase and elegant hall — if I had the money.

The clients loved the layout, but had doubts about the discreet colours. Hilary flicked at the screen, changed them to crude primaries, almost incandescent, and won his point. He passed on to display the state-of-the-art kitchen and the woman was enchanted. The man signed a clip of papers and they were given a copy of the video.

When Hilary saw them out he at last took account of the extra presence. 'Oh, S-S-Sergeant,' he stuttered. 'I'm so sorry. I . . .'

'Don't be. I'm impressed. Actually I wondered if I'd find Mr Halliwell here.'

'He was. But he got called away.'

'So if I wait . . . ?'

Hilary wriggled with discomfort. 'Actually, I couldn't say. He could be gone some time. It was an emergency.'

'Then maybe I could be of some help?'

'You mean as police? No, nothing like that. A friend taken ill at Heathrow. He just panicked and rushed off.'

Z couldn't imagine the urbane and smooth-tongued Justin Halliwell in panic. 'Was the friend catching a plane?' she asked. 'Fear of flying can be awful.'

'No. No, she was coming back. From Disneyworld.'

'With her family?'

'Alone.'

Now who goes to Disneyworld alone? Z asked herself. You'd surely beg, borrow or breed at least one child to take along. But

268

Disneyworld meant Florida. Flying out of Orlando. Or even Miami.

'How ill did she seem?'

'Just jet lag, I guess.' But at that Hilary clammed up. Any confidence he'd displayed with the clients had totally disappeared. He was frankly in a dither.

Z's curiosity had been centred on cocaine. So did this connect? From Colombia or Cuba illegal immigrants smuggle the raw stuff into Miami by sea. It's picked up there and flown to the UK in innocent-looking tourists' luggage. Or, at worst and sometimes fatally, swallowed.

There was plenty of that going on. Cabin crews on the long haul trip were warned to look for passengers refusing food for fear of defecating too soon. Customs and Immigration at British airports included medical back-up. One of their less palatable jobs was recovery and examination of faeces from stay-over detainees.

And sometimes the plastic containers for drugs, often condoms, burst while still inside. Not a pleasant way to die if you didn't get to a surgeon in time.

'I think,' Z told him, 'you'd better give me Justin's mobile number.'

'I'm not allowed to use it. Except in emergencies.'

'This is one, believe me. I've other ways of obtaining it, but that could be too late. You know she could die, don't you? And where does that leave you? Responsible.'

She thought then she heard his teeth chatter. He certainly knew of the traffic she'd suspected. His hands were shaking as he leafed through a notebook from his jacket pocket.

'Talk to him,' she ordered. 'Tell him the police are already on to it. And not to do anything stupid. He's to stay wherever he is and I'll send emergency services.'

She watched his stricken face as he pressed out the number. There was a babble of rapid speech at the other end, rising on a note of despair.

'He's in his car,' Hilary whispered. 'I think he wants to dump her.'

'Is she still alive?' Z insisted. She waited while Hilary cut through Justin's torrent of words.

'Unconscious,' he said.

'Tell him it's his only chance. He must keep her alive until we can get a surgeon to her.'

'Leave cover to the locals now,' Salmon snarled when she phoned to say Justin's girlfriend was in theatre at Hillingdon hospital having her abdomen explored. 'You've got a job here, remember? The Boss is expecting you to drive him to Bristol.'

Anna steered the Jeep along the twisting lane and in on the rutted track beside a country pub. The usual notice boards had been removed, packed for transport to the Moroccan site, but the wind sock was still flying, indicating a mild blow, south-south-easterly. Daniel, across from her in the passenger seat, appeared not to notice it.

She parked, backing on to a striped marquee, and waved the two men through an opening in the fence. Across the field something bulky was being manhandled off a flat-bed trailer. It was square and heavy.

'Good, we're in time to help,' Anna said complacently. They both started walking across the coarse grassland, Barley bringing up the rear. Ahead, a bulky metal object had also been unloaded and stood braced on four steel legs. Now, as they approached, an immense length of multi-coloured fabric was being drawn from a cube of wickerwork, like an outsized string of red, blue and orange handkerchiefs produced by a conjuror from a hat. Two men in charge ran out, dragging it behind like a great, gaudy, sloughed-off snakeskin.

'It's a ruddy balloon,' Daniel marvelled. 'Are we going up?' He was in there at once, helping pull open the folds, shouting to the others as outsize fans on the ground blew air in and the near end started to billow.

Again he was that complicated adolescent mixture of fascinated child and know-all male adult tackling technicalities. Anna went across to Jeremy who was testing the burners. He looked up and grinned, ran a hand over his cropped white hair. 'Good to see you, Squadron Leader.'

'Likewise,' she said. 'We've an extra passenger, Jeremy. My grandson's bodyguard. Did Caspar fill you in on the background?'

'He did. You have my sincere condolences, ma'am.'

DC Barley had drifted over to inspect the equipment. The two men shook hands. 'You the pilot?' They stood chatting, then together heaved the basket upright from the prone position.

'That's my section.' Jeremy pointed to the largest of five divisions in the basket, the central oblong. The others were square, forming each corner of the cube. 'Normally we take two passengers in each section, making nine, including the pilot.'

Barley examined the cockpit with its coloured hanging cords that controlled the upper panels of the balloon. Under the burners there wasn't a lot of space for a pilot, once mounted, because of the gas bottles.

'Flown before?' asked Jeremy.

'Just in holiday jets, and the Chiltern chopper. Did a bit of gliding off Booker airfield.'

'This is different,' Jeremy promised, busy fitting protective spats to the four steel legs of the superstructure. 'Total silence between burns, no engine, no straining fabric sounds, because we're wind-borne, not resisting the air. Too high even for traffic noise over the motorways. Peaceful, civilised.'

When the balloon was fully bellied and floating, they climbed in, using square toe-holds in the wickerwork to reach the breast-high rim. Anna and Daniel were to one side, the boy directionally ahead; Barley and a crewman on the other. Each in a separate section, balancing weight.

Jeremy ran through the safety precautions, indicated the security loops to be grasped, reminded them he'd repeat instructions directly before landing. 'You'll see there are no seats. That'd be a complication if anything went wrong. Which it won't.'

'OK then, everybody happy? We're off.' A groundsman loosed the moorings.

The burner roared above them. Slowly

they began to rise.

Anna turned and smiled at her grandson. His eyes blazed with excitement, his features taut. Then he smiled back, and her heart went cold. Such intensity, almost malevolence.

Dear God, don't let him do anything crazy.

Jeremy had said it was peaceful. It might have been so for Barley if he hadn't been uneasy about the boy. Silent it certainly was when, above nine hundred feet, Jeremy cut gas to the roaring burners. The last sound from below had been miniature cows lowing as they crossed unbelievably green pasture, driven towards a toy milking parlour. The River Chess snaked flatly, country lanes wriggled like kinky tape. As they rose still higher motorways began to look just as marked on the map.

They were progressing in a series of leisurely hops, soaring steadily as hot air filled the fabric, then, as the fire's roar was cut, more slowly drifting down until the burners took up again and they rose even higher.

In the late afternoon light, tapestry colours of autumn woods, lush fields and tidy country houses with turquoise swimming pools began to take on a harmonious overall blue haze. Long shadows drew bars across the valleys. The sky alone remained luminescent, immeasurable, with the sun sinking in a pearly silver towards the left horizon.

The DC looked over Jeremy's head as he squatted in the cockpit. Daniel, like himself, was in the forward basket section, on the far side. Out of reach. He was leaning far out, focusing on the chequered fields they were presently passing over. The old lady, behind him and separated by the breast-high wicker partition, was gazing back towards the disappearing village where they had taken off. She was smiling as she turned, leaning forward to speak with her grandson, one arm outstretched.

They were above the sun's level now, the balloon casting no shadow on a regimented pattern of buildings below. Barley took them for a military establishment, then recalled it would be RAF Halton: maybe a station at which the old lady had once served. Their altitude had wiped out ground contours and he barely recognised the flattened escarpment above the Vale of Aylesbury. Men appeared to be winching up a car upended half-way down the slope.

Fascinated, he could pick out villages he remembered driving through, half-familiar loops of waterways meandering like flat ribbons to lose themselves finally towards the Thames.

A startled cry made him straighten and turn. Across from the cockpit two figures were struggling, the woman's arms clamped about the young man, he fighting to get her off his back. Both out of reach because of the cockpit in between, and Jeremy's hands busy with the burners.

Bloody balls of fire! I should have kept close, the DC knew. Can't do a bloody thing from here. They should have warned me he was this crazy. For God's sake, what was the old girl thinking of to give him a chance like this? Did she want him to leap?

'Get down!' roared Jeremy, reaching out to grasp Daniel by the shoulder, but the boy swung back an elbow, thrusting him away. Anna Plumley, knocked off balance, gave a little grunt and fell back against the rear wall of wicker, one hand still clutching the boy's jacket which pulled down imprisoning his arms. Savagely he shook her off, like a terrier with a rat.

He reached out with something in his hand. For a brief second he held it over the void, looking down and then, too fast for Barley to be sure what the object was, he'd released it. Falling, there was a flash of metal as the low sun caught it. Then it was gone. Daniel drew back, turned a mocking smile on him. 'What's the sweat, man? Didn't you ever play Pooh Sticks?'

Jeremy was talking into his mobile, ordering up the truck to meet them, giving location of an emergency landing site. They were dropping steadily now, the fall decelerated with steady, short bursts of burning.

He ignored Anna's attempt to apologise for the scuffle. He repeated the landing instructions to them, twisted round to check all their grips on the safety ropes, watched them take up squat position for landing, heads below the basket's rim. The ground was getting close now.

'There will be one slight bump,' he said. 'Then a second slighter one, and we'll have landed.'

They barely felt a thing, then a little slither on grass, and cool evening air blowing on their flushed faces. The basket stayed upright.

'So what,' Jeremy asked grimly, facing Anna and her grandson, 'was all that about?'

DC Barley looked at the boy's closed face. He'd thought for a mistaken moment that Daniel had meant to jump. But it wasn't that. He'd risked killing someone below by dropping a metal object. So what had it been? Something he needed to be rid of? Evidence that hadn't turned up, despite fingertip searches of the murder site?

Like a sharp kitchen knife, or a small handgun? Who the hell was he protecting?

Jeremy was white with contained anger. 'Everyone out,' he ordered. He swung down and waited while the others clambered over the high edge of the basket.

When Daniel stood with his back to him he whirled him round. 'Did you need telling how dangerous that was? Any solid object falling from that height . . . You could have killed someone below. For all we know you may have done. Aren't you in trouble enough?'

The boy flushed, biting his lips. He was trembling with outrage. 'Take your hands off me. You can't speak to me like that!'

'Daniel, the pilot's in charge,' Anna warned him, coldly angry. 'What was it you dropped?'

'Just my mobile. I'll not be getting any more death threats on that. Let someone else pick it up. They're welcome to it.'

Which didn't ring true, Barley thought. The boy had been too focused on what he was doing. They'd been passing across water at that point. It looked like a stretch of the Grand Union Canal. If the dropped object had hit target, it could take days of dragging to retrieve it. And, anyway, it wouldn't have been his mobile: Barley had been in the job too long not to know a cover-up when he heard it.

Jeremy had given up on them and was phoning again, guiding in their pick-up. The collapsing balloon needed sorting. Anna joined the crewman who was dragging the sagged fabric out in a straight line, prior to beating out the residual air. They all lent a hand while Jeremy set about dismantling the superstructure.

A 4x4 with the flat-bed trailer appeared at the gate to their field, having tracked their route from ground level. Between them they gathered the fabric into horizontal folds and rolled it down tight, ready to fit again in the basket. The engine was hoisted alongside on the flat-bed. In the 4x4 there was room for them all, with bottles of drinking water provided.

Jeremy nodded to Barley. 'I have to log it for the police.'

'Likewise,' Barley confided. 'It'll be my head rolling. I should have kept closer.'

No, Anna told herself: my fault. A stupid idea. It was intended as a pleasant outing, to divert him. Now it's complicated life further for the wretched boy.

They were driven back in silence to the take-off field. The striped marquee had already been dismantled, ready for transport abroad with the other gear. There was just a temporary table there laid with glasses, a bottle of champagne and nibbles.

Anna insisted that, out of courtesy, they accept the refreshments, along with signed certificates for the flight. It should have been a celebration but had gone seriously flat.

Still Daniel hadn't thought fit to apologise for his irresponsible behaviour. He drank the champagne as if it was gall. Barley refused it. They said goodbye to Jeremy and his assistants, then returned to Anna's car. Barley offered to drive but was stared down.

A little more than half an hour later they were back at Fordham Manor. Alma Pavitt hadn't returned and Anna was obliged to put together a meal, since they all seemed disinclined to eat out in a pub. She covered ready-made pizza bases with tomato purée, mozzarella, ham and chives, while Barley tossed a salad. Daniel had disappeared upstairs, leaving them to discuss him if they cared to. Which they didn't.

Not a good day at all, Anna decided. I don't know what good I'm doing here. I've never been a success in dealing with family.

CHAPTER NINETEEN

News of her mishap with the car had gone before her. When he picked Z up from the railway station, Yeadings looked rueful. 'Are you up to the journey? Sure? In which case you drive. Best to get back in the saddle straight after a spill. We'll stop for a late lunch on the way and you can bring me up to date on the London end while we eat.

'That explains Jennifer Hoad's access to drugs,' he commented when she told him, 'and raises more questions about the firm in Knightsbridge. Young Halliwell will be lucky to escape a manslaughter charge if his "mule" dies.'

He sounded almost pleased. But then there wasn't much progress to report on any other aspect of the investigation.

At the Bristol foundry Yeadings and Zyczynski, with a video screen apiece and surrounded by a welter of paperwork drawn from Personnel and Wages departments, were both interrupted by calls on their mobile phones. For the superintendent it was a text message, which he read off without comment.

Z, recognising Anna Plumley's number, took her call. The news was interesting rather than startling. It seemed that no great harm had come from the boy's actions, but his grandmother was clearly upset. 'I'm mortified,' Anna confessed. 'I badly misjudged Daniel's state of mind, and I've let my friends in for a severe reprimand at the very least.'

Z sympathised. 'Has the bodyguard arrived yet?'

'A Charlie Barley, yes. He's a great deal more alert than he appears. Unfortunately we were both situated where we couldn't prevent what happened. We felt sure the object would have fallen into the canal, but couldn't agree on the exact location. Then again the DC disbelieves that it was Daniel's mobile phone he got rid of, but I'm quite certain it was. A compact metal object, smaller than any kind of handgun I'm familiar with, and too short for the knife you're looking for.'

'Don't worry,' Z told her. 'As promised, I'm dropping in this evening, and I'll have a word with Daniel. That should give him time to realise he's been acting very stupidly.'

'Boy in balloon?' Yeadings queried as she closed her mobile. 'I had Barley's version. He wasn't best pleased with himself. How's your list coming on?'

'Four fictional employees to date,' she told him, 'one metallurgical trainee, one furnace-man, two metalworkers in medium salary range. All with phoney National Insurance numbers. Somebody at this end has been seriously into creative bookkeeping.'

'I guess we'd better check with Inland Revenue. The taxman will be losing out on this as well. "O what a tangled web we weave . . ." I wonder was it worth it?'

'Someone's made a quarter of a million to date,' she reckoned. 'Kept up another year or so, Fallon, or another, could have bought himself a handsome country estate.'

'Or paid off a whole load of debts. We need local investigators to go into Fallon's spending habits. There could be a bottom-less pit he's been throwing money down.'

He flipped open his mobile and pressed in the contact number for DCI Salmon. 'Yeadings,' he announced himself. 'Hang on to Fallon until I get back. Ply him with tea and sandwiches first, then leave him under supervision. At that point you might let drop where I've spent the best part of the day. It should get him in the right mood for a heart-to-heart on my return.'

Their visit to the foundry had been unexpected and raised a certain amount of ruffled feathers, but nobody they'd met had appeared particularly uneasy. Before leaving, Yeadings spoke aside to a young woman in the human resources department, and Z assumed he'd sniffed out the informer.

Dusk had at first slid into starry dark. A nip of frost was in the air. When cloud cover began to obscure the moon there was little discernible rise in temperature. The girlie weather-forecaster with the local news was warning of sleet and snow over the Chilterns during the night with difficult driving conditions on motorways. Anna edged the central heating up a notch and checked that the second guest room was adequately prepared for the visiting DC.

Passing Daniel's door she paused, knocked and went straight in. In view of his attitude to bathroom privacy he could hardly object. But he did, starting up at his writing desk, then hunching forward to cover a sheet of notepaper with both forearms. He stared coldly over one shoulder at her.

'I'm serving Irish coffee downstairs,' she

told him. 'Come and join us when you're ready.' In the doorway she turned back. 'Oh yes, I've almost run out of reading matter. Can I look through your bookcase for something to fill the gap?'

He let her request hang in the air, then shrugged. 'Whatever.'

She knelt to review the titles she'd been through before. 'Aleister Crowley; that's a bit old hat. *The Exorcist,* m'm. Might try that, I suppose. There was a film in the Seventies, which I missed.'

'Load of rubbish,' he muttered. 'They're not mine; they're hers.'

'Jennifer's?'

There was a pause before he grunted. Anna took it for yes. He scowled, stabbing the desktop with one end of his pen. 'D'you think the hulk would let me try out the Harley?'

'With your track record? And then this afternoon's performance? What do you think?'

'What a bloody waste, though, on a loser like him.'

'I wouldn't write him off as that.'

'No?' He was looking superior, implying that she had been nowhere, seen nothing, was no judge of character. She decided to walk out before the desire to box his ears put her on the wrong side of the law.

'I noticed a snooker table in the gun room,' she mentioned, again at the door. 'Maybe DC Barley would give you a frame or two if you've nothing better to do.'

'Better? Like sprinting starkers down to the front gate and making their day for the paparazzi, you mean? God, I wish something would happen! I can't stand being penned in, and all this farting about over nothing.'

Nothing, Anna considered, going downstairs. How could he see all that had happened as nothing? One moment he seemed chillingly detached. The next he was almost in a cold sweat with fear. And then mocking everyone. Were his attitudes all accountable to the aftermath of shock? You'd think the boy was growing up a monster. Jennifer had made an even worse job of mothering than herself. Small wonder Freddie had been so worried about the boy.

She cheered herself with the thought that Rosemary Zyczynski would be dropping in later. She was young, attractive, hadn't the drawback of a family connection. Maybe he would play along with her, open up, start to get things off his chest.

'It's still not clear who's behind the scam,' Yeadings remarked as he took over the drive homewards. It had begun to snow by the time he dropped Z off by Fordham mini-market to pick up something for supper. When she emerged she saw Mrs Pavitt getting into her car at the pavement edge. She bent to say hello through the lowered window, sticky little snowflakes feathering her hair and the shoulders of her sheepskin coat.

'You on foot?' the housekeeper demanded.

'My Ford's in dock. I've a hire car booked at the station.'

'Best jump in then, or you'll get soaked. It's coming on fast. Snow in October! We don't need winter this early.'

She appeared in a chatty mood, clearing the passenger seat of bulging carrier bags and swinging them back behind her on the car's floor. Z stepped in and clipped on her seat belt.

'Poor old Huggett,' Mrs Pavitt said, inviting comment.

'What's he done?'

'It's what's been done to him. A brick through his front window. They told me in the post office. I guess that'd be Animal Rights nutters.'

'Why them?' Z asked.

'Oh, the badger thing, don't you know? Nobody ever made a fuss about him poaching, but baiting with savage dogs turns the stomach for most people.'

Z said nothing, wondering how word had got around about Anna Plumley's brush with the man. Huggett himself would be unlikely to broadcast it and Anna hadn't been out to the village earlier.

Mrs Pavitt's smile had a sly little twist to it. She could have picked up the story while waiting at table, and Z wouldn't put it past her to enjoy gossiping by phone. There were plenty agog for any titbits of news from the stricken manor house and Anna Plumley's arrival would have stirred up curiosity.

'I'll be calling on Mrs Plumley later.'

'Right. I'll tell her. I'm heading back there now.' For some reason she seemed suddenly uneasy.

Z glanced sideways, alerted by a change in the woman's voice. There seemed nothing to account for it. She was staring ahead, brushing steam from the windscreen with the back of one hand, then shot out into the evening traffic flow.

At the station yard she drew up alongside the courtesy car. Z thanked her, getting out. Some elusive half-observation disturbed her about the short encounter. Something Pavitt had said or done? Whatever, it wasn't coming through. It would remain one of those itchy little half-memories that wake you in the night and then you never get off to sleep again until morning.

Best to change gear mentally and allow it to surface in its own good time. There was enough to chew over in the update Yeadings had just given her. For the present she must visit Mrs Plumley and see how Daniel could explain his behaviour of the afternoon.

'Why that?' Yeadings asked Salmon, echoing Z's curiosity about the brick through Ben Huggett's window.

'Bit of lowlife flexing its puny muscles,' the DCI offered as his opinion. 'Must be plenty of folks have a grudge against the man. Done someone down over his poached rabbits, I'd guess.'

Yeadings rubbed his chin reflectively. 'More likely some connection with our having him in for questioning. It might be supposed he was grassing on someone. Maybe it's a threat to keep him stumm about something he'd observed on his nightly prowls.'

'Because he might try blackmail?' Salmon queried.

'Blackmail or pure spite. Anyway, it's worth having another word with him. Last time his wife came along too, as his ruling conscience. So, better if Beaumont runs into him in the pub when the man's relaxed, alone and more inclined to talk.'

'And the balloon incident; do we drag the canal?'

'The rusted ironmongery retrieved wouldn't cover the cost of divers over a matter of days. No, the boy says it was his mobile phone he dropped and his grandmother agrees. Barley is more ready now to accept their word for it. For the present we'll leave it there. Daniel Hoad has enough to answer for on the Ascot end, and I guess it's time I saw Fallon about our enquiries at the foundry.'

Bertie Fallon was seething. 'For God's sake,' he greeted Yeadings when he materialised, 'what right have you lot to keep me hanging about like this? A whole working day wasted over some daft idea old Freddie had buzzing in his head. And what the hell did you need to go down to Bristol for? I could have told your man anything you needed to know right here.'

'You were free to leave at any time,' the Boss told him. 'You're not under arrest. Have you had anything to eat?'

'I went to the canteen for lunch and they've brought me tea since, but that's not the point. I demand an explanation.'

Yeadings took the empty seat opposite and nodded Beaumont alongside. 'For everyone's convenience we are taping this interview. You will receive a copy at the conclusion and be asked to sign a receipt.'

Beaumont switched on the recorder, stated date and time, and they identified themselves for the tape.

Yeadings resumed. 'Now, Mr Fallon, I will repeat my colleague's question. What was the nature of Mr Hoad's phone conversation with you on Wednesday, October 18th?'

'I've told your Inspector Salmon ten times over. Freddie ordered a meeting for the following Monday. As you know, we never made it. He'd been dead two days by then.'

'Did he mention any agenda for this meeting?'

'It wasn't to be that formal. We'd have lunch together at a pub midway, where we've met before. I booked a table for twelve-thirty.'

'To discuss what?'

'God knows. Finance, I guess. He saw to the business side. My line's production.'

'You must have been curious. This seems to have come out of the blue.'

Fallon's forehead puckered. 'I did wonder. He asked me to bring records from Personnel. Well, Human Resources they call it now. He wanted it kept quiet that I was removing them from the office. I wondered whether . . .'

'Yes?'

'If he was running short of capital; was he going to put on a squeeze, demand whole-sale sackings.'

'Did you have any reason to think he had money troubles?'

'Not till then. He'd always seemed to be rolling in it. Whenever we needed to expand he'd usually look the plans through, ask a few questions, then OK them right away. Easy about further outlay. Then I thought — what if the family . . . Well, his wife was spoilt, always demanded the best of every-thing. Only she was supposed to have private income from her arty stuff. But I know that a couple of months back Freddie had removed his son from an expensive school and sent him to a local one as a day boy . . .'

'You were worried.'

'Wouldn't you be? Freddie had sounded tense, not a bit like himself, and he wouldn't give me any inkling over the phone. There's a long list of orders we're part-way through, and a good-sized workforce who could be thrown on the market if the firm goes bottom up.'

'I don't think there's any danger of that. In fact, Mr Hoad's worries concerned something going on at the Bristol end. You'd no hint of that yourself?'

'My end? God, no. Is that what your Inspector was getting at? Hang on, man. You mean Salmon was simply keeping me out of the way while you served a search warrant!'

Yeadings leaned back in his seat, head tilted as he suffered the man's explosive rage. Fallon's astonishment seemed genuine enough, but there was a lot to clear up before he could be let off the hook.

'I'll level with you, Mr Fallon,' he said. 'From what we discovered, it appears Mr Hoad was right to be concerned. He had received an anonymous letter suggesting there were irregularities at your factory, if not criminal activity. This is what we found . . .'

Fallon boggled at him. 'And you think I was behind this!' he shouted as Yeadings finished. 'As if eleven hours a day overseeing production isn't enough, without you'd have me falsifying other departments' paperwork!'

Yeadings sat back and waited.

'It involves a bit more than paperwork,'

Beaumont challenged. 'Somebody's raking in a fortune channelling salaries for fictitious staff. Small wonder Hoad wanted a word with you. And very convenient he got killed when he did, wouldn't you say, Mr Fallon?'

Fallon's jaw sagged. 'Oh my God? You're not thinking I . . . ? Me harm old Freddie? You're bloody stark staring mad! Who the hell was the informer, and why didn't he come to me about it?'

'Perhaps,' Beaumont suggested, 'because he, or she, was pretty sure you were involved in the scam yourself.'

Yeadings returned to his office to pick up his hat and coat. From a drawer he took out a copy of SOCO's report on findings at the hut. He scanned it again rapidly, grunting at the described mess of smudged prints, the only recognisable latents being those of the housekeeper, young Daniel and his dead mother.

So had the boy broken into the hut in the woods, curious about what went on there? Or had Jennifer invited her adolescent son to her funky partying? Even involved him as a novice in occult rites?

Daniel's dabs were clearest on one of the gilded masks, that of the ram. The goat head, with its prominent, slitted, pale eyes, revealed Jennifer's fingerprints overlaid by Alma Pavitt's. Whatever had gone on in that part of the woods began to look less innocent than orgiastic.

Several items had been in contact with cocaine, and smoking apparatus had been unearthed from below the floorboards. A few minute pieces of white grit appeared to be from prepared 'rocks' of crack; which suggested that the pure drug's mixture with bicarbonate of soda, and the microwave baking, had taken place there.

Pavitt and the boy, sole survivors of the Manor's carnage, would need to give an account of themselves, whether it was relevant or not to investigation of the deaths.

How deeply was the boy involved in the drug scene? Yeadings asked himself. Had Jennifer used him as a teenage distributor to a local outlet? And would that be a further motive for his ditching his mobile phone, if it contained incriminating contact numbers?

All those questions were for tomorrow, Yeadings decided. He'd have Daniel brought back to Area nick, to face himself and Rosemary Zyczynski, with the grandmother present as responsible adult when the boy was questioned. All softly, softly, and strictly according to the book. Certainly not an occasion to risk Salmon's bigoted impatience or Beaumont's black humour.

And he'd have Dr Abercorn, as profiler, watch from the observation room with radio hook-up to his own ear-piece.

Half-way home he remembered. Tomorrow, at midday, was the Hoads' funeral. There could be no questioning until that was over. Angela and her parents were to be buried together in Fordham churchyard. A service for the other child, Monica, would take place at Ashridge on the following day. Although there was bound to be a great turnout of villagers at the church, both interments were for family only, with press and sightseers excluded. But not the police. Yeadings, as Senior Investigating Officer, was to attend, plus the Deputy Chief in full dress uniform.

CHAPTER TWENTY

Anna Plumley, told in no uncertain terms by Daniel that he'd have nothing to do with arrangements, had called on the Vicar of Fordham, borrowed a Book of Common Prayer, checked on The Order for the Burial of the Dead, and decided that the full works went a bit over the top.

Freddie, like many a decent and unimaginative man, hadn't had a lot of time for formal religion. Nor she in her younger days. She remembered Jennifer's confirmation as a formality of white dress, costly gifts from the godparents and little else. For the youngster herself the sacrament had been water off a duck's back. As a married couple, Jennifer and Freddie had put in a church appearance at special festivals and times of national crisis and, according to the Reverend Piers Farrier, Freddie had covenanted generously. The children, although christened, had seldom attended church and never Sunday School.

'Something comforting,' Anna requested, 'and not excessive. But I still prefer the language of 1662. And a couple of hymns with tunes everyone knows, so we can roar any lumps out of our throats.'

'I'll do what I can,' the Reverend Piers promised. He had made it tolerable.

There was a modest buffet lunch arranged for afterwards at the Manor. Yeadings asked Z to drive him there. It would be a good time to buttonhole the housekeeper and Daniel.

In the event he found that the invited guests included Fallon, both Huggetts and the Bartons.

'By Graham Dent's request. On account of Freddie's will being read this afternoon,' Anna Plumley explained.

So my little diversion can wait until later, Yeadings decided.

At a sign from Anna, Graham Dent, the solicitor from Aylesbury, moved off towards the dining room where extra chairs had been brought in, and in twos and threes the others drifted after him.

He looked at them over his half-moon spectacles and gave a little nervous cough. 'I must explain that normally when a married couple are involved in any unwitnessed disaster it is assumed that the older of the pair has predeceased the younger. That would mean that Mrs Jennifer Hoad, outliving her husband by however short a period, would benefit from any provisions made by him, rather than vice versa.

'In this case it has been established by the police forensic experts that Mr Frederick Arthur Hoad was indeed the first of the family to be killed in the early hours of Saturday October twenty-first. It is his last will and testament that I am now about to read to you.'

He began with announcing minor legacies to the Parish Church, the Samaritans, Oxfam, old friends, workers at the Bristol foundry, then summarised. 'Provision has already been made for the future of the firm, all shares in the company passing to the only other member of the Board of Directors, Mr Norbert Fallon, by a separate deed which does not concern us here.

'I will not trouble you with complicated measurements and rights of way at this moment, only to explain that the estate and grounds of Fordham Manor House and Fordham Manor Farm have already been divided by conveyance into two private residences and a separate agricultural unit.

'The will continues thus, "To my trusted

friends and employees Edwin (Ned) and Constance Barton I bequeath the freehold property of Fordham Manor Farm with its surrounding five acres as designated by deed of conveyance dated February twentieth in the year two thousand and two to be theirs in common absolutely and without impediment."

'There is also a condition of sale on the agricultural land which requires further limited acreage to be sold at market value to Edwin Barton upon his request.'

He looked round at the amazed couple. 'This is something we might well pursue together at some later date.'

'Oh lordy,' Barton said, turning to Anna. 'When you mentioned the will, ma'am, I thought maybe a coupla hundred'd be nice. But this . . . !'

Graham Dent controlled a smile and continued with 'the property known as Fordham Manor;' which to further amazement was bequeathed, together with fifty thousand pounds yearly for life "to my dear friend and mother-in-law Anna Plumley in the hope that she may long enjoy it and maintain a second home for her grandchildren, Daniel and Angela".'

Anna's gaze swept to Daniel who sat with mouth agape, shaking his head in disbelief.

Dent waited for the murmurs to be stilled before continuing. ' "To my relentless poaching friend and more recent game-keeper Benjamin Huggett I give thanks for his comradeship and worldly wisdom. And I bequeath that part of Fordham Woods delineated in the relevant deed of convey-ance dated February twentieth in the year two thousand and two for his absolute use maintenance or destruction as shall be his will".'

There followed details of a trust fund for the two children, with 'the remainder of the estate whatsoever and wheresover be-queathed to my wife Jennifer Suzanne Hoad in the knowledge that this was all she ever expected of her inadequate husband.'

'Mad! He was right out of his mind!' Dan-iel shouted.

No, just sad, Anna thought. Poor dear Freddie, I hope he got some kind of pleasure out of putting all that together.

She looked up and saw Yeadings looming square in the doorway. She stood, thanked the solicitor and walked across to the detec-tive. 'You heard all that? I get the impres-sion you're not in any way surprised.'

'I came across his rough copy for this revised version,' he admitted. 'It was made less than three weeks ago. Almost as though he knew things were coming to a head.'

'But not the way they did.'

He nodded. 'Thank God for that, at least.'

The visitors began slowly to disperse while Yeadings and Z made themselves inconspicuous in a corner of the drawing-room. Neither missed Ben Huggett's departing gesture towards young Daniel. He patted one bulging pocket of the straining dark blue suit, withdrew a keyring and shook it meaningfully. They heard the jingle of metal across the room.

The boy flushed and started forward, fists clenched, then, realising he was observed, turned back. His gaze flickered towards the two detectives and after a moment's hesitation he made for them, chin defiantly outthrust.

'What was that about?' Yeadings asked amiably.

'As if you don't know! He's got access to some of the outbuildings. We'll see what Gran thinks about that.'

'He has a key to the hut in the woods?'

'The rave cave, yeah. That's where the will's reference to "destruction" comes in.'

'Maybe he'll just return it to its original use, and raise pheasants for future shoots.'

'Who cares? It's the house that matters.

You heard. It goes to my grandmother. I shall dispute it. As legally adopted son I'm his heir. The way he's set it up I'd be tied to her even after I come of age. And I'd have nothing but the trust fund.'

'Including your late half-sister's share, unless that automatically reverts to her natural grandmother.'

'You bet it will. She's got it all sewn up. She'll have been manipulating him for years on the quiet.'

'One thing I find interesting,' Yeadings pursued. 'Your housekeeper, Mrs Pavitt, wasn't present, apart from serving refreshments earlier. And no mention of her in the will. That's unusual.'

'Because he'd sacked her. She'd be going at the end of the month.' His voice was full of contempt.

'I see. So she was irrelevant, because your father wasn't expecting the will to be activated so soon.'

'It's all a bloody mess,' the boy broke out. 'And the Bartons getting the farm. That won't stand, will it, when it's disputed?'

'Are you sure you want recourse to the law? Haven't you a few matters to settle yourself before you go so far?'

Daniel closed his eyes. From flushed, he had gone sickly pale. 'I have to get out of here.' He plunged away.

Yeadings caught Z's reproachful glance. 'You think I was hard on him? He has worse coming. He needs to face up to the truth. All the truths. But we'll leave him until later. Let's round up the unfortunate Mrs Pavitt. She still has a few questions to answer before she departs.'

Nevertheless it was towards Mrs Plumley that he steered first. 'Did you have forewarning of the will's contents?' he asked.

She looked thoughtful. 'Not specifically. I knew he aimed to convey the farmhouse and a few acres to the Bartons, but as a deserved retirement home. As it stands, coming so soon, they're still fit enough to continue working, so I imagine the proviso for taking on further acreage will interest them.'

'If they can afford it.'

'Whoever takes on the working farm will still need someone experienced in everyday control. In that case Ned could still be earning.'

Yeadings regarded her keenly. 'You've got it all worked out. You intend buying into the farming estate yourself, don't you?'

She smiled ruefully. 'You're too sharp, Superintendent. I haven't considered any details, but I've always regarded retirement as dangerous to the health. And I feel the Bartons might agree. I'd no idea the Manor was coming to me, but Daniel will need a home, even if he returns to boarding-school. Also I can see dear old Plum pottering around, scratching the pigs with a stick, getting excited about calving and milk output.'

'And the housekeeper, will you be keeping her on?'

It was Anna's turn to face him shrewdly. 'I rather thought to ask your advice on that. I can't overlook how in playing up to Jennifer's irregular lifestyle she's contributed to the corruption of my grandson. And I don't care for the woman. But I think there's something yet to be resolved. Have you further interest in her yourself?'

Instead of answering, he put his own question. 'You knew she was due to leave at the end of the month?'

Her eyebrows shot up. 'So soon? I knew Freddie was advertising for a replacement, but he hadn't been in touch with me recently. Did she give notice or was she sacked? No, obviously, if she'd chosen to go she'd have mentioned it to me. There are only a few days left.'

'Daniel knew.'

'They don't get on. I get the impression . . .'

Yeadings waited.

'. . . that it's personal chemistry. Mutual distaste. No, it's something more than that. I just don't know. You haven't said if you need to question her further.'

'I'm about to do that now. Daniel seems reconciled to our knowing about the goings-on in the woods. She may be less so.'

He found that Z had run Mrs Pavitt to earth in the kitchen quarters where she was stacking used crockery in the dishwasher. As he came in she slammed its door, seized a sponge cloth, squirted cleaner over the work surface and began vigorously polishing. Since this enabled her to keep her back turned, he walked round to confront her.

'I'm sure that can be left for the present, Mrs Pavitt,' he suggested mildly. 'We need to talk with you for a moment. In particular about your future plans.'

The woman bent to squint along the surface she had polished, appeared satisfied and straightened. 'Oh, I couldn't possibly leave them in the lurch now, could I? How would the poor old lady manage? And Danny, he needs someone around he's used to. Don't worry. I'll be staying on. Auntie is all right for the present in her nursing home. By spring she'll be walking as well as ever and won't need any looking after.'

'I imagine some choice will rest with Mrs Plumley.'

'No problem. We'll rub along fine. If she doesn't make any unreasonable demands.'

'One hopes not. Meanwhile my sergeant would like to ask you a few questions about your position here in Mr Hoad's employment.'

'Jennifer's.' The contradiction was immediate. 'She was the one took me on. He had little enough interest in household matters. Well, being a man, he wouldn't care, would he? Mind, we got along fine, and Jennifer was more like a sister to me than a boss.'

'Daniel seems to think differently.' Z wondered aloud. 'Why would that be then? He says Mr Hoad sacked you.'

Mrs Pavitt set her fists on her hips and leaned forward confidentially. 'He's a strange child. Between you and me, I think this awful business has sent him right round the bend. Bit of a mummy's boy, so he's not been brought up to accept hard facts. And ever since Granny moved in he's been really on edge, against everybody.'

'Crack cocaine can't have helped.' A laconic suggestion.

For the first time a flicker of some emotion crossed the woman's face. 'Drugs? You mean he's into the hard stuff? Where does he get it? Maybe that manicurist girl he went out with the other day . . .'

'Get your coat on, Mrs Pavitt,' Yeadings broke in. 'We'll do this properly down at the nick. Our time's too valuable to waste on watching you play the innocent.'

There was more concerning the cocaine source awaiting them on their arrival. A Sergeant Batts from the Met had faxed in a report on Justin Halliwell's girlfriend who acted as his drugs 'mule'. A surgeon, fighting against time, had removed twenty-eight packages of pure cocaine from her intestines. Only one had split but it could yet prove as fatal as the entire load. She was still comatose in intensive care at Hillingdon Hospital with a forty-sixty chance of recovery.

The woman's purse was found to contain counterfoils for her flight ticket Orlando-Heathrow and for hire-car travel Miami-Orlando. She had been scrupulous about retaining details of expenses. Her main luggage had been opened and examined when passing through both airports.

It seemed that on-flight she had avoided suspicion by ordering normal meals, and then contrived to dump the food in her cabin bag. Its unlovely mishmash had been more securely sealed to protect the fine leather lining than the plastic bag which now threatened her very life.

Examination of flight records for three major transatlantic airlines showed she was a frequent traveller between Florida and various cities in mainland Europe or the UK. At each eastern arrival point she had been met by her 'fiancé' Justin Halliwell and provided with shared accommodation booked in his name.

This last fact destroyed the man's credibility as an innocently deceived and caring friend. In hope of lessening the charges against him, the Met had persuaded Halliwell to admit that Jennifer blackmailed him into organising that vital part of her import business. He claimed that revealing an undercover set of accounts for Miradec Interiors would exonerate him as principal in the drugs dealing. It had been Jennifer's own speciality, using the décor business as a means of laundering profits.

Which solved the whole shebang in one fell swoop, declared Acting-DCI Salmon. His knobby-potato face glowed with Damascene revelation. This maniac case suddenly made sense. Halliwell, impatient at ranking as number two, had dreamed up a fantastic scenario to take over the entire operation. Jennifer must be eliminated.

And, in achieving this, somehow or other the rest of the family got caught up in it. A simple explanation for a complex outcome.

CHAPTER
TWENTY-ONE

'One or two small matters to clear up,' Yeadings told Salmon, excusing his return with Alma Pavitt to the Area nick.

'We can leave those to Zyczynski, then.'

'As you say.'

Never having seen Salmon so near a state of elation, the Boss was loath to prick his bubble. He also secretly admitted to a slick of malice in not sharing his own preferred intelligence.

'If you're off to see the Met I may as well sit in on this with Z.'

Acting-DCI Salmon grunted agreement, patting his many pockets in a version of crossing himself. Spectacles, testicles, watch and wallet, Beaumont had once described the procedure.

'Who's got my pen?'

It was retrieved from an ashtray alongside assorted paper clips and drawing pins, then the CID office settled to comparative peace with his departure.

In Interview Room 1, Mrs Pavitt was offered a choice of tea or coffee, both of which she refused.

'Probably just as well,' Z remarked comfortably. 'They're from a vending machine. I can never tell the difference myself. Now, about this hut in the wood. Just what was it for, Mrs Pavitt, and how were you involved?'

The woman was clearly prepared for the question. 'It's been there for donkeys' years. Keepers used to raise game chicks in incubators. Mr Hoad didn't go in much for shoots, so when it fell out of use Jennifer thought she'd take it over for — well, for fun really. Crazy parties. She'd have friends down from London, and sometimes local people too who liked to act bohemian.'

'And where did you come in?'

'I did the catering, prepared the food at the house and reheated it at the Cave. We had a microwave oven there and a small fridge. There was music laid on too.'

'Cave. Is that what everyone called it?'

'The Rave Cave, yes.'

'And what kind of raving went on?'

'Oh, just like kids do. Only sometimes grown-ups want to let their hair down too, play the fool a bit. OK, so there was a bit of wife-swapping now and again. No real harm in it.'

'And dressing-up?'

'Jennifer got some costumes made, yes.'

'Animal faces and so on?'

'Things like that, yeah.'

'For rituals which included flaring torches and dancing outdoors in a circle? Almost witchcraft, would you say?'

'Only playing at it.' Her tone was contemptuous.

'But for you it was different?'

'I'm not a witch.' She sat straight, dark eyes fixed on the woman detective. 'I'm gifted. I tell the cards. I can see into the dark ahead. When she got to know that, she relied on me. I warned her: of something terrible coming that she couldn't escape. It seemed to excite her.'

Z shifted in her seat, not daring to glance sideways at the Boss. Things were moving too fast, important points omitted.

'When did Daniel start to join in?'

Mrs Pavitt sat silent, head bowed. Eventually she looked up. 'He must have sneaked in. We discovered him hidden behind a curtain. Jennifer was a bit doped up and she let him . . . Well, we all . . .'

They'd all been stoned out of their minds and the boy had joined the rout, wore a ram's head, been bestial with the rest of them. High on drugs.

'There were photographs,' Z claimed. None had been found, but surely, sometime, one of the revellers would have brought a camera. There had to be a record somewhere, and Pavitt must know that.

The woman started to shake. She brushed the back of one hand under her nostrils. It shone wet.

'Jennifer provided crack cocaine,' Z claimed. 'You were all out of your minds. Where did you think it would end?'

'Not like it did! Never like that!' Her voice was a shriek. She fought to regain control. She closed her eyes and ground out the words. 'Someone must have come back that weekend. Found the stuff in the house. Went right over the edge! Don't ask me who. I wasn't there.'

Yeadings nodded to Z.

'Thank you, Mrs Pavitt. That will be all for now. If you wait a moment I'll arrange for a patrol car to take you back.'

But was that all for now? Z asked herself, shocked at the Boss's cutting short the flow. Silently she followed him back to his office and, uninvited, sat while he refilled the coffee-maker. Her distraction wasn't lost on him. If she was troubled by some half-realised theory he could wait for it to surface complete.

Beaumont knocked at the door and looked in. Yeadings pointed to a vacant chair. The DS slid on to it, picking up on the prevailing mood.

After a moment's hesitation, 'I think I know . . .' Z ventured slowly, and became aware that the others were waiting for illumination.

'. . . know why Jennifer wasn't raped,' she ended lamely.

Beaumont nodded. He knew too, of course. All that bloodletting came from frustration. The killer was struck impotent. When it came to the climax — couldn't get it up; hadn't the balls. Hence the broom handle.

'Lack of the wherewithal.' Z felt obliged to finish her thesis. It left no impression on Beaumont. But the Boss was a step ahead. 'What you mean is that her killer . . .'

'Is a woman. Yes.'

At the Manor Anna had felt obliged to put together an evening meal in the housekeeper's absence. Daniel was out walking with Barley. This time downhill towards the river. When the phone trilled she had taken it for her own mobile. But it wasn't.

She followed the sound and unearthed the thing from a window-settle in the study.

'Hi,' Camilla greeted her, 'got over that sick do, Danny?'

'It's his grandmother,' Anna said. 'Thank you, Camilla, he is better. But when did he give you this new number?'

For a few seconds they were at cross purposes until it struck Anna this must be the same mobile he claimed to have dropped from the balloon. She explained that Daniel was out: Camilla should try again later to reach him, and curtly rang off.

Twenty minutes later the men returned. She heard them talking in the gun room, then Daniel came through to the kitchen, unimproved by his taste of fresh air, and still grumbling about his father's feckless handling of the bequests.

'Maybe it is a little hard on you,' she eventually allowed.

But was that actually true? Hadn't he started out as the golden boy, with everything showered upon him before he even knew any need? Yet the essentials had been missed out: a constant standard of care, back-up discipline.

Jennifer had been useless, so ambitious, and forever flaunting her sexuality. Only Freddie was present to listen, but the boy wouldn't have opened up to him; Freddie not his true father. That other man had long ago shrugged him off and gone his way. Early rejection followed by careless pampering were an unholy mixture for a child to take.

She tried again. 'Daniel, there's so much anger in you. You need to get it out. Can we try to deal with it?'

'Anger?' His voice was bitter. He turned away and rested his head on his arms, bent over the work surface. She thought the single strangled word that reached her was 'guilt'.

Her heart beat fast in her throat. Would he talk now about the poor girl whose death he'd caused? At last show some regret, even compassion?

She wanted to believe that. There were times when she'd thought he wasn't capable of any feeling for others; always glibly charming and shallow, half-way to a casebook sociopath. Perhaps now that image was breaking down.

But instantly his mood changed again. He slouched over to observe the carrots she was chopping into batons and took a handful to chew.

'Camilla rang,' she told him. 'On the phone which you did not drop in the canal.'

317

'I've got two. This is the new one.'

'No,' she told him evenly. 'I recognised the scratch on its cover.'

'So?'

'So what did you drop from the balloon?'

He sauntered round the room, very *beau jeune homme* and mocking. 'D'you know. Grananna, I think I'll tell you the terrible truth. I did have two mobiles, just for a while. Because I needed to send myself a message. Yes, the melodramatic threat: "U NEXT!"'

'Rather a clever idea, you'll admit. I picked up someone else's phone when I went in the pub to clean up after being sick in Camel's car. It was lying on a table by some spilled beer. If the filth wanted to trace the message back they'd simply find some dozy yokel who couldn't remember where he'd left the thing. That's the one I got rid of.'

His face flushed with sudden anger. 'Hell, nobody cared a damn about me. They should have known I was next in line to be killed! I had to get the message across.'

'You wanted pity? We were concerned enough and trying not to show it. And while we tried to understand your grief and shock you were playing stupid little tricks like this on us. Even at the risk of wasting valuable

318

police time.'

'They're so thick they couldn't — couldn't see . . .'

Anna carefully put down the knife she had been using and slid it under the bag the carrots had come in. A bid for pity? Or was it something else? An attempt to put them off the right track?

'Daniel, I'm not the great fool you think me. And I'm not blind. I've tried, God knows, not to believe what's staring me in the face. You were here that night, weren't you? All along you've been telling a string of lies.'

There was complete silence, broken only when the refrigerator started up an active cycle. Anna discovered that her hands and knees were shaking.

He straightened, beat a bunched fist against the wall. His voice, a refined whisper till then, roared in agony.

'He turned and saw me! I was startled. I never meant to shoot him. And then he was falling back, surprised. There was this black hole in his chest. The — the crack of the gun came after. But his shotgun went off, sprayed the cabinet. Glass showering like fireworks. She was laughing . . . howling with laughter. She's insane!'

Never meant to shoot? He meant Freddie!

Who else had been shot? Now he was claiming it had been him who . . .

'She?' The word was torn from her.

He shoved off from the wall, turned a terrible, agonised face on her.

'Who?' Anna insisted, but she knew anyway. There was only one woman in this. Jennifer. If Daniel could be believed, she'd watched him shoot dead the husband she despised, and she'd laughed out loud at it.

'No, this is all wrong. You dreamt it. You weren't there!' she protested. 'You were with that girl in Ascot.'

'I came back. I had to see her.' His voice was monotonous now, grinding out the words, inhuman.

'We needed each other. It was all arranged. But I had to get the gun. It was the pistol, not a rifle. That empty clip hasn't been used for years. I got the cabinet open and then, in the dark, a chair went over. He must have been awake and heard us.

'He started coming downstairs, and I hid under the table. The light came on, but he went right by me, to the open gun case, reached in for the twelve-bore.'

Daniel stopped there, almost laughed. 'I nearly wet myself.'

Anna drew a soughing breath. She had to believe him. The boy was reliving some real terror. It must have happened how he told it. He'd gone totally over the edge.

It had been Daniel who shot his adoptive father. Not an outsider breaking in, or someone Freddie had opened the door to.

The boy had only pretended to go away. His story of spending the whole weekend with the prostitute was a fiction and, being dead, she couldn't give it the lie. So many killled now. Who was left to be believed but Daniel?

So shooting Freddie was an accident? He had come back, to be with his mother because they 'needed each other'. A secret assignation with his own mother? For sex? Surely, even for Jennifer, that was too depraved!

Is that what the orgies in the wood were about? But he, at last pushed too far, had desperately intended to end it the only way he knew how. He'd gone for a gun. But why so desperate? 'Guilt', he'd said. Yes, over what his mother had made of him; not the crash with the bike. He didn't kill that wretched girl until the following night; part of a false alibi.

Whatever he'd intended, on the Friday it had all gone hideously wrong, and he'd shot poor Freddie. It was unbelievable, but the boy had said so himself.

She turned away, sick to her soul. There was nothing she could say or do. To turn him in was impossible. He was past counselling. She had presently such a horror of him — for him — that her mind was numbed. She needed time to regain sanity.

She walked out of the house, let herself into the caravan, sat with head in hands, mindless. When she raised her eyes it was as though, half-conscious, she sat before a wide screen on which the tragedy was being silently projected: Jennifer, in her nightdress, insanely laughing over her husband's bloodied corpse, at her son's anguish.

And then Daniel, filled with rage, going after her. There was a knife. Had Jennifer been holding it and he'd wrested it from her? Whatever, he'd not shot his mother. Caught up with her when she fled to the barn. Was it there they used to meet in secret, play at being lovers, commit incest?

And there he'd half-strangled her, then stabbed her to death. Execution. And mutilation. That awful detail with the broom handle. Revenge for the sex puppet she'd made of him? And then, totally out of his mind . . . gone back to stab the two little girls.

Anna rushed to the galley's sink and vomited until throat and stomach ached.

She wiped bile from her lips and chin with a harsh paper towel and went shakily out into purer air. In the distance she saw DC Barley striding up the hill towards the woods, out of hearing.

How long she sat slumped on the van's steps she'd no way of knowing, but dark had come on when she realised: dear God, he'd still have the missing gun.

She must go back into the house and ring Mr Yeadings before there was another death.

In the hall she halted, one hand reaching for the phone. There were sounds of someone moving on the floor above. Alma Pavitt. She had to prevent the housekeeper meeting Daniel in his present state. 'Mrs Pavitt,' she called and started up after her.

The woman must not have heard. She was going higher, towards her own room under the eaves. Anna, breathless, followed.

She was on the final flight when she caught the sound of voices. And, instant upon it, a choking scream.

A single shot. Then nothing.

'Do you still have doubts about Anna Plumley?' Yeadings asked Z.

'Not really. She seems genuinely concerned about her grandson. She said yesterday, "I believe all children pass through a vicious phase, however brief. Natural savages before they reach a more civilised state. Their own violence may scare them out of it early on. But staying that way too long — that can mould them into a monster".'

'So does she see Daniel as a monster?'

Z hesitated. 'I think she's trying not to. She knows he's deeply disturbed. And she loves him.'

She sounded uneasy at the admission.

Yes, awful, Yeadings silently agreed.

'I wish I knew how deeply he's implicated in whatever occult or immoral play the adults were up to. That's unnatural enough. And then crack cocaine plus an adolescent's overcharge of testosterone. A dangerous mix.'

'Those foolish women had a lot to answer for,' Yeadings grunted.

Women? Jennifer yes; but who else? Surely he didn't include Anna Plumley. She seemed to have interfered as far as she'd dared to keep the children unaffected, using what information Freddie Hoad had leaked to her in letters.

'The housekeeper,' Yeadings said, as if she'd questioned aloud. 'Alma Pavitt was heavily into whatever went on in the hut in the woods. Hers were the only fingerprints on the Tarot cards and the whip. She'd set herself up as a psychic, some kind of medium or priestess of the occult. And then the Manson book which Anna had found in Daniel's bookcase: those were Pavitt's initials inside the cover, not Plumley's. Both AP.'

'So Anna told the truth then: that she'd found it in Daniel's bookcase? I'd assumed it was hers because I saw her with it.'

'Milton's *Comus,*' Yeadings murmured as if to himself. Then, as Z glanced at him enquiringly, 'The rout scene. Drunkenness and bestial behaviour. Remember the animal masks SOCO turned up? God knows what depravity they got into. If Daniel ever came across that, and was drawn in . . .'

'It could account for his mental state now. But that doesn't connect with the murders. There had to be some outsider who decided it all had to end. How about Huggett? He could have come across something obscene when out poaching. His wife's a Pentecostal. She'd not have stood for it if she'd got a hint of what went on. And that brick through their window. More than a threat not to talk out of turn?'

Yeadings appeared not to be listening. She had lost him some way back. 'I think . . .' he began. 'Yes, I fancy a quick trip out. I don't think we've been told all there is to know. I want you along.'

He let her drive, heading for the M40 eastbound while he was occupied searching through his pockets and grunting with dissatisfaction as each slip of paper he found was discarded. They made a little pool of screwed-up post-its round his feet.

'Ah, got you!' he finally exclaimed and read out a Slough address Z hadn't come across. But the only Slough connection was the prostitute killed in the bike crash.

'Not their case, so they didn't pursue it,' he muttered. Meaning the Ascot police, she supposed. But our case, so what have we let slip through unquestioned?

Yeadings was now riffling through the pages of a street map and directed her to a narrow road with an alley off it. She ran the side of his Rover on to the kerb. They got out. She handed him the car key, flicking the doors locked.

At 57b, an appropriately red-painted door between a barber's and a sleazy café, Yeadings pushed the doorbell and left his finger on it. The brunette who eventually opened up was in snarling mode.

'Police.' He said as she opened her mouth to sort him out. 'And we haven't time to waste. So let us in.' He flapped his ID under her nose. She looked past him to Z and saw little support there.

'It's about Charleen, I suppose.'

'It is. And your name is . . . ?'

'Prue.'

'Short for Prudence?'

'Yeah, but not for long. That's got green whiskers on it. Every punter thinks he's the first to say it. You better come up. Happens I'm on me own at the moment.'

She seemed reconciled to their intervention. Involvement with police was nothing new. She almost felt at times she had mates among them.

'You must feel bad about what happened to your friend,' Yeadings said when they were in the cramped little sitting room.

'Miss her, yes. Her and her sloppy ways,' Prue allowed. 'I'd like to get my hands on that skunk what done it.'

'An accident, apparently. What did you make of Daniel Hoad then?'

'Never met him. Just read the papers. Spoilt rich kid, he sounds.'

'Were you away that weekend?'

'Nuh. My asthma was somethink awful. Had to stay in for a coupla days.'

'You were here all Friday and Saturday?'

'Yeah. Sunday too. Bloody inhaler ran out and I couldn't get a new prescription because the clinic was shut. They never think you may need 'em in a hurry.'

'Difficult,' Yeadings sympathised. 'Must have been a bit of a crush that Friday, with Daniel staying over.'

She stared at him as if he was stupid. 'He never did. It was Sat'dy he picked her up at the pub. Same day he got ratted and crashed his bike. Anyway we never have punters stay overnight. There's no room. Just one double bed and we both used that, me and Char.'

'I see. The pub potman got it wrong, saying it was Friday.'

She shrugged. No concern of hers. 'Now I gotta find someone to share with. Can't afford to pay for the flat on my own.'

Yeadings forbore to offer money. It could be misunderstood.

CHAPTER
TWENTY-TWO

Yeadings opted to drive back. On the way it began gently to sleet. Staring through the wipers' slow slog-slog across the squeaky windscreen Zyczynski tried to come to terms with Daniel as the killer, but something was disturbingly wrong with that.

The sleet changed to rain and intensified. Yeadings switched to fast-wipe. The change of rhythm broke Z's half-trance with the wipers' irritating screech.

'I meant to renew the blades,' Yeadings reminded himself.

'So did she,' Z exploded, sitting bolt upright. 'Alma Pavitt claimed she put in her car to have a new motor fitted for the wipers, so she travelled to Swindon by train. I gave her a lift back, but I never saw the return half of her ticket.

'She returned the favour yesterday, gave me a lift after you dropped me off. That's what was bugging me, but it didn't come through. Her wipers were still faulty.

'I believe she drove down to Swindon and left her car still parked there when I gave her the lift back. She must have gone to pick it up later, when Anna gave her the day off.'

'Phone her garage as soon as we get back,' Yeadings snapped. 'If she lied, there'd be a reason for it. With her aunt sedated that night after the fall, Pavitt could sneak out and return to Fordham. For whatever purpose.'

Anna Plumley reached the top of the stairs, breathless, and her heart racing. The door to the housekeeper's room was wide open. Mrs Pavitt was sprawled backwards across the bed, a black hole above her eyes, a mess of blood on the duvet under her head.

Anna stared at Daniel standing wild-eyed over her, the gun drooping from one hand. She realised he was stoned. He must have had access to more drugs all the time. The stuff had been stashed somewhere and, like the gun, the police search hadn't turned it up.

Her eyes went back to the body of the woman and her blood ran cold. He'd run amok. Past all reason. She herself was the next he'd turn on. But she had to try and get through to him.

'What have you taken?' she demanded in a low voice.

He smiled at her from a great distance. 'Dutch courage.'

'Drugs are no help. The only safe thing for you now . . .'

He was suddenly on a high. 'Who wants safety? That's for losers. The world's full of them. Where are the real heroes?'

In their graves. Dead, from leading charges against impossible odds, she thought. But you never say that to the young.

'No, Grananna. For me the buzz is living on the edge. Like kids on skate boards taking the Big Leap. You get older and bolder and you do it all bigger.'

'But not drugs, Daniel. Subsidising criminals to rubbish you. You're worth more than that.'

He advanced closer to her. The momentary bravado had gone. His hands were shaking. The gun fell on the floor between them and he seemed not to notice. 'That's the point. I'm not.' His eyes brimmed with unshed tears.

'You were, once. Despite mistakes, the real you is still there.'

'It's dead. I'm finished. What do you know about me? — the things I've done. That girl, just a trollop, but I had to. I needed an alibi.

Dead, she couldn't disprove it.'

Anna drew a deep breath. 'It was deliberate, then? No accident?'

'As if you hadn't guessed! I took the call when they phoned to cancel scout camp. Not that it made any difference. I'd always meant to come back, sneak in up here and spend the weekend in her bed. I'd been screwing her for weeks. Or, more like, she was screwing me. We had some of Jenni . . .' His voice broke.

'. . . some good stuff my mother got in London. We'd get high together, plumb the depths. There was nothing like it in the whole world. We were immortal.'

Anna came towards him, arms outstretched. 'What you do and what you are — they're not the same. There's atonement, forgiveness.' Desperately she knew she must keep him talking.

His laugh was harsh. 'Religious crap: hate the sin and forgive the sinner?' he jeered. 'I'd expect better of you than that, Grananna.'

'What's wrong with it?'

'It's not real. Even my father knew better, poor sod. He used to insist that you pay for what you get and what you do. Well, by now the price is too high.'

His voice was rising, then the treble

cracked into a man's hoarse shout. 'You don't realise what I've done. I killed my father!

'I never meant to. We got caught downstairs. Neither of us was supposed to be in the house. She wanted to rough the place up and steal a few trinkets, to make it look . . . Only, between us we knocked over a chair. We were both stoned. Then my . . . my father came down and we hid. I had the revolver from the cabinet. Not a rifle. He should have handed it in when they changed the law. I'd always wanted it and I knew he could never openly admit it was gone.

'Somehow it went off. It sent her right over the edge. She'd always despised my father, hated my mother, even when they slept together out at the hut. They had this sort of . . . Well, each had to master the other. Rivals, really crazy. Alma the psychic and Jennifer with the money, the access to crack.'

He had covered his face again, muttering between his fingers. Now he stood erect, punched the air with his fist.

'And now the Jezebel's dead! I should have cut her black heart out. Butchered her with a kitchen knife. Like she used on the others.'

His voice dropped to a whisper. 'I didn't

know until afterwards about them. Just that, after I'd shot him, she had to make sure he was dead. I sort of passed out and woke up under the cold shower. It was all over then and she was on a high. She said at first that I'd done it. With the knife. Only, later, she admitted . . . gloated.

'She drove me away, through the storm, with Jeff's bike strapped on to the roof rack. Seemed cold sober by then, dropped me off and I hid in a shed out at the quarry. Had to break in. Next day I rode over to find the girl in Slough.

'It was Saturday I met her at the pub, not Friday. The potman got it wrong. But she was a blabbermouth. Once the police got to her she'd have sold me down the river. By then it had all gone too far not to go on. Finish it.'

Anna stood silent, letting him tell her everything. But she had guessed. On the last flight of stairs she had realised it wasn't his mother he'd needed to kill. Over days all the facts had been coming together. It made sense of his reaction to this house, to the woman who served his meals, cleaned his room, who had to be avoided like the very devil. He could never meet her eyes.

And now, the last act was over. The full truth struck her the moment she reached the door of this room, saw him with the gun in his hand, smelled the cordite. He believed he had done all he must, had completed the nightmare.

But surely something could yet be retrieved. 'Dan—'

She broke off at the distant but persistent hee-haw of a police siren. She reached out for him. 'They'll find the front door locked and go round to the back. You must be quick. We haven't long.'

'We? What do you mean? You can't hold them off.' His voice was desperate. 'There's nowhere to go!'

He was right. Only the fire-escape. And the gravelled courtyard below.

Now a second siren joined in. In minutes the cars would be turning in from the lane. Police would pour out, covering all exits from the house. Someone would look up towards the roof, see the lit window.

One way or the other, he had to go down to them.

Inside she was all ice and flame, could barely breathe. She opened the fire-escape door on to dark night, gestured towards it. As he hesitated, she touched his hand.

'Your edge, Daniel. The one you always had to live on. It's out there.'

Briefly their eyes met. The shock of her

meaning reached him.

He pulled his hand away, unbelieving. 'I don't un . . .'

'You do understand.'

'I won't. You can't make me.' Momentarily the petulant child again.

'You're right. I can't make you. I wouldn't. Daniel, what else is there?'

Headlights swung up as the first police car started on the hill towards the house. Then a second. They were coming in force.

'Shit, no. No!'

They were already here, braked with engines still racing. Gravel scattered. Doors slammed. There were voices below now, blue lights pulsing in the dark. The front doorbell shrilled through the house.

'Oh God, I can't.' He blundered out on to the iron platform, gazed down at dark figures moving against the cars' headlights.

'Shit, no!' He looked back at her, his eyes starting from his head. He straddled the rail, stood on the outer ledge, leapt as though he couldn't reach out far enough.

The same shock was in DS Beaumont's eyes as he knelt beside the body and covered the boy's mad stare. He looked up at the eaves and saw the woman silhouetted in the attic doorway.

Anna slowly began the long journey down-stairs. She would tell the truth, the whole truth and nothing but the truth. Except for one thing: if he'd resisted, she would have thrust him bodily out there and turned the lock on him.

But at the end he'd chosen. A lifetime locked away would have destroyed what little was left of the innocent child.

And she had loved him.

ABOUT THE AUTHOR

Clare Curzon began writing in the 1960s and has published over forty novels under a variety of pseudonyms. She studied French and Psychology at King's College, London, and much of her work is concerned with the dynamics within closely knit communities. A grandmother to seven, in her free time she enjoys travel and painting. Clare lives in Buckinghamshire, England.

The employees of Thorndike Press hope you have enjoyed this Large Print book. All our Thorndike and Wheeler Large Print titles are designed for easy reading, and all our books are made to last. Other Thorndike Press Large Print books are available at your library, through selected bookstores, or directly from us.

For information about titles, please call:
(800) 223-1244

or visit our Web site at:
http://gale.cengage.com/thorndike

To share your comments, please write:
Publisher
Thorndike Press
295 Kennedy Memorial Drive
Waterville, ME 04901

LOGAN-HOCKING
COUNTY DISTRICT LIBRARY
230 EAST MAIN STREET
LOGAN, OHIO 43138